JOSEPHINE'S STAR

The Spiker's Instruments Book 1

WILLIAM K. MARCATO

Cover art concept, design, and artwork © William K. Marcato
Cover art graphic editing by Nicholas McInturff

Pendants inspired and used with permission by
Matt Schiermeier and Cameron Earnheart.
Instagram @schiermeierearnheart
Proofreading by Ginnie Leguizamon

Contact author at WilliamKMarcato@gmail.com
Instagram @spikersinstruments

In memory of
my mother and father

The good finally outweighed the bad.

JOSEPHINE'S STAR

The biggest fear I have is that eventually you will see me the way I see myself.

-

Anonymous

PROLOGUE

Darkdust. The Shardland was blanketed with it, a deep black snow that's only reflection was from its rough glassy edges beaming light as it mirrored Zyriah's candle flame. These fragments were freshly made, new memories from a new reality, and although they normally intergraded more quickly into the memory shards she commonly encountered, these particles only sat there, struggling against a new force against their assimilation. Zyriah waited and viewed over them. Her own mind continued trying to focus on even the slightest glimmer of unification. The mind of the inflicted had been unique, been infected. Zyriah had no images, no name, no address, and no location. She had almost given up, when the darkdust brightened and colorized into an endless field of red, orange, and yellow. The image would not unite, but the color indicated enough of the disaster at hand. Something was on fire.

"Zyriah!"

Evan's voice brought her mind back to Morgan's Ridge, the right half of a long ridge of hillside overlooking the valley of the town of Wilcox. She maintained her view, holding the pendant of her necklace in her hand. The burning home on Willow Road was a beacon in the late-night darkness only lit by a scattering of lamps in windows and streetlights. Zyriah, still holding her lit candle, looked down with a peering glare, awestruck by the fire's height but also to try to figure out the home's owner. The shape of the home was hidden by flames, making the house look much taller than the two-story country home of its owner, whose name had escaped her. Evan grabbed her right forearm, shaking her tall slender frame with his firm grip, driving her attention towards his face.

"It's the deputy's house. Allan Baker, his new wife, and his daughter," Evan exclaimed as she felt him release her arm. Her head moved back forward, and her eyes closed.

Allan Baker.

The Shardland was now more solid, more structured. She knew then he was not the inflicted; he was to be a victim. The fire continued blazing through the large, broken glass images. Zyriah scanned over them, piece by piece. A headpost of a bed with a light reflection close by, his hand twisting and turning against it. She focused her mind harder. The reflection, a shiny mirroring around the post and his wrist that the deputy's eyes were also fixated upon. Handcuffs. Zyriah watched through the shards as the man scanned through the burning room to his wife, half covered, struggling with her own handcuffed wrist. Her body was shaking beneath a white gown. His eyes stared over the room, and as she looked upon the images, her eyes lifted above the shards to a green cloud forming above the images. Shooting down from the cloud was a copper-colored linear bolt that landed immediately before her. Through her own will, she grasped the fiery chord with energy of her own chord, emerging from her pendant hanging below her chin and gripping the chord with fierce intention. From the chord, his voice had finally joined his vision in his memories that seemed to lapse from present day by mere moments. Normally, her ability was not like that of Evan's, who was able to combine the fragments and syllables at a much quicker pace. However, the word emerged so fast that Zyriah's eyes winced in sorrow and helplessness.

"SARAH!"

Sarah Baker.

The field of dust returned, no longer in a fiery color but once again of blackness. The green cloud overhead as well as the copper bolt shooting down immediately dissipated. Zyriah scanned over it, still not finding any shards or any sort of unification, but through the dust came a light, not nearly as bright and much more artificial. The light disappeared, and within a few moments reemerged, white and electrical. Zyriah knew the light from other Shardland viewings. The girl was walking past streetlights.

"It's the daughter. Her father yelled her name was Sarah. She set the fire. The parents are handcuffed in the bedroom and can't free themselves. It is her Shardland that's coming through as dust. She's coming here," Zyriah explained.

Zyriah's eyes opened, looking once again at the fire, hearing the piercing of a new fire truck's siren, as two long red trucks pulled up to the house. She looked over at Evan, who looked so overcome by the image that he might not have heard what she had said. She shook his shoulder, and his head turned to face hers. His eyes were strained with concern.

"Coming? How can you tell if you can't see her shards?" Evan asked.

"I'm telling you, Evan. She's on her way. Just stay quiet and don't move," Zyriah replied, slightly dazed from the rushing back and forth from the Shardland to the present.

Zyriah moved her eyes along the tree line just below them, and even in the darkness she could see a faint formation of October leaves and tree branches reflecting the clear sky's moonlight. Moving slowly back and forth, her head turned and scanned the edge of that grassy field until a pale nightgown emerged from the woods. Zyriah watched the small form walking in her direction. She extended her left hand forward and then her right hand as well to steady the candle in front of her, hoping the light would be a beacon for the small child walking forward with slow, heavy steps.

With a combination of the moonlight and Zyriah's candlelight, a little face became visible, a sweet young girl, her face stained with tracks of tears and sweat through the soot that covered her cheeks. With little hands, Zyriah saw she had a candle, an unlit long yellow candlestick partially melted at its top, and she watched the child raise it slowly, inch by inch almost with her footsteps. Zyriah watched her face closely, until the little light reflected showed the child's eyes to be barely open and lifeless, yet her body still moved forward. Closer.

Within a couple feet from Zyriah, the child stopped and raised her head, but her eyes remained slightly open as her unlit candle rose between them in the child's little hands. Zyriah, realizing the child was going to light the long yellow candle from her own, lowered her own candle to make the lighting easier. Once lit, the little hands of the girl lowered her candle closer to her face, as Zyriah looked at her matted dark brown hair encircling the small round face. The child's eyes began to open.

Zyriah saw them, those little dark eyes fixated by the candle flame when the flame of her candle began to stretch horizontally at a quick pace into a new shape of a four-pointed star. Almost instantly, the child's eyelids rolled back along with a huge inhale of air that made her chest under that shell pink nightgown heave high. Those eyes, Zyriah recognized, were the eyes of fear and terror.

The young Sarah came to full alertness at that moment with a deep heavy scream, as she stared from the fire, up past Zyriah's face and into the sky, and her little body collapsed into the dewed grass. Zyriah and Evan moved in, Zyriah grabbing the long yellow candle and blowing the last of its fire out, while Evan collected the girl into his arms and turned to face her.

"No more of this," Evan said, his voice swelling into sorrow. "No more of this, Zyriah. You've waited long enough for this. Go and bring him here. I will not let this hurt a little girl or anybody else, do you hear me? Go and bring him."

Zyriah nodded. She walked over to him, holding her candle once again in her left hand and brushing the little Sarah's hair back from her face to see a sleeping child in Evan's arms. His chest rose and descended with the seriousness with what he had said. She nodded again and looked into his eyes which seemed to comfort his shortening breaths.

Zyriah looked at him with a deep intent, only to show her words yet to be spoken were truthfully said. She felt that although so many years had passed, this was the beginning of the journey that was unavoidable. Lenora Spike had seen to that years ago, and Zyriah knew her offspring was meant to return.

"It's time for Joshua to come home," Zyriah agreed.

CHAPTER ONE

The thunderclaps had continued throughout the morning during the rainfall. In his second-floor studio apartment, Joshua struggled to comb his hair and get dressed for the auction through the slight shakes of the weather booming outside the windows. He focused on the bathroom mirror, parting his hair with a forceful brushing, turning his head left and right to make sure his brown locks were well-groomed. He took a small brush he used for his short beard and brushed it evenly to try to control the curling hairs. His mind was focused on his painting and the hopeful sale of it in the next couple hours when a knocking at the door overwhelmed the sound of the thunder.

"JOSHUA SPIKER! ANSWER THIS DOOR RIGHT NOW! I KNOW YOU'RE IN THERE!"

Answering the door was unavoidable, Joshua knew. He took his clothes hanging on a coat hanger on the bathroom's doorknob and carried them to his bed, draping them carefully across the mattress. He adjusted his bath towel so that it was riding around his waist, making sure he was wrapped properly as he went to answer the door. He almost snickered imagining the facial expression of Miss Amos when he opened the door half naked, and as he predicted, her awkward smile did not disappoint when he opened the door.

"Oh, my goodness! I am sorry. I didn't realize you were getting dressed," Miss Amos exclaimed with an embarrassed tone. Her eyes dropped to the floor and began shifting side to side until they rose slowly to meet Joshua's face. Her short, stout frame swayed with nervousness, but Joshua stood confident in that blue towel. He liked how her feeling of being uncomfortable could work to his advantage.

"It's not a problem, Miss Amos. I was just getting ready to go. What can I do for you?" Joshua asked.

"The rent and utilities are due, Joshua. I left you a letter under your door a few days ago. I still do not understand why you will not invest in a telephone," Miss Amos replied.

"Oh, the rent? I almost forgot. I had written you a note for your mailbox, but it has been such a busy week, I think I left it on my desk," Joshua explained, turning to look over at his desk of papers for the note that did not exist and looked back at her blushing face staring at his chest. "I'm auctioning a painting today which will definitely cover my bills. To answer the telephone question, the thing gives me a headache. Plus, I doubt you want me wasting all my money on one phone bill when I need to make sure I keep a roof over my head."

"Mr. Spiker, this is the third time this year the rent has

been late." Miss Amos flipped through her little clipboard of papers for Joshua's bills. Just a few pages of payments needing made, but Joshua knew he was flat broke until this auction hopefully produced some type of income. "The rent of course is $500, the water bill comes to $32.18, and the electric is..." She adjusted her bifocals to look down at the small print of electric bill statement "...$55.13. Now, I do realize that the end of your lease is slowly approaching, but I certainly hope you don't think your security deposit will be used to cover these expenses."

Joshua looked into her eyes as they returned to his with an arrogant smile, then her eyes lowered down scanning over him. He stretched his arms upward to grab the doorframe, the towel lowering an inch. Although he knew teasing a woman that was many years his senior was not appropriate, Joshua also knew moments like this could be a step-by-step effort and necessary.

"Oh, I know it has been a tough month since this auction got rescheduled from last month. I have practically been living on canned soup for the last few days, but that check will be in your little hands this Monday, Miss Amos. I can promise you."

"Monday? Mr. Spiker, I am sorry, but that just won't do right now. I need to get these payments in the mail immediately."

"Today? A Saturday? Now you know that they will not process any checks at the bank until the beginning of the week. Please, just let me drop that money off to you first thing Monday after I cash the check for the painting I am selling today. I am sure that it will be selling for a good amount."

"You have a definite buyer then?" Miss Amos

questioned firmly. "This is something I need your absolute word on."

"Of course!" Joshua affirmed

Of course, Joshua knew he had not had a decent buyer for one of his artworks in months. There was little chance of covering his bills with just this one sale, but he had to keep this apartment. He smiled suggestively at Miss Amos, who was still slightly swaying in an uncomfortable rhythm. She had been wanting him since he signed his lease, and he knew that. It helped him out of a few close eviction calls. He knew that too.

"Well, if you are sure it won't be an issue, I suppose I can wait until Monday morning." Her smile looked like that of an embarrassed girl in her grade school years instead of a grey hair lady in her golden years. "You must promise me though that I'll receive it Monday before lunch. I'll leave the leasing office around noon and drop the mail off at the post office before I eat."

"Not a problem, ma'am. Now I'm running late if I'm to get over to the gallery. I hope you don't mind if I finished getting ready. Thank you so much for stopping by," Joshua said cordially.

He closed the door slowly enough that he was sure Miss Amos saw a rear view as he dropped his towel from his waist to the floor. That was enough, he thought, to make her speechless and not ask for any more money. He had moments like this previously that he felt some shame at this sexual tactic, but today he had to use it to his advantage if he was to guarantee a roof to sleep under.

Joshua looked at the clock and realized it was 10:17 a.m., so he rushed to finish getting dressed. He grabbed the socks and underwear from his dresser drawers, and he quickly put them on as well as the khaki pants and white buttoned shirt he had ironed the night before for this occasion. He slipped on his leather shoes and looked over his attire in the full-length mirror in the studio's corner. He smiled then scanned over his studio, which was neatly cleaned for a single man with everything organized except for his desk, which was covered in stacks of paperwork and unread mail. He went to the apartment's door just as another thunderclap shook the building and the rain beat against the windows with another wave. After grabbing his large black umbrella from where it was leaning in the corner behind the door, he left for the gallery.

Once downstairs, he looked out on Delaware Avenue, shook his umbrella open and crossed the street, noticing a beautiful red sportscar parked and still running against the curb directly across from the building entrance. The car was new, with the rainfall beating against its highly waxed surface. He tried for a moment to see the figure behind the wheel, but he turned back towards the direction of the gallery. He was going to be late.

Joshua reached Austin's Art and Gallery within a few minutes from the apartment building. It was not that long of a walk down Charleston's downtown streets, and even through the pelting rain, his stress level over this auction drove his feet forward even quicker to the gallery doors. He was excited to see how many cars were parked along the street and saw a few well-dressed people walking into the building before he reached the doors himself. West Virginia had its share of amateur artists for an auction like this, but he tried not to discourage himself. He knew it would only take one buyer, and he needed the money.

"Joshua Spiker. Good to see you." Glenna Austin strolled right to him as he walked into the foyer, depositing his umbrella near the hanging coats. "I made sure you have a great wall on the upper level. Go ahead up. I've not had the opportunity to make it up there. There's just so much happening today."

"Upper level? The front room?" Joshua inquired.

"Oh, no. Jack Haines' new piece is in the front room. He did not put it up for sale, but he was willing for the exhibition. Take a moment to look at it. It's wonderful."

"Jack Haines? I'll definitely take a look," Joshua said.

He walked leisurely away not to show his disappointment. The downstairs' showrooms were a better place to get the immediate eyes of prospective buyers. The only decent showroom upstairs was the front room with its large windows for natural lighting. He walked up the wide wooden stairs to the right of the downstairs' main hall, listening to the chatter from the crowd talking about various paintings that had their interest so far. Not once did he hear his name.

Joshua parted through the people in the upstairs hall toward the front room, partially roaming room to room looking at the paintings, but also heavily involved in listening to polite social conversations. Unexpectedly, there was three people looking at the Haines' painting, so he walked up beside them, looking over the work but also jealous of how well the light coming from the windows through the rainstorm lit the piece. It suited the work, a chaotic piece of a burning building. It was a bit abstract, with fiery purple flames shooting from a tall, stoned structure and blue flames coming from three windows in a vertical line. It was well done, and he admitted that to himself. Looking down at the title card to the lower right of the painting, he saw the title was The Tower, then he left the room with a quickened stroll. He knew that although his painting was good, it was not to the level of Jack Haines. Luckily, the Haines' painting was not for sale that day, so Joshua roamed room to room until he found his painting, in an unpopulated room with a cushioned bench sitting in front of it. He looked back down the hall at all the people roaming with liveliness then he looked back into the empty viewing room. He sat down on the cushioned bench and took a deep sigh.

The title card that sat on the lower right of the painting read Joshua Spiker's Untitled. Joshua thought that may have been a drawback. He had a difficult time with naming his artwork, especially this painting. The painting consisted of a lady in a yellow dress standing on large brown stones near a waterfall, five kites flying in the distance over a background of pines. The lady was shown in reverse looking up at the kites, and the yellow dress blowing sideways in the light wind. He looked at the painting, quantifying the brushstrokes as to the time he took to paint them. He loved painting landscapes, enjoying the water and the trees, but so rarely did he include a person in the work. He remembered back to the night he dreamed the image, just a few months ago in the springtime. For him it was never an image of simple beauty. The woman was waiting there, standing on the stone and looking at the kites, but what was she waiting for? A man? Her children? He thought the image left the answer to the viewer, so he left it untitled, thinking the title would have answered the question he did not want to answer. It was a beautiful painting, and Joshua was proud of it.

He would have felt better if there was more of a buzz about the work in the building, people discussing it or wondering who this "Joshua Spiker" was. He had sold other paintings before at the gallery, but he never received any more than a couple hundred dollars. It was just a hope that this would be more of a seller, due to a much larger size and brighter colors than what he normally had painted. He sat on the bench, slightly shifting to hear the talk in the hallway where people still were walking by chatting about random subjects, but he heard no mention of his painting or his name. He started to think about which canned soup was still in the cabinet back in the apartment that he would choose for dinner.

Joshua came early just for that reason, in order to listen to those conversations. He was determined to be hopeful. It was always an exciting idea that once he was downstairs in the main auction room, that a bidding war would start over one of his works. He longed for a great starting bid that led to a bigger bid, then back and forth fighting with bids and money until a grand figure would result in the auctioneer yelling "Sold!"

He had heard it numerous times before, even when he had not entered a painting himself. He had attended several auctions over the past couple years, just to get a better feeling of what types of artwork were selling. It seemed popular trends were even maintained in artwork. Some auctions were more into his types of landscapes and colorful images, while others were more abstract and difficult to conclude the artist's intentions, like the Jack Haines' painting down the hall. That tower painting. Was that the current trend? Artwork showing destruction and agony through color and abstract images?

If that was the current trend, his painting was the exact opposite of that concept. He sighed again, looking at his watch, and realized it was fifteen minutes before noon. He stood from his cushioned bench and slowly walked through the crowd to the downstairs' auction room, hoping to find a decent seat to view the bidding.

Joshua took the back left-corner seat for the best overall viewing, and in that auction room there was a great number of things worth observing. Whether it be the black and white floor tile that extended halfway up the wall or the various artworks of local artists that represented many different West Virginia landmarks, the room was full of elegances and colorful images. The silver and crystal chandelier hung low with hundreds of crystals that acted like prisms, painting the room with rainbows as the track lighting penetrated them. The chairs were heavy maple with green velvet cushions that made him feel comfortable as he eased into his seat. Yet, his ears and eyes were set on the many conversations from those around him, until Glenna Austin walked in from the foyer door across to the center podium and greeted the room.

"Good afternoon, one and all, and welcome to the October Local Artists' Sale Auction here at Austin's Art and Gallery," Glenna announced.

She smiled as the room applauded, while some people dispersed from their conversation groups and into their seats. Joshua noticed several numbered green bidding paddles in many people's hands, and as they sat down, they laid the paddles onto their laps for the future bidding. Glenna's smiled, waiting for the applause to conclude, slightly adjusting her simple but elegant mauve cocktail dress on her shoulders, and began to continue her opening remarks. Joshua shifted slightly, preparing himself in case the opening speech would be longer than he anticipated.

"I'm truly delighted to see so many familiar faces today. Old friends are welcome friends. Plus, I've had the opportunity to meet new people today from out of state, from Kentucky, Ohio, and even Pennsylvania and Maryland who came to join in our festivities today. Please enjoy your experience with us today, as I hope you enjoy the works we are presenting today as much as we have enjoyed presenting the works to you. Now, I would like to introduce to you our auctioneer, who has been with us now for nearly fifteen years. Please welcome, Mr. Oregon Pyles." Glenna announced.

Glenna walked from the podium to a chair in the front row to allow the auctioneer to utilize the podium. Joshua knew Oregon Pyles, a tall, balding lanky man with bright and wide eyes that never needed a microphone due to his bombastic voice. His black and red plaid flannel shirt and blue jeans made Joshua uncomfortable. He did not want the auction to have a look of inexpensiveness. Still, he used that microphone, which made the crystals in the chandelier plus any available eardrum erupt in constant vibration. Joshua noticed his voice even jostled his wavy white hair, or what little hair he had.

"Good *aaaffffttteeeerrrnoooon,* one and all," he blared out, a full toothed grin to hopefully compensate for the loud introduction. "I'm so happy to be here with, y'all. I'm hoping we all have a great day, and y'all are looking forward to a fun afternoon. So, get those paddles out and let's see what we're starting with today."

Out from his shirt pocket he pulled his silver framed

glasses and put them on, then shuffled through the deck of title cards he used to announce the paintings on the auction block. To his right, a screen lit up from a projector was ready to show the represented work to be bid upon. The first was a starry nightscape from an artist named Nuzum which Joshua did not recognize. The work was rather beautiful and simplistic, a multitude of stars over a darkly painted river scene. Joshua heard several sounds of awe once the painting was shown on the screen, and he knew the painting was wanted. A few people began trying to bid before Pyles even opened the bidding, including a man in a brown suit in the second row who shifted in his seat and pulsed his paddle up and down in little movements waiting for Pyles to acknowledge his bid. A lady in a floral print in the fifth row was pulsing her paddle as well, slightly shifting in her seat waiting for the bidding to commence. Joshua noticed her bright red hair swaying as she rocked back and forth.

"Our first piece today is entitled The Starbridge by Shirley Nuzum. Nuzum, a native to Phillipi, West Virginia, has entered this as her first entry into our local talent auction," Pyles said, preparing for his opening bid. "Do I have a bid for…one hundred?"

Immediately, the lady in the floral print raised her paddle with a fully up stretched arm for an opening bid for one hundred dollars. The man in the brown suit followed, offering a bid for one hundred fifty almost immediately. Joshua smiled as the bidding exchange began, two hundred to three hundred to three hundred fifty to three hundred seventy-five dollars. Finally, the lady in the floral print bid four hundred, nodding her head as she lowered her paddle, confident it was her final bid.

"That's four hundred dollars. Going once. Going twice. Sold!"

Pyles pounded a maple wood gavel onto the corner of his podium. "To the lady in the lovely pink and purple floral dress. Thank ya kindly Mrs. Goff. Pleasure to see you." A little round of applause for the first buyer emerged, which seemed to be a custom at these auctions. Joshua just sat and observed quietly, remembering he had not asked for the order to the auction so he was unaware when his painting would come onto the auction block.

Joshua looked around at the random faces until in the back center of the room, he saw a tall blond woman staring at him. She smiled and refocused on the auctioneer, peeking her eyes quickly to Joshua's gaze then returning her stare to the front of the room. She did stand out to him, the only lady dressed in bright red, which he admitted to himself looked very striking on her. Yet, with all the faces in the room, she seemed to stand out more. He thought she had too much class for this room, which he interpreted as she was from out of town, maybe from Pittsburgh or Philadelphia. He knew she was overdressed for the occasion, perhaps even intentionally overdressed.

The auction seemed to go rather quickly, with satisfying bids coming for each work in very little time. The bids were countered once or twice a painting it seemed like, but overall, the paintings were not being purchased for nearly the amount he needed for his bills. The lowest bid he heard was a painting sold for seventy-five dollars, and he hoped his painting would go for far more than that. He sat patiently, and as the called numbers for the artwork reached into the twenties, he wondered when or even if his painting was going to ever be called. Finally, upon reaching the call number twenty-one, he saw a familiar image emerge on the projector screen.

"Ladies and gentlemen, we now have entry number twenty-one, an untitled piece by the local artist Joshua Spiker." Pyles looked up from his auction card to a relatively quiet room. Joshua noticed the lady with the red hair turning quickly around looking for something or someone. Her eyes met Joshua's briefly, and she squinted for a better view before facing forward once again. Oregon Pyles shifted his stance slightly for his opening bid amount. "Let's start the bidding at fifty dollars."

Joshua gasped. Only fifty bucks? He needed way more than that. He looked quickly around the room, just as the same man in the brown suit he noticed at the beginning of the auction raised his paddle, bidding fifty dollars.

"I have fifty. Do I hear one hundred?"

A man raised his paddle from the back corner of the room. Joshua's eyes shifted back and forth like watching a tennis match, from auctioneer to bidders as the bids steadily increased. His hopes made his blood churn. He began quietly clapping his hands together in anticipation, somehow thinking that the gesture would raise the bidding. He knew the biddings needed to increase, and his heart pulsed more urgently from bid to bid. Finally, the bidding seemed to stop at three hundred seventy-five dollars, the bid belonging to the man in the brown suit. The room was quiet. Pyles, looking around for raised paddles and not seeing one, began his final calls.

"I have a bid of three hundred seventy-five dollars. Going once. Going twice."

Joshua grew instantly disappointed and scanned the room. Surely, he could get a higher bid than that. More importantly, he knew he needed a higher bid than that. He wanted Pyles to not rush the bidding and let the people have more time to think. More time meant more money, he thought. His hands increased in sweat, which he stopped his steady clapping for a wringing of his palms and fingers, wiping them on his pants legs. He was not going to pay those bills with that bid. He thought quickly of the amounts Miss Amos had given him in his doorway. He needed more.

"I bid five hundred ninety-one dollars and fifty-four cents," a voice called out.

His breathing momentarily stopped, wondering if he had heard that correctly. Even with the turning of those around him to see the bidder, Joshua was frozen momentarily. He forced a quick breath and took a few quick blinks, realizing his focus had dried his eyes with all of the staring. He looked back at the rear of the room, seeing that same woman in the red dress lowering her paddle she had raised during her bid.

He could not understand it. He was happy for the bid amount. He was more than happy. The bid amount, however, was strange. Apparently, he was not the only person in the room with those feelings. Numerous people continued turning and shifting in their green velvet seats to see the face of the woman, giving her a questioning glare.

The woman with the red hair who had purchased the first painting turned the fastest Joshua noticed. Her face was fiery with a still glare, looking back at the woman who just purchased Joshua's work. The lady rose from her seat, nodding politely to Pyles, and left the room.

Joshua looked back at the woman in the rear of the room that just made the purchase. She stood firm with a confident expression looking at Pyles, who himself was looking as if he had misunderstood the bid.

"Ma'am, I'm sorry. Can you repeat that please?" Pyles asked.

"Certainly. I would like to bid five hundred ninety-one dollars and fifty-four cents," the woman responded with a determined tone.

Joshua joined the rest of the people in the room from looking at the woman repeating her bid back to Pyles, scrawling the amount on a small piece of paper. He had adjusted his glasses while writing, then pushed the glasses back higher on his nose to face the audience. He took a quiet sigh, smiled, and finalized the bidding.

"I have a bid of," Pyles began reading the total amount from the small piece of paper, "five hundred ninety-one dollars and fifty-four cents. Going once."

Joshua looked around the room, seeing people whispering to one another about how unusual the bid was. Part of him even forgot to hope for a higher bid, merely due to the oddity of the bid total. He looked back to the blond woman in the red dress. Her eyes were focused upon Pyles, and she smiled slightly. Joshua wondered if she knew he was watching her.

"Going twice."

Joshua's eyes were focused on her now even more, and internally he felt an odd wave he could only define as relief. It was a moment, and inside Joshua felt that the situation had become something for him to remember. Although he could not understand why the situation felt more important than just having his bills paid, Joshua knew there was more to it. He could feel it.

Through the thoughts in his mind, the mental control

forcing him to remain looking at the woman was staying strong. Her eyes quickly looked over to Joshua, and with that same slight smile she had given previously, she nodded. Joshua knew she knew that her purchase was his artwork. She was now the purchaser, and more importantly, he knew his bills were paid.

"Sold."

CHAPTER
TWO

Joshua took a long breath and closed his eyes, happy with relief his apartment bills had been paid, but that purchase price of his painting did not make sense to him. Every auction he had ever attended always had bids for even dollar amounts, so the fact his purchased price was including quarters and pennies confused him. Still, the issue of being in debt to Miss Amos was no longer a problem, so he sat in his back row seat with a high level of satisfaction.

"Joshua?"

Joshua felt a gentle hand on his shoulder giving him a little shake, and he opened his eyes and realized it was Glenna standing behind him along with the blonde woman in the red dress. He smiled and stood up facing them, still with an overwhelming sense of relief but also curiosity. He extended his hand to Glenna and finally to his mysterious bidder.

"Thank you both, and especially you for that wonderful bid. I really do appreciate it," Joshua said with a nervous strain of the vocal cords. The excitement was welling up inside.

Glenna said, "Oh yes, that bid will definitely be talked about for some time to come. Joshua, Miss Flint asked if I would introduce her to you. Joshua Spiker, this is Zyriah Flint."

Joshua shook her hand gently, but her grip was surprisingly strong. Her dress was very lovely, but he immediately noticed a diamond and ruby ring along with her matching droplet earrings. Obviously, she was a woman of money, but he observed no wedding ring. He had a habit of collecting clues to conclude certain facts about people, but this woman was certainly a different sort compared to people he had met over the years at these affairs.

Although she was certainly pleasant, her eyes had more behind them that Joshua recognized as type of deliberate intent. Even the soft flow of blond hair that occasionally blocked her view did not prevent her eyes from making Joshua feel there was some intent behind them. Still, he remained happy about the painting being purchased.

"You did a fine job with your piece Mr. Spiker," Zyriah remarked. "It certainly shows you have much potential in you. It's certainly worth noting."

"Joshua, please," Joshua requested, smiling a prideful grin from her praise. "Hearing I have potential truly means a lot to me."

"Joshua, excuse me. I do have a tendency of being a bit formal in speaking," Zyriah smiled. "I asked Glenna here to introduce me to perhaps get the opportunity to talk to you for a few minutes."

"Oh, I'm sure that won't be a problem," Glenna

interjected. "I'm sure Joshua will be happy to, especially after that fine bid on his painting."

"Sure," Joshua said. "I wouldn't mind." He extended his hand to the neighboring chair. "Would this be ok?"

"Actually, I had a little business still with Glenna over this sale. I was hoping we could talk outside. Possibly that little coffee shop I saw on the corner?"

"McClenndon's? Oh, I don't turn down a good cup of coffee," Joshua laughed. "Should I wait here?"

"It shouldn't take any more than fifteen minutes to get this payment settled, wouldn't you think, Glenna?" Zyriah looked back to Glenna, smiling with an eager politeness.

"Oh, ten minutes maximum I'm sure. Joshua, you sit here, and I'll take care of this little matter of money with Miss Flint in my office. She can meet you back here. Give us just a few minutes," Glenna instructed.

Joshua retook his seat as the two women quickly left the auction room, and he began to wonder. It was not uncommon to meet buyers after the auctions at these events, but this was the first time a buyer had asked him for a personal meeting immediately after the purchase. He thought it was possibly about questions concerning this particular painting and to even request another painting if she liked the style.

In the back of his mind, he was seriously hoping this was not her attempt at some type of romantic opportunity. It was an odd thought, he admitted, but there was some strange tone to how she had used the word potential. He thought about it only for a few moments and disregarded the romantic motive.

He watched the remaining people exit the room until he was the only one remaining, but within a few minutes, both

Glenna and Zyriah Flint entered the room. Joshua noticed Glenna's smile was even broader than it was just minutes ago. The sale obviously went well, but he immediately noticed a white envelope in Glenna's hand. Just as his eyes focused on it, she approached him, raising and holding the envelope's top corners with her fingertips. The envelope had his full name written on it.

"Mr. Spiker, I do believe this is for you," Glenna said as she handed him the envelope. "Miss Flint here has already paid our auction fees as well as delivery fees, so this bid amount is completely for you."

"Really?" Joshua smiled. Normally, Glenna charged just a small fee for the auctioneer's fee, but Joshua had usually talked her out of the fee payment. "Thank you so much, I really do appreciate it." He felt the coins inside the envelope with his fingers. "Cash?"

"Cash isn't a problem is it?" Zyriah asked.

"Cash? Oh, I like cash," Joshua snickered in a sly giggle. "Saves me a trip to the bank."

Zyriah laughed. "I figured as much. It's the weekend, and a little cash in the pocket is always nice to have."

"Oh yeah, absolutely," Joshua said as he folded the envelope and put it in his front pocket.

"Well, don't let me interrupt you too, but I do need to talk to the auctioneer about some business matters. If you will excuse me," Glenna said politely as she excused herself and left the room.

"Well now, how does that coffee sound?" Zyriah asked.

"Sounds great actually. I do have to question first. Why the meeting?" Joshua questioned. "I'm sorry, but it does feel a bit out of the ordinary."

"I have some information that I need to share with

you," Zyriah said, informing Joshua of a new type of intent.

"Information? What kind of information?" Joshua was immediately puzzled.

Joshua watched Zyriah's chin stick out in confidence as her right eyebrow perked upwards. Something had told him this was not just about his artwork. It took only moments to confirm his thinking. Her demeanor remained pleasing, so he felt comfortable even though he had just met her minutes ago. Part of him was intrigued by the mysterious air of the situation. The two began walking to exit the gallery.

"I need to discuss some financial matters concerning your mother," Zyriah explained.

"My mother? My mother died when I was eight, and my foster dad took care of me the rest of the time. He passed away a couple years ago, but the lawyer said all their bills were taken care of now," Joshua remarked.

"Not your foster mother, Joshua," Zyriah explained further.

Joshua, who had been steadily walking towards the front door and had just grabbed his umbrella, now had stopped all movement and looked into Zyriah's eyes. She was firm, professional, and unwavering in her delivery of the revelation.

It was shocking to even think of the words, so he stood there quiet and waited for the stranger who just put all that money into his pocket to finally state her intentions. When the answer did not come immediately, Joshua finally felt forced into a question.

"I don't know anything about the woman who gave birth to me. Now, you're saying to me you have information about her," Joshua, feeling slightly frustrated, said with conviction. "Who are you that you would have any information about her?"

Zyriah paused only for a moment to make eye contact with Joshua, and he felt the determination and the formal tone of her response.

"I'm the executrix of her estate, Joshua. Your biological mother's estate."

Joshua watched Zyriah walk out the gallery's front doors and realized the rain had stopped, allowing sunbeams to trace along High Street as he quickly followed. Suddenly, all the common questions a child would ask about his biological parents that he had never met had completely escaped him. He had never known much information other than his parents had died around the time of his birth, and he had been immediately placed in the foster system. His foster father, Jim Groves, had said only that he was not born in Charleston. Melissa Groves, his foster mother, never mentioned much of anything that was of importance. He remembered only her love for reading and family meals. However, she did tell Joshua that he had been born in the north central part of the state just below the Pennsylvania border. He always remembered the name of the town was Wilcox.

"So how did you know my mother?" Joshua asked, questioning this stranger's new revelation.

"Let's just sit down here and I'll tell you more," Zyriah answered as they crossed the street in the direction of McClenndon's café. "I almost forgot. I need to put change in the meter."

Joshua recognized the vehicle in a quick instant. It was the same red car parked across the street from his apartment when he left for the auction just a few short hours ago. He watched Zyriah remove change from her small satin red purse and put it in the parking meter, close her purse, and smile back at Joshua. He admitted to himself that she did have good taste in cars. He watched as she walked towards the café's front door with a steady confidence, not admiring the remodeled building, the red and white signs, and sidewalk sandwich board advertising the business. He thought this was not her first visit or first cup of coffee at this coffeeshop. His mind went back to her car that he remembered and admired.

"Wasn't your car parked down on Delaware Avenue this morning?" Joshua asked.

"This place looks quaint. I'm in desperate need for some ice water." Zyriah said, pushing open McClenndon's front door and walked inside, ignoring Joshua's question about the car. Joshua quickly followed her in. The front window table was free, so the two sat across from each other, Joshua quickly taking a brief overlook at Zyriah, and they both waited for a waitress. The morning had been almost a continual morning of surprises, and Joshua felt unprepared for any more surprises he was sure would come.

Netta came to see what they wanted, a slender older woman with curly short brown hair and a small-printed plaid dress. Joshua knew her well from the previous times he had been a customer, but she was so focused on work that he never got to know her as a person. If it was not for a little silver nametag saying "Netta" he probably would not have known her name. After Netta took their order, Joshua's coffee with amaretto and Zyriah's water with lemon, Joshua and his painting's owner began to converse.

The wait was filled with silence, Joshua looking out the window at the car and admiring its high-gloss finish only to occasionally stare back at Zyriah, who sat properly with hands clasped and observing the café's decorations, hanging plants, and chalkboard sales sign. Her eyes did not appear to look with the interest of a new visitor to the establishment. She had a look of familiarity, with a slight smile in between her glances as if she was remembering the location and recalling memories within its walls. Netta brought their beverages, which they both took a large drink from. His last question about her statement concerning his biological mother was still unanswered. He wanted the answer.

"So, how did you know my mother?" Joshua inquired.

"Your mother was a good friend. Had been for years. She was one smart lady. Always wanting to know more things and do more things. Pretty difficult to get her to stay still long enough for a talk sometimes, but she always was a hard worker. She had her own ideas of success and what it would take to achieve it," Zyriah revealed.

"What did she like to do?" Joshua wondered.

"Oh, many things," Zyriah said smiling, taking a sip of her water and clearing her throat. "She collected a lot of little antiques and things from around the area. She always said she was on the hunt for good conversation pieces, so if she found something with a story behind it, she would probably buy it. She was so busy with work usually, but she made the time to go 'explore shopping' as she called it."

"What did she do for a living?" Joshua inquired.

"Job? She was a therapist. Worked with all sorts of people. She worked a lot with young people and their depression mainly. She would never specifically talk about patients, but she did mention that it was a lot of children, families, and couple's counseling. She did it for years," Zyriah responded.

Joshua listened and drank his coffee, which helped his alertness and questioning. All these general questions about her interests and employment, he remembered there was one question more than any he wanted answered. He took a deep breath.

"What was her name?" Joshua asked with a deep stare.

"Lenora. Named after her grandmother she said. Lenora Louise Spiker," Zyriah revealed.

"And my father?" Joshua questioned, wanting to know more.

"I barely knew him personally. He was always out of town working, and your mother went to spent time with him on occasion. I was never that close to him," Zyriah explained.

"No. I meant what was his name?" Joshua asked, feeling that her slightly shifting position in her chair was showing a level of uncomfortability with questions about his father.

"Elijah," Zyriah responded. "Elijah Burrows. There had been a good deal of love between them once. Both were really involved in their careers I guess you could say, so they never officially married."

"Was he a therapist too?" Joshua asked but felt it was a definite possibility.

"Oh no. Elijah was investor and did a good deal of public motivational speaking. He worked with small companies and investor's wanting to buy stock and build businesses. That was why he traveled so much. He was from Wilcox, though, just like your mother," Zyriah explained.

"So, they grew up together?" Joshua continued questioning.

"No. They both just lived in the same town." Joshua watched as Zyriah sipped her water again, this time consuming more than before. He could see the unease in her, so it was no surprise to him when she changed the conversation's topic. She did look like there was urgency. "Joshua, I need to talk to you about why I'm here."

"There's more than the auction?" Joshua wondered.

"There is much more. That was just a clever way to get the opportunity to talk to you. I wanted to talk to you about your inheritance," Zyriah explained.

"My inheritance? She left me something?" Joshua asked with immediate excitement.

"Oh, yes yes yes. I've been holding onto this property since her passing. There are conditions in her will that we need to discuss," Zyriah continued to explain.

"Conditions, huh? I figured there would be a catch of some sort.," Joshua said with disappointment. His right eyebrow began to rise with skepticism.

"Catch?" Zyriah laughed. "There's no real catch. Your mother just stated that she wanted you to receive your inheritance on your twenty-first birthday."

"Twenty-one? I'm only nineteen. I've got a little ways to go." Joshua said, with his excitement beginning to fizzle out.

"That's part of the reason why I wanted to discuss this with you. I wanted to take the opportunity to meet you and invite you to Wilcox to talk about these assets. I have a feeling this could possibly be resolved earlier if you're willing to help me," Zyriah detailed.

"What kind of help are we talking about here?" Joshua

asked with a uncomfortable quality in his tone that matched his skeptical squint of his eyes.

"Well, we need to look at all the assets, and you can make a decision about what you want done with them. Perhaps, we can go to your mother's attorney and get this will taken care of at an earlier date," Zyriah suggested.

"Well, what kind of assets are we talking about?" Joshua did not want to sound greedy, but he finally had to ask the question. "Is it something sizeable that you think I would need to be concerned with?"

"I'll be happy to show you all your assets, if you are willing to come to Wilcox to see them."

Joshua shifted in his seat. "Ok, this whole thing is sounding stranger and stranger to me. I just met you, and you tell me you know my biological mother and father. Now, you're expecting me to drop everything and go to some town that I've never been to with a woman I've never met. Why should I?"

"You're right. The situation is odd and it will sound more and more odd as we go. In the end, it will be worth it to you. I can see your interest. I can see it in your eyes," Zyriah pointed out.

"And how do you know this? Are you psychic or something?" Joshua asked with a snicker. He did not like the conditions of this deal. He felt there was something else about Zyriah though. His thoughts did not dismiss the offers being made. He just did not like the approach.

Zyriah pulled out a small piece of paper and a pen from her purse and began writing. Across the table, he could see that she was writing words and numbers, but he could not make out what it said. She looked up at him twice with a slight curl of a smile as she wrote, quickly returning her focus to what she was jotting on that paper. She finished her writing, and pushed the paper towards him, and his eyes got large when he read it:

Rent-$500
Water-$32.18
Electric $55.13
Total 587.31

"Wait, what is this? Did you go ask my landlord about how much I owed?" Joshua questioned with a demanding tone. It was becoming more uncomfortable conversing with her, and if it was not for the fact she had paid his bills, he would have left. He looked back at the paper and read over the words and numbers briefly and returned his stare in Zyriah's eyes.

"Absolutely not," Zyriah chuckled. "You asked if I was psychic, and I answered your question."

Joshua looked over the paper again with his bill totals on it. He thought she had to have gone and asked Miss Amos about how much he owed her, but he quickly realized there was a mathematical error and began laughing. He watched as Zyriah finished her water, and she stood to leave. She had a confident air about her, in her red dress that looked suddenly inappropriate for a small corner coffee shop. Joshua thought of how the entire morning she seemed to be in control of the situation, and perhaps even him. He had found a gleaming error in her math, and he could not wait to point it out.

"Your bid this morning was five hundred ninety-one dollars and fifty-four cents though, Miss Flint. Your total written here is five hundred eighty-seven dollars and thirty-one cents. That leaves you a balance of…lemme see here,"

Joshua said, subtracting the bill total from the auction money in his head. He felt the confidence in how Zyriah presented herself, but he wanted to make clear he was not an easy mark to be manipulated. At that moment, he wished he was faster with math.

"Four dollars and twenty-three cents," Netta exclaimed, announcing the total of his order while placing the order ticket with a register slip stapled to it in front of Joshua. He had been so focused on doing the math in his head, Joshua had not even seen Netta approach.

"Huh? I'm sorry?" Joshua lost his concentration and looked at the waitress, realizing the coffee shop total matched the amount he had just subtracted in his mind.

"That's your total, sir. Cash or credit?" Netta asked.

"He's got the cash, Miss." Zyriah giggled. "Joshua, I'll wait for you outside."

Joshua took out the envelope of auction money, gave the waitress a ten-dollar bill, and waited for his change. His thought of how was all this possible was becoming more unclear. Zyriah could have gotten the total of his bills from Miss Amos, but there was no chance that she would know what he would order from the coffee shop. His thought that this woman was a psychic or at least trying her best to prove it, but the situation along with all the information so far about his parents was overwhelming him. All he knew for certain was that he needed to know more. Once Netta brought back the change, he went out the door to see Zyriah standing confidently against her red car.

"How did you do that? How did you come up with that auction bid?" Joshua inquired with a inquisitive stare.

"There's a lot of answers that I'll need to give to a lot of questions, Mr. Spiker. How about we take this baby over to your apartment and talk a little more?" Zyriah offered with a grin.

"What makes you think I'm getting into your car with you?" Joshua immediately questioned.

"My car?" Zyriah laughed. "It's not my car, Joshua. It's yours."

Joshua unzipped his luggage on his bed and began searching through his dresser drawers and closet for clothing that would get him through a few days. He thought of the craziness of just leaving so quickly, but his mind continued to focus on that automobile. While Zyriah had driven him back to his apartment, he looked over the black leather interior and loved the sound system. He realized he could not even remember the song that was playing or even if Zyriah had spoken to him during the drive. He had never owned his own car, and this was too perfect of an opportunity for him to have his first. At least, that was his hope.

"So how many days do you think this will take?" Joshua asked.

"Oh, I have no idea. That car has a nice large trunk so don't be afraid to pack heavy," Zyriah explained, looking around his apartment with her hands clasped behind her. Joshua noticed her deliberate attempt not to touch anything and just look around the room observing. In truth, there was not much to steal, and he knew it.

"Anything in particular you think I'll need?" Joshua wondered.

"Oh, I would probably take a nice outfit for the lawyer meeting. It is October, so you never know how warm or cold the days will be. I would just take a little of everything, including this," Zyriah suggested with a sound of instance in what she was looking upon.

Joshua paused to see what Zyriah was referring to and realized she was looking at a small painting he had placed over his cluttered desk. He had painted that piece last winter, thinking that the warmth of the painting would bring him a better feeling than the chilly weather that was outside with a season of ice and snowfall. He walked over to look at the painting with Zyriah.

"Why take this?" Joshua asked, reaching to take it from its place on the wall.

"It's lovely. A nice sunset. A pretty tree-lined hill. It's very beautiful. I like artwork that leans more to the abstract sometimes," Zyriah explained.

Joshua looked at his work, recognizing the geometric shapes of half circles and diamonds used for the sun itself. It was, in his opinion, a bit elementary. He continued that style in lines and angles through the trees, the hilltop fields, and even in the scattered clouds. Overall, it was not his best, but once he had that image in his mind that cold January day he decided to paint it, he was determined to get it achieved in the style he envisioned it.

"It's not a style I normally paint, but overall, I thought it was effective for the work," Joshua said.

"And the inspiration?" Zyriah asked smiling. Joshua could feel there was an intention in her tone.

"Wishing the heat would stay on," Joshua laughed. "I painted that in January, and I wasn't sure if I had enough money to keep the electric up."

Zyriah laughed, stepping in closer, and Joshua noticed she had a particular focus on that sun. Basic coloring, he thought, of golds, oranges, and reds and he thought it could have been a little darker in its hues. He watched her continue to smile and examine. He wondered what she saw in it. She seemed to have a keen interest in something on that canvas, and he failed to realize what she was seeing.

"It's really not that great of a painting. Why take it?" Joshua asked, setting the painting on his desk.

"Oh, I think it's a fine piece. So, it wasn't inspired by any specific location?" Zyriah asked, and Joshua felt the oddity of the question. He began focusing on the oddity in her and her random questions and way of thinking. Perhaps this is just her way of communicating, he thought. He just could not see where the conversation was leading.

There was a knock at the door. Joshua reached for the knob and opened it to find Miss Amos, smiling and politely gesturing with opening hands in a welcoming expression. Joshua was a little disheartened that she was coming for her bill money so quickly.

"Oh, Mr. Spiker. I heard the painting sold rather well today. Congratulations!" Miss Amos said, smiling widely.

"How did you..?" Joshua tried asking, but he stopped as Miss Amos interrupted.

"Oh, Glenna Austin is a member of my church. I just called the gallery asking her a question about Sunday service, so I had to ask her about the auction. She said the bid was a rather odd one."

"That odd bidder was me," Zyriah chuckled, overlooking Joshua's shoulder.

"Oh, I'm sorry. Should I do introductions?" Joshua said smiling, determined to prove Zyriah had met Miss Amos earlier to find out his bill amounts.

"Patty Amos, and it's a pleasure to meet you. I'm sure Joshua here has been very excited since your exceptional bid amount," Miss Amos said with politeness as the two women shook hands.

"Oh, I think it made his day to be honest," Zyriah laughed. "I'm Zyriah Flint."

"Pleasure to meet you," Miss Amos nodded and looked back to Joshua. "Glenna also happened to mention that the payment was made in…."

Joshua reached into his pocket, grabbing the envelope, and placed it in Miss Amos' hand. "Here, before you even ask. It's all there. You don't have to count it."

"Count it?" Miss Amos laughed with a touch of sarcasm. "Now you know I would never do such a thing."

"You'll have to excuse us, Miss Amos. We have some important things to discuss," Joshua said, already closing the door.

"Well, it was a pleasure to meet…" Miss Amos tried to finish her statement, but Joshua closed the door.

"Fine. She didn't know you. So how did you know how much I owed?" Joshua questioned, disappointed that his attempt to debunk the situation had failed.

"You asked that question before, and I thought I answered it," Zyriah responded.

"What are you trying to tell me here?" Joshua said with a puzzled tone. "You're really psychic?"

"To be honest, I never liked the word," Zyriah said, walking over to the bed and looking at the clothing he had already placed in his luggage. Joshua continued to grab random clothing from his closet, not really paying much attention to his selections, then grabbed a small black bag from the bottom of his closet. He carried the bag and walked into the bathroom to collect his toiletries.

"So, what would you call it then?" Joshua questioned

loudly, placing his bathroom items in his bag. He began thinking of the car. He struggled to find a reason to go through with this plan, but the car made it simpler. He needed the car.

"I'd call it a mental gift that doesn't need a label," Zyriah defined.

"A mental gift?" Joshua said, emerging with a full toiletry bag and placing it the corner of one of his open suitcases. "Bunch of trickery I call it."

"Trickery?" Zyriah asked with a smiling smirk.

"C'mon there's no such thing as psychic ability. You can't see the past, and you can't tell the future. Are you also going to try and tell me my biological mom was into this stuff? Or even better, was she psychic too?" Joshua questioned with a sarcastic tone.

"I don't think you're ready for this answer," Zyriah said, which Joshua immediately interpreted the answer as affirmative. "Things like this take a little time to explain. It's very common for these things to occur in people, and it's even possible for the gift to run in family trees."

"Family trees?" Joshua asked, zipping the last of his suitcases closed and walked toward the front door. He watched as Zyriah carefully took the painting of the sunset from where Joshua placed it on his desk. "I hate to disappoint you, my new friend, but I can tell you now that I have never and I doubt will ever have any type of psychic ability. Just because my family tree has some craziness to it, it does not mean I'm the nut on the branch waiting to fall."

Zyriah laughed.

"What's so funny?" Joshua asked with a skeptical arrogance. It seemed like a strange battle of wills between the two of them, and he was determined to win. Still, he was not completely sure he could succeed.

Zyriah turned the painting facing him. He looked at his work and looked back at her with a questioning expression. He was not ready her response, but his ears waited to hear it.

"I know where this location is, Joshua," Zyriah revealed.

CHAPTER
THREE

J oshua sat in the car, looking through the passenger window at October's foliage colors of reds, oranges, and yellows while thinking of a long list of questions. Zyriah had just called him something he never considered himself, a psychic. It was true that she did not use the word directly to describe him, but he thought her saying that his sun painting was a painting of an actual location he had never seen made him assume what she was implying. Personally, he never had much of a belief system about anything. He thought much of it was due to his never being officially adopted as a child. He had many dreams of a perfect family and a happy life, but no tree seemed to bear fruit that was sweet enough for his taste.

He knew the drive would last a couple hours, according to the information Zyriah provided initially once they got into the vehicle. The drive was supposed to be a "straight shot" according to her description, but Interstate 79 was anything but a linear travel road. It curved, rose, and dipped repeatedly through valleys and hillsides of West Virginia, and although he had enjoyed the drive before on other trips he had taken in his youth, his mind was transfixed upon more serious matters. However, when he began conversing, he decided to take a more general approach to find out more information about his chauffer.

"So, what is it that you do for a living?" he asked, turning his head to Zyriah, whose eyes were focused on the twisting path of the road.

"I'm a freelance journalist, novelist, and researcher. I taught secondary education for a number of years, but once the writing began paying off, I decided to focus on what I enjoyed," Zyriah explained

"And what is it that you enjoy?" Joshua continued to question. He admitted to himself he did like communicating with creative people like authors and artists. Still, he wanted more information.

"People," Zyriah smiled, turning quickly to see Joshua's face then back to watching her driving. "I was determined growing up that I was going to find a job that would help people. It was just a question of how to do that."

"What do you normally write about? Anything in particular?" Joshua wondered.

"Psychic abilities and phenomenon," Zyriah responded.

"I thought you didn't like the word 'psychic'," Joshua said with a smug tone, thinking once again he caught Zyriah in a falsehood.

"Well, when I get a question like that, sometimes it's easier to explain things in terms people are more familiar with," Zyriah expounded.

"So, what do you do exactly," Joshua snickered. "See ghosts?"

Zyriah laughed. "I would describe myself as a channeled

automatic writer with short-term retrocognition."

"And you think those terms I'd be more familiar with?" Joshua jested.

"Well, retrocognition refers to seeing the past, so short-term would be things that happened recently in a person's past."

"Short term? Well, how useful would that be then?" Joshua asked cynically.

"Well," Zyriah giggled, "it's helped me find my car keys from time to time."

"I don't really see the joke," Joshua said in a deflated tone. He had a tendency of getting frustrated by people that would not discuss things in a serious manner.

"You don't?" Zyriah said, taking a quick glance at Joshua which did not make him feel any more at ease.

"I mean I don't really believe in all this. I don't see how anybody could do anything like seeing the past or seeing the future. Only seeing short term to what just happened to somebody doesn't really sound that exceptional," Joshua admitted.

"It just depends on the circumstance. Maybe the automatic writing will sound more interesting," Zyriah offered to explain.

"Ok, what's that?" Joshua asked, willing to give her the opportunity to persuade him.

Zyriah took a deep breath, and he watched her shift slightly in the driver's seat before she provided the answer. "I let the dead use my hand to write."

"Ah ha! You are telling me you see ghosts then," Joshua said triumphantly.

"I never said that. I suppose you could say that when that time comes, I blank my mind and let my hand, holding a pen or pencil, begin writing whatever it wanted," Zyriah said explaining the process.

"Blank your mind?" Joshua questioned. The terminology of the conversation was confusing to him.

"It's a technique to clear your mind of thoughts and feelings. The reason why this type of writing is controlled is that I focus on one individual rather than leaving myself open to anybody and anything," Zyriah attempted to define.

"Why is that important?" Joshua asked for more information.

"It's dangerous to leave your mind completely clear. You never know who or what may enter it," Zyriah explained.

"Are we talking possession here?" Joshua questioned, remembering horror films he had seen in the past. His cynical side touched his questions with a deliberate sarcasm.

"It's just a way of protecting yourself. The dangers of doing anything involving any ability like this is being too open for anything. The most important thing is to learn control," Zyriah instructed.

Joshua looked back out the passenger window as they crossed a bridge, looking down at the river flowing underneath them until they quickly passed over it. He was initially considering having more of an open mind to the possibility of these abilities, but now he was more confused than curious. Then, he thought of a good way to perhaps understand exactly how Zyriah's mind worked.

"So, the auction bid then. How did you come up with the total?" Joshua asked, beginning a line of questioning.

"Oh," Zyriah laughed. "That took a little bit of doing."

"I can imagine, but I really want to know how you did that. It could really help me figure this whole thing out," Joshua said, attempting to discover the truth.

"Well, I was sitting outside in the car when you were getting ready to leave for the auction. I guess you can say I hijacked your landlord's memories this morning," Zyriah admitted.

"Hijacked?" Joshua exclaimed, feeling a strange sense of violation.

"Just a figure of speech. I just focused on her looking through your bill totals before she decided to go and visit you to ask where your money was. Wasn't much to it," Zyriah explained with conviction.

"So, you don't need to be in the room with the person in order to do this?" Joshua inquired.

"For me? No. I've never had much of an issue as long as the person was in a relative vicinity to me. For some people with retrocognition, they need to be much closer. When I first realized I could do it, I definitely needed the person to be closer to me. After all the years of practice, I suppose I got better at it," Zyriah explained.

Joshua thought for a moment and realized something was not making as much sense. Perhaps, she did have this ability and she did "hijack" Miss Amos and her dwelling over the money, but it did not explain how she knew the other part of the bid total, which he was quick to point out. He felt as if he had uncovered her deception. Part of him enjoyed a good mystery, and he hoped to be successful in solving what was occurring.

"Wait, wait, wait. You said you saw things in recent past," Joshua reminded.

"That's what I said," Zyriah agreed.

"So, it could be a few minutes or maybe an hour?" Joshua asked, feeling more like a detective as he proceeded.

"Oh no. It can even go back sometimes a few days or almost a week," Zyriah explained.

"That's the past you're seeing, and not the future though," Joshua said, seeking confirmation.

"Yes?" Zyriah looked at him quickly with a questioning expression. "What's your point here?"

"I didn't order the coffee and muffin at McClenndon's until after the auction was over. The bid amount included the money for that coffee and muffin. If you only see the past, then how did you see the future?" Joshua asked confidently. He began feeling like the mystery was beginning to be clearer.

"Oh, I didn't need to see the future for that," Zyriah explained.

"Huh? How do you figure?" Joshua asked, unable to see why it was not necessary.

"You're a creature of habit, Joshua. You got that same cup of coffee and muffin two times in the last week. Both times the waitress told you it was four dollars and twenty-three cents."

Joshua grew silent.

"So," Zyriah smiled. "What other tests you have for me?"

The interstate's road signs to Wilcox were sparse. Slowly, the signs began counting down the miles to the Wilcox exit as they passed one sign after another. Joshua did not bother to further test his driver and focused more on the foliage outside the window. Occasionally, he would look around the car admiring it, reminding himself that the vehicle belonged to him, but part of him still questioned it. The entire trip was a risk, and he knew that. Desperation for money had become a driving force in his actions, and his hopes remained high. What he did question about his driver had increasing became disproven, so he quieted himself to avoid conflict. Finally, looking out at the trees, he saw the sign that said, "Wilcox Next Right."

The road curved slightly right as well, and once they were off the interstate, the traveling was rather bucolic, he thought. Country homes, large maples, the occasional flowing creeks and streams enveloped the picturesque scene, and he saw a particular beauty to it all. The houses seemed to be more on the upscale financial end of things, with well-kept flowerbeds and freshly painted sides and trims. The occasional resident working on their lawns looked clean and freshly dressed. There was a level of pride in their dwellings, and Joshua liked the wholesomeness of the view.

"I am getting rather hungry," Zyriah said, interrupting his thoughts. "How do you feel about something for dinner?"

Joshua looked at the clock on the car dash that read a few minutes after five p.m., and he had to admit his stomach had been feeling a rumble. He thought for a moment how food was sometimes a concern for him, trying to make sure he had enough money to afford it. He did not like going to soup kitchens for handouts, but he was forced to on occasion.

"I could definitely go for a little food. You buying?" Joshua jested, knowing that once all the bills and the McClenndon's coffee and muffin were paid for, he was pretty much broke.

"Oh, I think I can handle it," Zyriah, looking at him and smiled, turned back to finish the drive. "I've been starving the last few hours. Plus, I wanted to show you a popular place around here for a quick bite."

"Not fast food, I hope. I'm not really in the mood for burgers and fries," Joshua insisted.

"You are in West Virginia, you know. There's a little place up here that has a couple West Virginia staples of eating I'm thinking you'll enjoy. It certainly hits the spot when you have an empty stomach," Zyriah remarked with a friendly tone.

"All I know is I could eat anything about now. I'm thirsty too. We should have picked up drinks for that drive. I'm dry as a well," he explained, feeling a pastiness on his tongue.

"Well, here's the place to fill you up then," Zyriah said, pulling into a small parking lot next to a grey and white painted building with an orange neon sign saying "Soccer's" near the side of the road. A couple cars were already in the parking lot, so they pulled in the parking space between them. Joshua got out of the car, stretched his legs, and glanced around at the nearby homes. Zyriah walked around the car toward the restaurant's front door, and Joshua followed behind walking inside the little establishment.

The restaurant was small, and Joshua felt it resembled more of a diner with its booths and long counter with stools lining beside it. The wall beside the booths was decorated with numerous framed pictures of all sizes, showing what appeared to be landmarks and young people playing various sports. Joshua smiled, thinking the youngsters must be local athletes and this was a pride wall showing off their accomplishments. He could see why a parent could be proud.

There were not many people there, a waitress and an older thin man behind the counter making food, opening hot dog buns and placing hot dogs in the buns with a fork. A couple men stood appearing to wait for their orders wearing green and brown clothing that Joshua believed were hunters. Two men appeared to be in conversation, one well-built brown-haired man and a thinner red-haired man talking jovially. After a moment of laughter between the two men, the red-haired man turned to see Joshua with Zyriah entering and spoke to the other man, drawing his attention to the front door.

"Looks like you have company," the red-haired man said. "I better get back to work before mom throws a fit."

"Looks like you're right," the other man replied. "I'll try and catch you later, Brier. The boss here might have me staying busy the rest of the day."

The two men slapped their hands together in a firm handshake to say goodbye, and Joshua stepped to the side to allow the man with red hair to pass him upon exiting. The man grew quiet, appearing to politely nod to Zyriah in acknowledgement. Joshua made a mental note of his hair. The brightness of his red locks reminded him of the red hair of the woman that left the auction early. He had never seen such bright red hair on anyone before them.

"Can I bother you for a second, Brier?" Zyriah asked. "I wanted to do a quick introduction before you left so you could meet Joshua Spiker."

"Joshua Spiker? From Spiker's Knob?" Brier questioned, extending his hand to grab Joshua's into a handshake. "Well, it's a surprise to see a Spiker back in town, Joshua. I wasn't really sure if you there was any left. It's a pleasure to meet you."

"Thank you," Joshua replied, with a strange feeling after the sudden introduction. "I'm sorry, but I just got into town."

"Oh, you're fine," Brier said. "I don't mean to cut you off, but my mom is going to be expecting me back at work. Glad to have met you. Trust me, I won't forget the name."

"Nice to have met you too," Joshua said, watching Brier quickly open the front door and leave.

"Well, don't you think you're just a little overdressed for hotdogs?" the man seated asked.

The young well-built man sitting in one of only five booths in the restaurant had looked up and recognized Zyriah. He was clean in his appearance, with curly brown hair and a black t-shirt and jeans. He took a hotdog, covered in hotdog sauce, from his plate and took a bite. He seemed to have a large appetite.

"Don't you think you should be working?" Zyriah smirked sarcastically.

"That yard looks impeccable, Miss Flint. I kept my promise. Everything is ready," the man confirmed between chews of his food.

"That's what I wanted to hear," Zyriah sighed, letting Joshua pass her and waved him into the booth seat across from the man. She sat down beside Joshua, and he then remembered this entire time she had been wearing those high heel shoes.

"I never got how women can drive in those things," Joshua remarked, looking down quickly under the table, then turning back to face her. "It has to hurt."

"Years of practice, years of pain, years of compliments.

I always thought it was worth it," Zyriah explained with a smile.

"Trust me, my friend. It's a rare thing to see her out of the things," the man smiled and took another bite from his hot dog.

"What can I get you all?" A young girl with an order pad had walked up to the table to take an order. Joshua noticed a small silver nametag with "Nikki" printed in black letters attached to her shirt. She was petite, and her hair had been dyed an unusual shade of light blue.

"Let us have four, hot with everything and a large roll with cheese, peppers and hot as well. Chocolate milk ok?" Zyriah turned to ask the final question to Joshua, who was confused about the strange food order and nodded to the drink selection. The young girl wrote the order down and walked back behind the long counter, lined in the front with little metal counter stools that Joshua finally took a closer look at.

"Not sure what you just said, but I hope it's good." Joshua said, rolling his eyes.

"That's years of ordering and eating here. You'll catch on to the ordering lingo. Soccer's has been serving up hotdogs and pepperoni rolls for years," the man responded, grabbing a napkin and wiping a spot of mustard from the corner of his mouth.

The man, finishing his meal, wiped his hands with a napkin and extending it to Joshua for a handshake, seemed more than familiar with the ordering etiquette. His grip was firm, as Joshua expected from the man's muscular appearance. However, his smile was pleasing, which help Joshua ignore the squeezing of his fingers that gave him a momentarily discomfort.

"I'm Evan Scott, Mr. Spiker. I guess I should've said that sooner," the man greeted.

"Name is Joshua," Joshua laughed, hearing his name said so formally.

"Good. Calling Miss Flint 'Miss Flint' can be a tough thing sometimes, but it's what I was requested to do," Evan explained with a grin.

"Only when it's appropriate Evan. You know that," Zyriah commented.

"I know. I know. I'm just an employee," Evan explained. "A minor player in the big production."

"You're his boss?" Joshua questioned.

"Actually Mr. Spiker, you're his boss." Zyriah giggled, reaching past Joshua for napkins from the chrome napkin holder at the table's end. "I'm just the middleman in the situation."

"Well, she signs the paychecks, so I don't have a problem with showing a little respect," Evan explained.

The waitress returned with a large plate with four hotdogs and a smaller plate with a large pepperoni roll covered in melted cheese. She left and returned with two pints of chocolate milk, giving one each to Joshua and Zyriah. She was young, but Joshua heard the deliberate professionalism in her speech and tone. Even as a waitress, she appeared to want to do her job well.

"Anything else I can get for you?" she asked.

"No, but it looks delicious Nikki. Your hair is looking lovely today," Zyriah complimented, and Joshua watched the girl smile and walk back behind the counter. "Now, dig in. I hope you like it."

Joshua took half of the pepperoni roll and bit into the heat of the sauce and the peppers. He was not really prepared for the spiciness and the heat, and he quickly drank part of his chocolate milk. The heat quickly resolved, and his mouth returned to a less burning feeling. His tongue continued to tingle as he took a relieving breath.

"I get now why you need the milk," Joshua laughed.

"Oh, you get used to it." Zyriah smiled, passing a napkin, and returned holding her already half eaten hotdog. "Pretty soon, it doesn't even taste that hot. But does it tastes good?"

"It's great," Joshua agreed, reaching for a hotdog to try after placing the partially eaten pepperoni roll down on the plate. "I told you I can eat anything right now. These are really good."

"Good. I'm glad you like them," Zyriah said, and they returned to eating. It was a matter of minutes that the two of them ate and emptied their plates, while Evan sat in quiet letting them eat. Joshua was full by the meal's end, but he had a slightly burning stomach. He drank the last of his chocolate milk.

"The hotdogs could have used a little ketchup though," Joshua added.

"KETCHUP?"

Joshua turned seeing the short older man behind the counter, standing in front of a long counter with a cutting board. He was slight in frame, black hair peppered with grey, but there was a strong glare emerging through his brown plastic framed glasses. Joshua noticed quickly that in front of the man were the ingredients to make his food. There was a yellow bottle of mustard and a large cup of chopped onions. There was a large steaming table with pots Joshua assumed contained the various sauces. However, he did notice that a red ketchup bottle was not on that table.

"Is there something wrong with ketchup here?" Joshua asked, looking at Evan and Zyriah.

"In this place, yeah there's a problem," the man exclaimed. "Stick to the sauce or you can go outside and stick to the road. There's no ketchup in this place and their never will be." The man turned back to his counter and continued filling orders.

"You have to forgive Russell over there," Evan said quietly. "He has his own way of doing things around here."

"He must have worked here a long time, I guess," Joshua assumed.

"Worked? He owns the place," Evan corrected. "That's Russell Lloyd, and his daughter Nikki is the waitress waiting on us. His dad, Soccer, opened the place, and Russell took it over after his dad passed away. He kept all the Soccer Lloyd's traditions though. In this place, there's a simple rule: No ketchup. Best thing to not even say the word."

"So, what if somebody ordered a couple hotdogs with ketchup to go?" Joshua wondered out loud.

"I've seen it happen," Evan said, continuing to speak quietly but now had a slight giggle. "Young girl walked in here one time and ordered exactly that. Russell was a bit more polite, probably because she was a child. I watched him spoon out hot sauce on two plain hot dogs, wrap them up, crammed them in a paper bag, and set the girl on her way."

"So, what are you telling me here?" Joshua asked, beginning to giggle at the situation. He wondered why such a trivial issue would be so important to these people.

"No ketchup, my friend," Evan replied. "I wouldn't even try it."

The conversation was comical to Joshua. He thought of how every town had their stories and quirks. He was just beginning to know the little things that made Wilcox what it was. For a moment, he began to feel slightly more interested, seeing how even this hotdog place had its own personal charm.

"So, what does he know so far?" Evan asked, returning the conversation to more important matters.

"I think we have a little time before we get into the details. Joshua and I have talked a little about the basic stuff. I thought you could take him for a little drive before taking him home. I need to stop by my house to change these clothes, and I can meet you up there," Zyriah explained.

"You're leaving?" Joshua said with a slight concern. His main guide the entire time had been Zyriah, and he felt a little feeling of abandonment. Evan seemed nice enough, but still he had only known him a few minutes. He preferred her to stay.

"Just for a little bit," Zyriah said attempting to calm him he felt. "I'm just going home to change clothes and check on a couple things. I'll be up at your house before you even get there. It won't be too long. Evan, let me talk to you for minute."

The two stood, and Joshua watched them walk to the end of the counter, Zyriah taking money from her small purse and giving it to Nikki the waitress to pay for the meal. The two talked quietly, Evan was nodding, and they both returned standing beside the booth. Joshua began thinking more about what Zyriah had just said. He paid the most attention to the idea of "his house" and how the inheritance may be way more than he expected. The possibilities began entering his head.

"I'm going to go ahead and go," Zyriah said, touching Joshua's shoulder for a moment. "I'll see you in a few minutes."

"Ok, see you in a few." Joshua said and watched her leave, returning his eyes back to Evan.

Evan smiled.

"What?" Joshua asked, thinking there was something behind that smile he saw.

"Ready to get out of here? I've been asked to show you something."

"Show me what?" Joshua asked.

"C'mon." Evan continued to smile, speaking to Nikki again asking for two chocolate milks to go. She put them in a small bag, and Evan took a few dollars from his pocket and laid them beside the register. "I'll catch up with you tomorrow, Nikki." Joshua followed him outside.

Evan walked over to an old grey pickup truck and got inside the driver's side door. Joshua walked to the passenger door, opening it, and quickly looked around surprised how neat and clean the inside was. He still felt slightly uncomfortable getting into another stranger's car, but the conversation while eating had helped put him a little more at ease but there remained just a small bit of fear.

"C'mon buddy. I wanna get out there before it gets too dark," Evan said, waving Joshua to come inside the truck.

Joshua jumped in on the passenger side, shutting the door behind him. He noticed that his slight feeling of fear had been replaced by a feeling of excitement. He watched Evan open the paper bag, and he passed Joshua a chocolate milk. Joshua opened it, took a drink, and put the pint bottle into the truck's cup holder.

"So, where are we going Evan?" Joshua inquired.

Evan smiled. Joshua didn't like how quiet and secretive people were being, but Evan made things intriguing.

"Seriously," Joshua smiled with curiosity. "Where are we going?"

"On a little adventure," Evan said, pulling the old truck out of the parking lot and slamming on the gas pedal jolting Joshua back into his seat.

Joshua could tell they were trying to outrun the sunset, which was slowly coming but still coming soon. The road shaded the hillsides as he watched Evan twist and turn the steering wheel to match the winding road. The colors from the leaves hanging still on the trees streaked by the window like brushstrokes, and Joshua was happy they had not seen another car on that road blocking their journey.

He tried to enjoy the view, but Evan was driving so quickly. It was too soon after his arrival to suddenly have a car wreck. His eyes moved back and forth hoping to not see a deer.

"Can't we slow down just a little bit?" Joshua requested, gripping the inner handle of the passenger door.

"Now what's the fun in that?" Evan laughed, slightly accelerating even more, but Joshua realized Evan knew that road better than he did, so he hoped Evan knew what he was doing. He hoped.

"Well, it's only my first day here," Joshua said with a slight loss of breath on a quick right turn of the tires. "I'd like to make sure it's not my last."

"Oh, you'll be fine. We're almost there anyway," Evan explained, bouncing his left knee with an excited twitch. Joshua could feel the suspense growing.

"Where?" Joshua questioned, realizing his breathing had become slightly rushed with nervousness.

"I can't tell you. Zyriah said keep it a secret and you'll know it when you see it," Evan said, looking at Joshua with a quick, excited smile.

"When I see it? I've never been in this part of the state before. How am I supposed to recognize anything?" Joshua asked.

"Trust me. You'll know it," Evan said confidently.

"You trust Zyriah, then?" Joshua asked. He wondered, even while on this erratic drive if the man was comfortable enough to say the word "trust" regarding Zyriah. Evan had known her longer than Joshua had, although Joshua was not sure exactly how long the two were friends. Still, Joshua put a great deal of weight into the word "trust", so if he could hear it from someone that had known Zyriah longer, he thought he would feel more comfortable with the situation.

"She knows what she's talking about," Evan said, slowing the truck as they approached what looked like a river on the left side of the vehicle. "I have a good feeling this will prove it to you."

The road quickly turned into a parking lot. Evan dropped the speed significantly and drove closer to the lot's front. He found a parking space close to a paved trail that led into the trees, and Joshua saw a family emerge with the remnants of a picnic. He could see a blanket and basket being carried out by a family of five. Three little children closely walked with their parents with drooped eyes that looked like naptime was overdue. Evan opened his door, jumped out of the truck, and Joshua watched Evan waiting for him by the trail to exit the passenger side. Joshua left the truck, locking the door behind him, and joined his reckless chauffeur.

"We came to see a trail?" Joshua snickered, almost mockingly commenting. "Got some great squirrels around here?"

"C'mon. Let's take a little walk.," Evan commented, ignoring Joshua's sarcasm.

The trail, like the road, was curved and travelled up and down with the terrain of the land. They kept walking until Joshua saw an unused railroad track that the path crossed, and they both walked across the track, stepping over the rusty rails, and continued their walk on the other side. Joshua knew the area was new to him, but he began to feel a small amount of familiarity. Something to him was becoming way too familiar.

"Is it far?" Joshua asked, feeling the anticipation in his mind and body begin to slightly tingle.

Evan started to slow his steps, but Joshua continued moving forward. He could see a parting in the trees ahead, and slowly he heard a quiet roar that only increased in volume. Louder and louder the roar grew, and as he recognized it was water flowing and crashing, Joshua's pace increased. He turned for a moment to see Evan walking behind him, smiling, urging him forward with an open hand gesture. Joshua turned back to what was ahead of him, and slowly the sight confirmed the familiar feeling he felt. The stones that emerged, large brown rocks smoothed by the wear of the rushing water, led into a crashing low waterfall, with a hill on the other side of the river, high and tree covered. The location was more than too familiar. He knew it all too well, as if the memory of his painted brushstrokes still was lingering in his fingers.

"Wait," Joshua exclaimed while taking in the sight of the area, amazed by the beauty but beginning to be more confused as to what he was seeing. It was the setting of the painting, the woman in the yellow dress and the five colored kites in the sky. The painting that Zyriah just bought in the auction in Charleston that morning was now in a full reality that he had only thought was his imagination. The painting he visualized in his mind and basing it on no location he had ever visited was now in full reality in his view. This was that waterfall.

"Look a little familiar?" Evan joined him on his right side, but Joshua's head remained forward absorbing the sight.

"I don't understand. How's this even possible? This was all in my head. How can this be real?" Joshua questioned with a sense of awe.

"Well, I can't vouch for what all was in your head, but I can promise you Rock Falls is definitely real, my friend. Beautiful place, really. I love coming down here in the summertime.," Evan explained, rocking back and forth from heels to toes and taking in a deep breath.

"No, no, no. You don't understand. I painted this place. This stone we are standing on, that waterfall, and those trees. How did I do this?" Joshua questioned, his confusion battling with the fascination of the moment as he spoke.

"I think Zyriah is going to have to answer that for you," Evan said. "Let me give you a minute. I'm going to look around a minute."

Joshua continued looking at the site of his imagination becoming reality. He had no answers. Nothing was making sense to him. His mind sat in a confused state, then slowly that confused agony that was welling up in him eased into a more comforted feeling. It was real, he knew that, but what was better to him is how beautiful the area was. He felt a level of amazement how well he had captured the color of the stones, the rush of the falls, and the fullness of the trees. His painting had a new value to him, some unexpected increase in personal worth to him that he was able through his own artistic expression to encapsulate the wonders that were around him. He had created true art, and he felt it was special.

The questions slowly started to enter his brain once he began thinking about Zyriah's words about his apparent abilities. He questioned his own mind wondering if what she had said was true. Perhaps, there was something within him, some ability that made all this possible.

Truth became mixed with possibilities as he thought, and his thought of discovering such a talent within him began to overwhelm his senses. However, Joshua always wanted to know more facts. He wanted educated. Knowledge would be a key to all this. If any of this was true, there were answers he needed. He turned and walked back to Evan, who by then was waiting a few feet back behind him once again on the paved trail.

"I need to talk to Zyriah." Joshua said.

"I'm betting she is already back at your house by now," Evan responded, looking at his watch, then back towards Joshua.

"Then let's go there," Joshua insisted. He was more mystified than ever now that things were being revealed.

The walk back to the truck seemed like a fast one with all the ideas Joshua continued thinking and trying to analyze. Everything that had happened that day just seemed to add upon itself into a strange and curious world.

Once in the truck, Joshua realized the fullness of what Evan had said on the path, and a new reality had entered his mind. He did not need to have the constant worry of a roof over his head or Miss Amos to answer to when the rent was due. He was going to be able to sleep without worrying about a roof, walls, and a floor encircling him that he could call his own. Joshua had his own home. He could not wait to see it for the first time.

The road away from Rock Falls back into town did not feel as curved and twisted as Joshua sat in that old grey truck with Evan driving a little slower now. Joshua sat there quietly thinking and becoming increasingly unaware of his surroundings even as the trees on the side of the road switched into homes and buildings as they entered the town. The sunset was slowly completing, and the darkness was beginning to blanket the community with a increasingly shaded calm. The streetlights blinked on and lights from the homes shined through the sheared windows as they drove farther into the little town.

"The town isn't hard to figure out once you get use to the streets," Evan said breaking the quiet truck ride. "The main road is right up here and pretty much all the streets somehow connect with it."

Joshua's eyes refocused from his deep thinking toward the brick and wooden homes on the street that grew in size and height into brick and stone buildings the closer they got into the main part of town. Finally, they had reached a stop sign, and Joshua looked up to the little green street sign with white letters saying "Treeclimber Drive" on top of a long street pole. Joshua felt the truck turn to the left, seeing many businesses, a little grocery store with the name "Michalski's Market" printed on the store front, pharmacy, a bank, a produce market, a shoe store, many businesses of different types in brick and stone buildings on either side of the street.

"Treeclimber Drive?" Joshua asked. "Strange name for a street, isn't it?"

"Well, when the founders made it to the area, the main guy that envisioned the town told them that it'd be a great place to start a town except for all the trees that would need to be cleared out. You'd pretty much have to be a tree climber to see the potential. At least it's how the story goes," Evan explained.

"Oh," Joshua nodded. "Then the name fits it rather well."

"Treeclimber Drive is pretty much the spine of the town, dividing it right down the middle and leading right up to the Knob and the Ridge."

"The Knob and the Ridge?" Joshua asked.

"Yep. It's two parts of the same long hillside. At the top of this road, you go to the left and you'll be on the Knob. You go to the right, and you'll be on the Ridge," Evan detailed.

"What if you stay in the middle?" Joshua giggled, trying to be amusing.

"The middle?" Evan smiled and turned his face quickly to see Joshua's expression. "Well then, my friend, you'd be driving straight through your front door."

"I live on the middle of a hillside?" Joshua said, trying to visualize it as Evan explained.

"Trust me, Joshua. It's a great house with a great view. You're gonna love living there," Evan said confidently.

"Is it much farther?" Joshua asked. He was enjoying the tour, but he was wanting a certain view.

"Your house?" Evan said. "All you got to do is look straight ahead and up."

Joshua followed the directions and peered through the streetlights and darkened shadows of the evening and let his eyes follow down Treeclimber Drive and upward toward what should be the hillside according to the description given, and his eyes caught a view he did not expect. His eyes widened, and the farther down the street they went and began inclining up the hillside to a house, Joshua wondered if what he was seeing was his. A three-floored building stood at the road's fork up ahead, and it had a unexpected feature. Joshua's eyes became fixed upon a large and unique window on the building's second floor. Stained glass and large, a half circle and five diamond-shaped window all colored with an orange and yellow blend of color was the focal point of the house's roadside appeal, and Joshua's mind went to that painting Zyriah had insisted they take from his apartment in Charleston. Once again, he realized that another of his paintings was an actual location, and he was even more perplexed how both paintings were from a single area of West Virginia. He looked for small details, remembering when he had painted individual trees and even the house's signature stained-glass window. His jaw stiffened in the awe of it. He had painted his own home before ever seeing it in person, and he could not explain it. It was his sunset, the one he painted with the colors and the shapes he used almost to the exact hues of his artwork.

Evan pulled up beside the building on the left side to a two-floored brick garage behind that familiar red car he had arrived in town in with Zyriah. Joshua immediately jumped out of Evan's truck once it stopped, not saying anything to Evan, and ran to the front of the building looking up at that window. His body began slightly shaking with nervous excitement, that once again his painting had been made real again in this little town, a town he had never been. He was so focused that when Zyriah, now in black slacks, red blouse, and a black suit jacket, emerged from the front door of the home, she surprised him. Evan quickly joined her to meet Joshua where he stood looking upward. Her greeting was warm and most definitely welcoming to Joshua.

"Welcome home," Zyriah said with a smile.

CHAPTER
FOUR

Joshua looked over the home and thought this was definitely more than a house, it was a three-floored building. The entryway was a center door outlined by two display windows with large flower boxes of red petunias accompanying each window at their base, similar to a couple storefront's he just saw on two business front's on Treeclimber Drive. The corners of the building were columned with bricked corners, with white vinyl siding underneath the flower boxes that continued around the side of the building. He walked to the right of the building, seeing the vinyl siding cover the entire side as well as a few sporadic windows. A long flowerbed filled with colorful petunias and greenery lined the entire side of the building. He walked back to the front of the building, seeing Zyriah and Evan still standing in the entry way allowing him the opportunity to look at the home. He walked to the left side, seeing the driveway where they had just parked with another long flower bed along the house's base and more scattered windows on that side as well as a red bricked chimney. The garage, from what he could see in the evening light, was a brick garage with two floors with a staircase that came out from the rear of the building. His eyes looked back upwards to the higher levels of the house, walking slowly back to the front, and to the window he now was sure was representing a sunset.

"You have a lot of explaining to do," he said, indirectly addressing Zyriah with a lack of eye contact.

The questions began refilling Joshua like they had at Rock Falls about how even this location was already used in his artwork, and still it was another location he had never seen before. Evan had told him though that she would have answers, and at that moment maybe more than another other that day, Joshua felt he really needed the answers.

"Explaining?" Zyriah asked. "Don't you like the house?"

"A house? It's an entire building. This place is enormous. But that's not what I need to know," Joshua explained with an increasing level of impatience.

"You're talking about Rock Falls and this window I take it then," Zyriah said, stepping out of the entryway and getting closer to him. "They look pretty familiar don't they?"

"Familiar? They're more than familiar and you know it. How did I paint these things? How did I know about these places, and I've never been here? Why can't you just give me a simple answer?" Joshua questioned with frustration.

"Simple?" Zyriah asked, touching his shoulder for a moment. "There's nothing simple to this, Joshua. I have several things to tell you. This is going to take a little time, and you're going to really need an open mind to understand these things."

"So, you're telling me you aren't going to answer me," Joshua said with a disappointed tone. Clarity was not going to be an easy goal to achieve.

"Oh, I'm going to answer, but I can't explain everything in one minute, Joshua. Let's just get you situated, and then we can talk," Zyriah responded with a calming tone.

"Well, let's empty the trunk really quick so we can talk," Evan interrupted.

Zyriah laughed. "Evan, will you grab Joshua's things from the back of the car and bring them upstairs please?" She reached into her pants pocket, grabbing the car keys, and gave them to Evan. "I'd like to take him inside and show him around a few minutes."

"Oh, I can help carry the bags in," Joshua said, stepping in the direction of the parked cars.

"Heck no, you don't have to do that bud," Evan said. "This is what I get paid for."

Joshua walked toward the front entrance of the building, Zyriah following, while Evan went to retrieve Joshua's belongings. Once he reached the doorway, Joshua grabbed the handle. He took a deep breath, opened the door, and walked inside. He took a moment to wonder what was inside. The inside of the first floor was almost as unexpected to him as the outside of the building was.

The floors were beautiful dark-stained hardwood that led throughout the long room, but the walls were solid white and almost seemed like a maze of corners and turns. There was leather chairs and a leather sofa in the front room with a solid wood coffee table and track lighting shining throughout the area.

He walked slowly through the space, realizing that this was previously used for some other reason besides somebody's home. The structure was far too large.

"What was this place?" Joshua asked with curiosity in his voice.

"Most recently? Office space. Your mother used it for her counseling practice," Zyriah explained.

"But where are the doors? It looks more like a gallery space here than a shrink's office." Joshua laughed.

"Oh, your mother didn't want any doors on this floor. She thought it helped the patients feel more comfortable not having anything locking them or binding them in any way," Zyriah responded, walking forward throughout the floor leading Joshua onward.

"Well, I got to admit, it's a really nice space." Joshua smiled, happy to what he had seen so far within his home.

"Plenty more to see if you just walk this way," Zyriah said as she began leading him to the rear of the building.

The staircase at the end of the corridor was truly a unique one. Wooden and spiral with no center support beam, the staircase filled an open area at the end up the building, and when Joshua looked up, he realized it spiraled not only to the second but also the third floor. The wood appeared to be maple and stained a light color on the steps and a darker color on the slats and handrail. Taking another look at it, Joshua thought it looked like an unraveled spring, but its elegance and workmanship was one of the best woodworking examples he had ever seen. Unfortunately, a dark purple velvet rope blocked the stairway's entry.

"We can't walk up the stairs?" Joshua asked.

"Oh, no. That staircase was a rare piece that your mother specifically had installed, and she had it further extended to the third floor by the same company that built the initial staircase. It's for looks more than use. Besides, there's a more inventive way to get upstairs right over here." Zyriah answered, pressing a small black button on the rear left wall, opening an elevator. Two brass doors that Joshua had not paid attention to due to looking upward at the stairs then opened.

"An elevator?" Joshua exclaimed.

"It's a unique one as well," Zyriah explained. "I had an extra key made already for you." She dug into her pants pocket once again, producing a brass key on a brass circular keychain.

"All aboard" she laughed, and Joshua followed her into the elevator,

The inside of the elevator was the same dark stained maple as the handrail of the stairs, with a control panel of three black buttons and a keyhole for his key. Joshua watched the elevator door close slowly in front of them, and he touched the walls feeling their smoothness. He took a deep breath, trying to let this new environment sink into familiarity.

"Now what?" Joshua questioned, sounding more excited.

"Simple. Insert your key right here below the floor buttons. Turn the key and while keeping it turned, press the floor button until the elevator is in motion," Zyriah explained.

Joshua followed Zyriah's instructions, inserting his brass key into the keyhole, turning it, and pressed the button for the second floor. The elevator lifted upward, and the smoothness of the ride made him feel like the elevator was ran on a fine hydraulic system. The elevator lifted like a smooth liftoff from an airplane, and even as it stopped on the second floor, there was no sudden jerking motion of the motor or any of its parts. It stopped gracefully, and the door opened. Joshua thought having an elevator was already oddly comfortable.

"Now you can turn your key back to the starting position and remove it," Zyriah further instructed, and Joshua did as he was told. Both of them stepped out onto the second-floor entryway, tiled with large white and grey square tiles. Looking to his left, Joshua looked at the second-floor opening of the stairwell, also roped off with a purple velvet rope to both the stairs going down and up to the third floor. Zyriah guided Joshua to his right into a dark room, except a light coming from the bottom of a door on the opposite end. In the dimness, he could see Zyriah walk to the right wall to a row of light switches that she brought her hand up to, and she turned her head to face him.

"And this is your living area," Zyriah announced, and began turning on the many switches, exposing a room Joshua was unprepared for.

Everything, from the square tile from the entry hall that stretched and covered the entire floor, to the counters of the kitchen, to the appliances, to the cabinets, to the dining table, to the living room furniture all appeared to be brand new merchandise. The room stretched almost the full length of the building, and it was decorated with color, unlit candles, and flowers throughout. He could feel the elegance of the space and smiled over how clean and fresh everything appeared.

"I hope you're not unhappy that I thought the place needed some upgrading," Zyriah remarked.

"Unhappy? This is amazing. Everything looks so new and incredible," Joshua responded in awe.

"Well, it is pretty much entirely new. I thought with a

new owner, you should have it as if the house and you were both starting fresh. I took the liberty of doing some grocery shopping as well, so the cabinets and refrigerator are well stocked. You have plenty of cookware and utensils as well," Zyriah explained.

"I guess I need to learn how to cook then. Well, I need to learn how to make more than canned soup and boxed spaghetti," Joshua laughed.

"Lucky for you, Evan and I are both really decent in the kitchen, so ask away for any cooking advice," Zyriah offered.

"I'll be asking a lot of things. You don't have to worry about that," Joshua said, further walking into the living room, noticing the large screen television, the two comfortable looking recliners, and an oversized plush sofa.

"I picked the dark grey furniture, the chrome and glass end tables, and coffee table to add a touch of elegance. Plus, they went so well with the floor tile," Zyriah remarked, and Joshua could tell she was proud of her decorating efforts.

"It looks wonderful," Joshua said, so transfixed by such a large television mounted on the high wall, that he finally looked down and noticed the white brick fireplace.

"A fireplace?" Joshua smiled largely as he had forgotten seeing the chimney when he was outside.

"And in full working order for those upcoming winter evenings," Zyriah explained.

"But what about the…you know…" Joshua questioned in an immature tone.

"The bathroom?" Zyriah smiled.

"Well, yeah." Joshua said with a slight blushing. He always had a weird time talking about restrooms.

"That corner door on the right," Zyriah pointed past the fireplace to the door in the corner of the room. Joshua walked to the door, peeked inside, shut the door quickly, and turned to Zyriah and smiled.

"Are you alright?" Zyriah laughed.

"A clawfoot bathtub," Joshua sighed with almost a tone of ecstasy. "I'm never leaving this place."

He turned and reopened the door, walking into a full bathroom with a large double sink area, a walk-in shower, and a large white clawfoot bathtub. The brass handles for the water looked like they had been freshly polished. He noticed how clean everything looked. He just kept reminding himself this was not a hotel or a place he was visiting. This was his new home.

"Hey, can anybody give me a hand here?" Evan's voice yelled from down in the entryway, and Joshua took a second to almost respond to it. Zyriah and he both emerged from the bathroom, and they walked to the entryway seeing Evan unloading all the suitcases and Joshua's painting from the elevator. Immediately, Joshua decided to carry the painting himself and one of the suitcases. Evan, he thought, could handle the remainder.

"Well, nobody said you had to bring up everything at one time," Zyriah said.

"Hey, it's nothing I couldn't handle," Evan said, even though Joshua could see the sweat begin sliding down his forehead.

"Now, that's one question I forgot to ask," Joshua said, almost forgetting one logical question. "I was so focused on the bathtub that I forgot to ask. Where do I sleep?"

"Pretty simple actually," Zyriah giggled.

"It's the only door you haven't opened yet. The other

door in the living room facing the front of the house.,"
Evan instructed.

Joshua turned and walked to the door, turning the
doorknob, and walked into a beautiful sight. Almost the
entire facing wall was the sunset window, almost stretching
the full length of the wall. It's orange and yellow stain glass
glimmered in the reflection of a small chandelier in the
center of the ceiling, brass with a stained-glass shade that
looked like a collection of yellow teardrops. To his left was
a large bed, maple headboard and footboard, with navy,
tan, and mint green pillows. Underneath the pillows was a
navy comforter, with the appearance of being deliberately
placed evenly and stretched over the mattress with a
crispness Joshua imagined of the sheets on a soldier's bed.

A little matching maple nightstand with a collection of
candles matching the colors of the pillowcases stood to the
left of the bed, with a tall brass floor lamp in the room's
corner. To his right, a hand carved dresser and a spacious
closet, with a full-length standing mirror in the corner. The
floor was now hardwood instead of tile, slightly darker than
the wood of the furniture, but shined like it was covered
with a heavy gloss.

The room was relaxing Joshua's mind almost
immediately. All the details seemed to offer a level of
comfort than made him feel like it was his personal room.
Even the mint green pillowcases, his favorite color, added
a touch of his personality and made the room his own. He
sighed, recalling the memory of his stressful time worrying
about his lack of money. That lack of security no longer
seemed important now.

"I don't know what to say," Joshua whispered in a
humbled voice

"Well, I hope you like it," Zyriah said with a note of concern.

"Oh, I definitely do like it. It is just so overwhelming," Joshua said, with a smile and slightly watery eyes. "This is really my room? Really mine?"

"It is yours," Zyriah said, stepping up beside him, grabbing his hand, and guiding him to the bed. "Would you like to lay down? Just to see if its soft enough?"

Joshua sat down on the bed, hearing no squeaks or creaks, and laid back with his feet still on the floor. He never liked a bed that was so soft that he sank into it or a bed so hard it felt like laying on a tabletop. Yet, this bed was just enough support and comfort that his back's tension released and diffused. He could not wait for a good night of uninterrupted sleep, without worrying about a bill collector's letter in the mail or Miss Amos knocking for a rent payment.

"Don't go to sleep yet buddy," Evan laughed. "Can we sit in the living room for a minute? I think Miss Flint wants to talk to you."

"Let him enjoy the room a minute, Evan. It's something new and different, you know," Zyriah responded.

"I know, I know. I just wanted to give him my present," Evan added.

"Present?" Joshua jerked his head forward, and he quickly sat up straight. "Sure, we can talk all you'd like."

He was in no hurry to fall asleep just yet. He still wanted to look through the home and get his bearings. It was so much space, but so grand in its style that he was not sure what he wanted to do first. Still, if Evan was offering a present, he was not going to stop the gift giving. He stood, quickly walking into the living room, and fell into the plush comfort of the sofa before Zyriah and Evan had even followed him into the room.

"I take it the sofa is comfortable?" Zyriah questioned.

"Seriously, you don't have to ask me if I like this place," Joshua said. "I haven't seen anything I haven't liked yet. This place is amazing. I just cannot believe it's mine yet."

"Give it a day or two. Trust me, you'll get more comfortable to it," Evan said, walking into the kitchen, opening a corner drawer, and pulling out two small gift boxes wrapped in navy blue paper. He relaxed himself into one of the recliners, passing the boxes to Joshua, while Zyriah sat in the adjoining chair. Joshua, after thanking him for the gifts, quickly opened the first package.

"Ok, now I'm confused," Joshua giggled, looking at a present with a whimsical humor. "A deck of playing cards?"

"Oh, trust me buddy, a deck of cards comes in handy on a boring evening around here. A good game of solitaire is fun, or I'll play cards with you sometime," Evan offered.

"It's been a long time since anybody has ever asked me for a card game," Joshua smiled. "Thank you."

"You still have another present, you know," Zyriah said, pointing at his lap at the remaining wrapped gift.

Joshua quickly opened the remaining box to reveal a pendant on a silver chain. The charm was some type of crystal, cloudy white in its color and topped with a silver bail. Around the bail was some type of artwork, geometric with rectangles, diamond shapes, and lines encircling the cylindrical stone. The bottom of the stone had been cut to a slanted side point. A small silver chain had been placed through the hole in the bail at the pendant's uppermost point.

He took it out of the box, holding it by the chain's clasp, and rotated it slightly back and forth for a better examination. He admired how, even though cloudy in its coloring, it was still reflecting the light in the room with flashes of light as he turned the stone.

"I'm not sure exactly what this is, but it's really nice," Joshua smiled, thanking Evan for his second gift. Immediately, Evan pulled out from under his t-shirt a necklace and pendant just like it, and Zyriah pulled her pendant from her blouse as well. Joshua giggled under his breath, thinking he just gained membership to a little club.

"The stone is called selenite," Evan explained, turning his pendant's chain in the same way Joshua had just done. Joshua watched his stone, seeing it was just as reflective as the one he had been given. "It's a stone of energy and protection."

"I like it, but why do you both have one too?" Joshua asked, looking back at his pendant for an even closer inspection.

"Oh, the idea was…" Evan attempted to explain.

Zyriah interrupted Evan. "It's just a local novelty. They make these at a shop in town."

"Well, I do like it, but are you implying I need some type of protection?" Joshua asked, clasping the chain behind his neck and letting the new gift hang belong his chin and over his chest.

He thought the stone had a weight to it, but he also wondered its significance. He returned his sight to Zyriah and Evan, who looked as if they were trying to come up with an answer to his last question. He took a deep breath, taking a closer look into both Zyriah and Evan's eyes, and began asking questions instead of waiting for an answer to his last one. He had many, many questions, yet he felt so empty of answers.

"So, why am I here?" Joshua began.

"Don't you like the house?" Zyriah asked with concern.

"I told you I really do like it. I really do appreciate the fact you brought me here, but I need to ask why. It's been such a long day of surprises and things I don't understand. I still am not sure how you really knew how much to bid this morning, how I painted that waterfall or that bedroom window, or how any of this is even possible. I'm just really confused," Joshua admitted.

"Everything happens for a reason bud," Evan interjected. "Sometimes we know why things happen, and sometimes we spend way too much time trying to figure out why. I think tonight it's best to just relax and enjoy it. Tomorrow is going to be a long day, and we can explain even more."

"Yes," Zyriah added. "Tomorrow we can answer in a great deal more detail, but I don't think we need to rush anything. There's plenty of time for all that."

"Zyriah?" Evan's head turned to look at her, and Joshua noticed that for the first time Evan's expression was more of urgent concern. While Evan had seemed to want to wait to give more information, there seemed to be a momentary need to not wait that long.

"Let him rest," Zyriah said, looking at Evan with a calming look in her eyes, then back to Joshua. "There will be plenty of time to discuss more things tomorrow. I will be bringing the lawyer, Mr. Burke, by in the morning so you are able to sign a couple things for the house and the car. It won't take long. Then, we can talk more and perhaps see a little more of the town. Will that be alright?"

"Sure," Joshua smiled. Although he had plenty to ask, slowly he began to get a little tired. He did not feel the need to go to sleep for the night just yet, but his mind definitely needed a break from his curiosity. However, it was rather difficult for him not to want to ask all the questions he had. He often had difficulty sleeping due to overthinking things, and he hoped he would have had all his questions answered before he went to bed.

"Now, Evan here lives in the upstairs apartment above the garage, and he takes care of all the outside maintenance, plus anything you think you made need fixed here inside the house. If he can't fix it, we can find somebody that can," Zyriah said.

"Don't worry. If I can't fix it, it can't be fixed," Evan laughed.

"I seem to remember a water pump issue on the water fountain last summer," Zyriah said with slight sarcasm.

"Hey, another fifteen minutes, and I would've had it," Evan pointed out.

"A water fountain?" Joshua asked.

"Oh sure, there's a big one out in the backyard," Evan smiled. "It looks great in the moonlight."

"But for now, gentlemen, I really need to head home. Tomorrow morning comes early, and there's a number of things I need to do before I go to bed. Evan? Can you handle things here?" Zyriah asked.

"Oh, sure. Break out the beer, and let's have a little housewarming party." Evan laughed.

"He's nineteen, Evan. You two behave yourself, and I'll see you first thing in the morning. Is there anything else you need, Joshua?" Zyriah wondered.

"A pinch?" Joshua said smiling with slightly sleepy eyes.

"It's real. It's all real, I promise you. Just give it a little time. Goodnight gentlemen. I'll see myself out," Zyriah said excusing herself. She turned walking to the entryway, entered the elevator, and she was gone.

Joshua placed the gift boxes and unwrapped navy-blue paper on the glass coffee table, opening the box of playing cards, replacing the two jokers and instruction card back into the card box, and placed the card box on the table as well. He remembered for a moment being a child, learning how to shuffle playing cards from his foster father, and he smiled from the memory. He began shuffling the cards, looking at the cards at first then over to Evan, who sat back in the recliner in a more relaxed position once Zyriah had left.

"So," Joshua said, hearing the familiar ripping sound with his card shuffling, "Let's talk about a few things."

"Sure. What do you want to know?" Evan asked. Joshua noticed he was carefully looking at the way he was shuffling the cards.

"To be honest, I'm not even sure where to begin," Joshua admitted.

"Well, just go through the questions in your mind, and when you're ready you can just ask." Evan looked up from the cards, and Joshua noticed his smile. "You're really good at shuffling that deck. Do you like card games?"

"I've played a game of solitaire or two," Joshua agreed. "It's just been a while since I've played."

"Still thinking of what you want to ask me?" Evan inquired.

"Still thinking. This is all so new to me that I don't really know what to say. I suppose there's one question more than anything," Joshua admitted.

While several questions stirred within his mind, one in particular was in the forefront. Joshua thought that this could be a test of what he had been explained so far.

"Don't say it yet," Evan continued to smile. "Just keep thinking it until you're really ready to ask it."

"I'm not sure I'll ever really be ready to ask a question like this," Joshua said, still shuffling the cards, trying to stay focused.

"But are you thinking about it right now?" Evan asked, leaning slightly forward.

"I'm thinking about it. I'm thinking about it," Joshua laughed. He finished shuffling the playing cards and placed them beside the gift boxes on the coffee table. "Give me a minute, will you? I need to go to the bathroom."

"Sure," Evan replied.

Joshua stood and went to the bathroom, closing the door behind him. He really did not need to go. He just needed a minute by himself. He thought of that question again, sighed, and went to the linen closet in the corner of the room in need of a washcloth. Once opened, he looked at the array of soaps, shampoos, and various toiletries all neatly arranged and organized on the high shelves. Towels and washcloths were stacked on the lower shelves. Once again, all the towels and washcloths were that color, mint green. He was not going to complain about all these things that were being given to him, but seeing that color repeatedly just raised his curiosity.

He took a washcloth from the closet and walked to the double sink and looked at himself in the wide mirror. His hair was slightly disarrayed. He still felt presentable, but his eyes were showing signs of exhaustion. He turned on the cold water, rinsed his washcloth, and held the cold cloth to his face, especially the eyes and forehead to cool himself.

Joshua thought of that question concerning Rock Falls, the sunset window, and the entire day in general. Perhaps he did have some little trickle of an ability of some sort. Something, he thought, had to explain how he painted those locations before he had even seen him. He wondered if he did have some sort of mental gift, as Zyriah called it. He questioned if he was psychic. He placed the washcloth on the sink counter and went back to the bathroom door. He slowly opened it, not sure why he was doing it slowly, but he saw something strange once it was cracked open enough to see Evan and what he was doing in the living room. The pendant hanging from his neck felt momentarily heavier.

Joshua watched Evan, looking at the cards he had just shuffled that were now place in a strange array on the table. Not many cards, maybe a dozen, but he saw they were face up and placed in some sort of deliberate order. Evan was bent slightly over them, turning his head in quick movements from one card to the other, occasionally tilting his head in a questioning position or nodding like he was answering something. Joshua stepped back into the bathroom, reclosing the door.

"What time do you think I should be up in the morning?" Joshua said loud enough to ask the question so Evan could hear him through the door.

"Oh, I'm betting eight a.m. would be early enough," Evan said. "That lawyer will be here at ten, so don't forget."

Joshua thought that whatever Evan was doing with the cards would be interrupted by him speaking so close to the door. He assumed it was enough of a warning that he was returning to the living room. He slowly opened the bathroom door, seeing that the playing cards were restacked on the table and Evan was facing him with a smile. There was a knowledge in Evan's eyes which made Joshua feel that his eyes much have appeared vacant.

He was not sure exactly what Evan was doing with the cards, but he had an idea. He knew fortune tellers read people's cards to tell their future, but then he imagined Evan in a draping fortune teller's outfit with a large colorful turban. Without much warning, Joshua burst into laughter.

"I'm so sorry," Joshua began to calm down the outburst. "Got something funny stuck in my head."

"Hey, it's the first big laugh I've heard for a while, so I'm not complaining," Evan responded in a friendly tone.

"It's just been a long day," Joshua explained, finally calmed down with tired eyes. "I'm starting to get tired, but I'm not sure how I'll ever get to sleep with all these thoughts in my head."

"Oh, that's easy," Evan said, gesturing Joshua back to the plush sofa. "Let me show you a little trick. I've always had a hard time trying to figure out a way to fall asleep. That's when that little charm can come in handy. If I turn it back and forth with the right light catching it, it almost has a pulsating, metronome quality. Try counting the flashes, and it'll be like counting sheep. I've fallen asleep like that quite a few times."

"Well, I don't want to accidentally drop and break it, right?" Joshua asked.

"Oh, don't worry about that," Evan replied. "That selenite is hard as a literal rock. Dropping it accidentally won't break it. I promise you."

"Thanks again for the pendant," Joshua added, taking another look at the stone, holding it in his hand.

"To be honest with you bud," Evan sighed and stretched his arms above his head. "I'm getting pretty tired myself. How about we continue this little talk in the morning?"

"Actually, I was thinking about trying out that bathtub," Joshua smiled. "I've always wanted a bathtub like that."

"Those clawfoot tubs are like mini-swimming pools. I've got one in my bathroom too," Evan said, while standing up to go. "Well, you go and enjoy a swim around the tub, and I'll see you in the morning, alright?"

"Sounds like a good plan," Joshua said. "Thank you for all your help today." Joshua followed him to the entryway and pressed the button for the elevator, hearing the soft sound of the motor, and waiting for the elevator to arrive.

"It's not a problem, Joshua. Glad to have a new neighbor. If you need anything, I'm either in the apartment or around the house somewhere usually. But I'll see you in the morning. C'mon down to the back patio whenever you get up, ok?"

"I have a back patio?" Joshua asked, realizing he never walked to the rear of the building.

"Oh, sure. Nice little patio. You can check it out in the morning. Looks even better in morning light. Trust me," Evan said as the elevator door opened. He stepped in, pulling his elevator key from his pocket, inserting it, and turning to look at Joshua. "One more thing, that question that you had? The one I told you to think about when you were shuffling those cards? The answer to the question is yes." Evan smiled.

"What?" Joshua asked with instant curiosity and a twinge of fear. "What did I ask?"

He knew the question, to whether he had some type of

psychic ability, but how did Evan know that, or did he? Was he just guessing? Was this all some kind of trick? More and more, Joshua began believing this was more real than he expected.

"Goodnight, Joshua," Evan said, not responding to Joshua's curiosity. He pressed the elevator button to go down, and the door to the elevator closed.

The long bath in the clawfoot tub felt so relaxing that for a moment, Joshua could have fallen asleep, but the questions in his mind reemerged to startle his drooping eyes. Still, the overwhelming satisfaction of having his own home was much more pleasing, just as pleasing as the warm bath water that he soaked in. Once out of the water, he finished getting ready for bed, retrieving his bags from the entry way, and put his things away in his closet and dresser. Dressed in a shirt and shorts, he eased into bed, and he quickly remembered he had taken off the pendant before his bath and had left it on the bathroom counter. He brought it back to the bedroom, draping the necklace over a trio of candles on his nightstand, with the pendant facing where his head would be laying on the pillows. He reached over and held the necklace between his fingertips an inch above the bail and began to rotate it. He enjoyed the moment for a few seconds of attempting to count the reflective flashes before returning to getting back into preparation for his night's sleep.

After rolling the sheets back, Joshua entered the bed, covering himself with the sheets and blankets, and he adjusted his head into the pillows for comfort as well as to see the flashing light. He knew he had a difficult time sleeping, and with all that went on that day he felt the bombardment of new information would consume his thinking through the night. However, he wanted his first night's sleep to be a sound, soothing, and relaxing one. Admittedly, with all the ideas of how the day had transpired and all the eventful moments he had experiences so far, Joshua knew that trying to calm his mind would be a tricky venture. Perhaps Evan's advice of using his new pendant would help.

The bed was more than comfortable, and he eased his body, shifting slightly back and forth to find the best sleeping position. He laid on his right side, facing the nightstand and the light. He reached for the pendant and began turning it to count the flashes as Evan had advised, not counting the numbers out loud but in his mind in a steady rhythm. The increase in numbers was matching the increase in steps towards being asleep, and although he was filled with so many thoughts and questions, they all seemed to dissipate into a sense that rest was needed more than answers at that moment. Counting and drifting, Joshua, with pendant still in hand, fell asleep.

Trees. Many trees. A dirty path on a dark hill at night. Unfamiliar path. Unfamiliar location. Turning to see the glow of an enormous housefire. Looking forward again at leaves and sticks around his feet, but the feet were too small to be his. Small hands, like that of a young girl. Matted hair. Pale pink nightgown. Ash and dirt-stained face. A girl. A distance voice. An unknown voice. A quick flash of light. A name.

Sarah Baker.

CHAPTER
FIVE

The breakfast made by Evan on the back patio was unexpected. The eggs, bacon, toast with blackberry jam, and orange juice was satisfying, but Joshua continued to think of the previous night's dream. There was something real to it, and as he looked over the remnants of his meal, he wondered if there was more to the images in his head. Even the grand circular concrete fountain in the middle of the back yard did not seem to impress him. The copper statue of woman with a flowing gown with an upraised dagger in one hand while spouting water in four places into a pool of blue was not enough to relax his mind. Evan sat with him on tan metal porch furniture, looking around with patience until Joshua finally pushed his empty plate forward and wiped his mouth with a napkin.

"Did you get enough to eat?" Evan asked, collecting the glasses and plates.

"It tasted great. Thank you," Joshua said solemnly.

"Let me take these back into my apartment, and then

I'll be right back," Evan said with a tone of concern. He took the dishes back up the rear steps of the garage to his apartment, and he was back sitting at that table within just a couple minutes.

Silence.

Joshua waited, thinking of the little girl and the trees from his dream. He thought of the realness of it. He had dreams similar to this before that seemed so real, and within a few days those dreams seem to come true, as if he was mentally preparing himself for future events. Once again, this was a dream of a location he was not familiar with, and although that would not usually concern him, it did concern him now. The way he painted Rock Falls and the sunset window had made any dreams or thoughts of a location he did not recognize a strange and worrisome occurrence. He was not sure what it meant. He was so involved into trying to rationalize the thoughts that a conversation with Evan did not seem to take much priority.

"Did you sleep well?" Evan asked.

"Not really. A new place. A new bed. It's going to take some time to get adjusted," Joshua explained.

"Did you try the pendant? That usually knocks me out pretty quick," Evan said with a calming grin.

"Actually, I did, and I fell asleep without a problem. I just had dreams," Joshua said, concentrating his stare towards the fountain.

"Dreams? What kind of dreams?" Evan asked with a quick note of concern to his voice. He moved his metal chair forward closer to the patio table, focusing on Joshua's words.

"Oh, it was nothing. Just bits and pieces of things. It really didn't make much sense to be honest. Usually my dreams are more complete, like my brain is telling me a story. This one just seemed more like a broken jigsaw puzzle that I can't put together," Joshua said with a sound of frustration.

"What did you see in the pieces?" Evan asked, with a curious tone.

"It was nothing. Trees. A house on fire. A path. A little girl I didn't know. The strangest part was I heard this voice I didn't recognize saying a name. Well, it wasn't so much that I heard it as much as felt it. Sarah Baker," Joshua detailed, focusing his gaze on the raised dagger of the fountain's statue.

Evan sat back in his chair, mouth slightly open, and his eyes widened looking back at Joshua with an expression of amazement and a little shock. Joshua kept looking at him, knowing that he said something that triggered the reaction, but he was not sure what it was. Evan knew something more than he did, Joshua was sure. He needed to know more. Those pieces of the puzzle needed to be put together.

"Ok, what is it? Evan, I can just tell by your face that you know something," Joshua said, returning his concentration on looking at Evan's face for some type of information.

"You...are...impressive," Evan responded, with a vocal rhythm Joshua felt was almost like a pulse. His expression slowly turned into a relieved smile. "You coming here is going to be a good thing. I can tell."

"What do you mean? Because I dreamed something? I just keep getting more and more questions, and I get less and less answers. I really want to know what's going on here," Joshua said urgently.

"Zyriah and Mr. Burke will be here in a minute. Let's get the paperwork out of the way, then we can talk about all this. I know it's a lot to think about, it but the answer is really going to take a while. I just think Zyriah is better at answering it all than I am. If anything, after all this time, she should be the one responsible for giving you all the necessary details. I just hope you can help," Evan explained.

"Help? Help with what?" Joshua asked.

"See? The more I talk, the more questions you get. I'm really sorry I can't just spit it all out. I'm not even sure Zyriah can answer every little detail you have. We're learning more and more as the days go on ourselves. I just have a feeling by the end of the day after you get caught up with what's been going on, you'll feel a lot better. Trust me, it will be a lot of information to take in. Best thing is to save all the questions until the end," Evan affirmed.

"Well, I can tell you now that my will to speak is way too strong. When I don't know something, I'm pretty quick to ask," Joshua stated with a firm confidence.

"That's not a bad thing at all, Joshua. Just wait for Zyriah to get here, alright?" Evan requested as he was looking around the patio and back yard. "Do you like the scenery back here? I tried to make sure it was all clean and neat before you got here."

Joshua nodded.

"They should be here really soon. I'm going to do a few things in the apartment. I'll be back once Mr. Burke leaves, so you all have a little privacy. Good luck with everything this morning," Evan concluded.

Joshua watched him walk away and felt a bit of nervousness about meeting somebody new with this lawyer coming. Really, all these people were new to him, and he began to wonder if the need for the home and the car was truly going to be worth all the mystery. Something made him uneasy, something unknown. He took the time for some deep breathing for relaxation before the expected arrival of his guests, looking at the flowing water from the fountain and the statue once again. He just hoped the business of the paperwork would not take too long.

Soon, he heard the sounds from a car, maybe two cars pulling into the driveway, and he continued sitting at the patio table in case he was wrong. Once he heard the engines shut off and two car doors opening and closing, he was sure his guests had showed up. He combed his fingers through his hair with hopes he looked presentable and waited.

"I have a feeling they're around the back. Fine morning like this, and I'm sure Evan had him eating on the patio," a voice said.

A familiar voice Joshua recognized as Zyriah's slowly increased in volume as he heard approaching footsteps. He waited patiently for them to turn the corner, and they did. Zyriah, dressed rather professionally in a red suit jacket, white blouse, and long black skirt, came around the rear to the patio area with a short man, rather rotund, with gold rimmed glasses, a blue suit, and a black leather suitcase. Joshua had forgotten to dress well for this moment.

"Well, good morning Joshua," Zyriah greeted. "How was the first night here?"

"Pretty eventful actually," Joshua responded. "How are you today?"

"Just fine. Just fine. It's been a busy morning already. I met up with Mr. Burke here for a little talk, and we came right over. Enoch Burke, I'd like for you to meet Mr. Joshua Spiker," Zyriah introduced.

"Mr. Spiker?" The lawyer extended his hand, shaking Joshua's with a stern grip. "It's a pleasure to meet you. Talk about a meeting that's been long overdue."

"Nice meeting you, Mr. Burke," Joshua said cordially.

"Oh, call me Enoch, son. No need to be prim and proper around this town. I think everybody's on a first name basis except Miss Flint here. I think it came from the years of school teaching," Enoch said, pulling out a patio chair for Zyriah to sit, and then sitting down himself. "I wouldn't worry. All this will be done rather quickly." He placed the suitcase on the table, unlocking it, and quickly opening it looking through files and papers.

"Quicker the better I always say. Nice to meet you, Enoch," Joshua said with an emphasis on the first name. "You have to forgive me, but all this has been a lot to take in. I just met Miss Flint here yesterday morning, you know."

"And he's been a pleasure getting to know ever since," Zyriah said while addressing Enoch but looking back to Joshua with a pleasant smile. "I'm sure you'll make this process as painless as possible, Enoch."

"Oh, just a matter of a couple signatures," Enoch said, opening a folder of documents. "Now, Joshua, I have explained to Miss Flint just a moment ago that I have had time to review your mother's will. In accordance with your mother's wishes, I cannot legally let Miss Flint sign away her full rights to the property in question until your twenty-first birthday. However, as agreed upon by Miss Flint and myself, I am willing to extend to you the ability to be listed as a secondary on all property and accounts in question.

This will make the transference of the property easier once you become the required age. Let me explain in a more simplistic way. You will be listed as co-owner of this property, the car, and co-holder of all accounts, to which Miss Flint will remain the primary. Is this clear?" Enoch asked.

"So, I can still live here and drive the car, right?" Joshua said, with a slight laugh, but he wanted clarification.

"Absolutely, Joshua," Zyriah interjected. "You'll just be a co-owner with me until you reach the age according to your mother's will."

"How's that sound to you?" Enoch smiled.

"I think I'll take it." Joshua smiled in return.

Enoch, from the papers in the file folder he riffled in, took out forms for the house deed, the car, and forms from the bank, each having his typed name along with Zyriah Flint's name with X's marked for Joshua's signature.

He read over the forms, carefully and slowly, and the reality that all this was now coming true impacted him. He took a long breath, closed his eyes and reopened them, then realized he was missing something.

"Got a pen?" Joshua laughed.

"I wouldn't be a lawyer without one," Enoch smiled, removing a silver ink pen from his briefcase and passing it to Joshua. "If you agree with all terms presented, all I need are signatures beside the Xs on each indicated line."

Joshua signed the forms slowly, making sure his typically mangled signature was clearly legible. He took a moment for himself to look over the paperwork then passed the forms and pen back across the table to Enoch. He now had his home and car officially, or at least he was now a co-owner.

"One more thing, and that comes from Miss Flint here," Enoch said, turning toward Zyriah. "Do you have some keys for this young man?"

Zyriah pulled a brass key ring from her coat pocket with multiple keys on the ring. She extended her hand, dangling the keys like pocket watch, and Joshua opened his hand underneath. She dropped the keys into his hand with a happy sigh. Joshua felt the coolness of the metal on his skin and made a mental note to himself.

"Keys to all the doors, including the garage, Evan's apartment, and the car, young sir," Zyriah said smiling. "If you need help figuring out which key is for which door, I'd be happy to show you. I don't think that it'll be too difficult. The key with the black rubber around the head is your car key. I have a feeling that it's the one you wanted to know first."

"Actually, I'm happy with all of them," Joshua exclaimed.

"Well now," Enoch said, organizing the paperwork back into the file. "There's a couple things here I need to file at the courthouse to make things official. Then, I can let you all know when your copies of all these will be available. Is that fine with you, sir?"

"It sounds perfect," Joshua answered, slightly amused being called "sir".

"Now, Miss Flint, is there anything else I can help you with this morning? I do have some appointments that I need to get ready for this afternoon," Enoch inquired.

"I think you've taken care of everything Enoch," Zyriah said smiling. "Let me walk you to your car."

"No need for that. You just sit back, and you two can enjoy your morning. I can show myself out. Pleasure meeting you, Mr. Spiker. I'm sure I'll be seeing you soon," Enoch said, locking his suitcase, and quickly he walked around the rear corner back to his car. Joshua could hear his car door open and close, the engine start, and it quickly pulled away as the sound of the engine vanished.

"Now, that wasn't bad at all was it?" Zyriah asked.

"Not bad at all. I thought it might at least take an hour or two to be honest," Joshua admitted.

"That's part of why I went in early. He definitely knows what he's doing. He usually has the paperwork practically done before you even walk into his office some days," Zyriah explained.

"Well, thank you for these. I'll be sure to ask if I can't figure out which key goes to what," Joshua said jingling the keys on the key ring before putting the keys into his pocket.

"That's what I'm here for," Zyriah said, turning to look towards the rear of the garage, "I actually thought Evan would be out and about this morning."

"I'll be out in a minute," Evan yelled from an open window. Zyriah turned back to Joshua giggling.

"He must have some great ears," Joshua laughed.

"I heard that," Evan shouted, running down the rear garage stairs and onto the patio. "How did everything go?"

"Well, you officially have a new neighbor," Joshua said. "You better keep the noise down."

"Well, yes sir," Evan said saluting sarcastically. "How are you this morning Miss Flint?"

"I'm just glad to get all that paperwork taken care of. It's certainly a weight lifted," Zyriah expressed, taking a slight sigh.

"Well, when one problem gets solved, another is soon on the way," Evan said with a tone of concern.

"Problem? What sort of problem?" Zyriah asked as her left eyebrow arched. Joshua had the sense that Evan had disappointed Zyriah before.

"I think I might have made a little mistake," Evan said, dropping his eyes for a moment.

"What sort of mistake? Joshua has only been here one night so far," Zyriah said sounding disappointed.

"Well, it was his first night, and he had a lot on his mind," Evan explained, dropping his eyes a few more moments, "I recommended that he use the selenite pendant to help him get to sleep."

"What? Why would you do that? You know he's not ready for something like that without one of us being present, most of all me. Did something happen Joshua?" Zyriah asked with heightened concern.

"Just a strange dream. It's nothing important. It was just strange," Joshua said dismissively to try to avoid making it a stressful moment.

"Why was it strange? What did you dream?" Zyriah asked insistently.

"It was nothing," Joshua said, trying to understate the dream and relax Zyriah's concerns. "It was just a girl walking through a path in the woods."

"There's more," Evan interrupted. "He knew somewhere there was a fire."

"A fire?" Zyriah focused into Joshua's eyes with an intense stare. "Did you see a fire?"

"Only for a moment. I mainly saw a little girl on the path that had some ash and soot on her," Joshua detailed, trying to speak completely. "It was just a dream. I only remember parts of it."

"Miss Flint?" Evan interrupted yet again. "There is

something else. He heard a voice saying a name."

"Name?" Zyriah continued looking intensely. "What name did you hear?"

"Sarah Baker," Joshua said unwittingly. "I didn't actually hear it though. It was just a strange feeling that was in my mind. Does that mean anything?"

Zyriah stood and turned to think. Joshua looked at Evan, and he saw Evan's concerned expression. There was apparently something more to that dream than it just being a dream. There was something relevant. There was something important. Joshua knew the instant concern in both Zyriah and Evan was a concern that needed addressed. He still did not understand why a simple dream could cause all this importance. He remained quiet until Zyriah turned back and looked at Evan with disappointment.

"You knew better than to tell him to use that pendant without us. That's not what it was meant for," Zyriah dictated in a strict manner.

"I'm sorry, but how was I supposed to know he'd zero in on something so fast?" Evan apologized. "I knew you said he had something, but I didn't know he can do that."

"What did I do?" Joshua finally spoke up. "It was just a dream, right? What is everybody so upset about?"

"I'm upset because I didn't want you to start any kind of training without me, Joshua," Zyriah said, slowing her speech to more of a concerned and articulate tone. "It's very important that you understand all things in a steady and progressive way."

"Exactly," Joshua said, finally standing his ground. "I came here trusting you to help me, and thank you for all the help you both have given me. I've received more in twenty-four hours than I have in years, but I know you're keeping something from me. You want me to believe you're really here to help me? Then why do you keep talking about that I need to understand things? What is this training you're talking about? What the hell is going on around here?"

All three of them grew quiet. Joshua's tone was definitely stern, and it seemed to him that he momentarily stunned them. He had tried being polite, smiling and being courteous, but he was not going to wait any longer with questions when these two people were keeping the answers. Zyriah, looking away for a moment, appeared to be collecting her thoughts in some type of understandable order. Evan looked at her and back to Joshua, with a slight smile and nodding his head. Joshua could tell Evan understood why he vented in such a way. He was confused, and he needed to know more.

"You're right, Joshua," Zyriah said with a sigh. "I've just been putting this off, and I guess I've waited long enough. There's just so much explaining to do, but you deserve to know what's happening here."

"Yes, I deserve that much," Joshua said. "Please, can you tell me now?"

"Can we step to the front of the house, please?" Zyriah stood and stepped to the same rear corner of the building that Mr. Burke had just exited from. "There's some things you can see from there that will help you understand what is going on."

Joshua stood and moved over beside Evan. He was ready for an explanation, but at the same time he knew that it could be more than he could handle. He just had all the satisfaction of getting a home and a car, and now he was afraid that what would be said would put all of that into jeopardy. Instantly, he felt blame as his dream seemed to have caused the urgency of the issue.

"Can you at least tell me it's not my fault?" Joshua requested. "I didn't mean to cause all this trouble just by dreaming something. Just tell me I didn't do something wrong."

"I know whose fault it is, Joshua," Zyriah said, crossing to face him and putting her hand on his shoulder. "Believe me, the fault isn't yours."

"If it's not my fault then whose fault is it?" Joshua asked.

"The fault lies with your mother, Joshua. In a way, your mother is the reason for all of it," Zyriah explained.

In the daytime, Wilcox unfolded like a balanced scale, the buildings and the houses behind them on the left of Treeclimber Drive mirroring the right-hand side of the road. There was steady traffic, and from a distance the people looked like parts of a model, reading their newspapers, walking along sidewalks and across crosswalks, or just standing to look at the beauty of the day. Joshua's new home, standing high on the hillside, towered above the town, and the fact that he was the newest resident, sitting on the highest pedestal of the little town gave Joshua a slight feeling of unease.

He looked to the left of the hillside, a long field with a dead-end road surrounded by maples and pines, then to his right seeing a large home with an above average sized parking lot with many cars. Realizing the building was some place of business with a large sign on the edge of the parking lot that he was unable to read from the distance,

Joshua wondered what a large home like that, two stories with a long-curved porch, could have been remodeled into.

"What is that? That building over there?" Joshua inquired.

"Peaceful Days Senior Center," Zyriah said, standing beside the petunia filled flowerbox in front of the front window. "It's assisted living for the infirmed and elderly."

"Well, they picked a beautiful location with a beautiful view," Joshua said, trying to remember what part of the hillside that was. He remembered Evan had given the hillside two different names, but he was unable to remember what they were. "What name did you give that part of the hillside?"

"That side is The Knob," Evan said, stepping over to the other side of the building, standing opposite from Zyriah. "The other half with the field is Morgan's Ridge."

"I'll have to get use to the names of things around here," Joshua said, sitting down on the front step that led to the front door. He thought random questions might help ease the intensity of the conversation on the patio. However, he knew he could not pass the opportunity to uncover the secrets he was about to absorb.

"Are you ready?" Zyriah asked.

"To hear what all my mother did that caused all these issues you two seem to have?" Joshua responded with his own question. "To be honest, I won't know until I hear the explanation."

"Well, it all wasn't intended from the beginning. Your mother, Lenora, was always so inquisitive. If she didn't know the answer to something, she researched the subject until she got a firm grasp on the subject. So, when she decided to write a paper on the psychology of the psychic mind, she sought me out in college. I was fairly known for doing a reading or two, although tarot cards were never my thing. I hadn't developed my automatic writing ability yet, so I was an amateur. Still, she was interested in the research I had done on the subject and sought me out. To be honest, I was pretty flattered by somebody wanting to know more about me and the topic of my psychic ability. That was the point when she and I began working together," Lenora explained.

"But I don't understand what that has to do with me coming here," Joshua said, feeling the long backstory was going to take too long to get to the point of his concern.

"In the process of researching her paper, she became more and more interested in discovering her own abilities. I always told her and anybody that ever asked that if the mind is willing to experiment and try new things, any person could uncover some sort of either innate or learned ability simply by allowing their minds to be open to the experience. Your mother learned rather quickly that she could use different techniques to not only envision the recent past but also the near future. Very similar to the abilities you've demonstrated so far," Zyriah continued.

"I'm not exactly sure how I've demonstrated anything," Joshua interrupted. "A few lucky coincidences on some paintings I painted and a dream I had doesn't make me a psychic wonder."

"It does show that your mind is open to the possibilities of training those coincidences into a true mental gift. The problem with your mother was that she continued to desire to strengthen that ability, perhaps far too quickly, in order to see even farther in the past and further into the future than she was prepared for. It almost became a mental addiction once she realized that the coincidences you referred to weren't coincidences at all. She was using the gifts she had but pushing the limits of her range far too early. So, when she discovered that certain things could assist her in that endeavor of going farther in either direction of the timeline, she went out on her own to pursue those artifacts, without proper planning and training. I would have been happy to do further research with Lenora anytime she would have asked, but unfortunately she kept those details of her life to herself," Zyriah explained.

"Let me ask this then," Joshua questioned. "If you and Evan and God knows who else has these abilities, then why weren't you able to see what she had been doing? Doesn't that just show that your gifts, as you call them, are faulty?"

"These artifacts have a unique characteristic," Zyriah explained. "Whenever they're being utilized, our abilities don't seem to be able to see them in operation."

"Well, that's a very convenient explanation," Joshua smirked, not wanting to be cruel or bitter, but he did not like when the answers were easy.

"That is until your dream last night," Zyriah continued.

"What's his dream prove?" Evan interjected.

"A couple of things," Zyriah explained to Evan, while Joshua listened. "Not only does it demonstrate Joshua's ability to see past events, in this case events that happened days ago, but it also shows he was able to see the instrument, or artifact, in action. I couldn't do it. Evan, you couldn't do it. Joshua was able to see Sarah Baker on that pathway through the trees that night, and at that moment that little girl was in full control of the Star. I'm betting, with a little training, he can see even more."

"The Star?" Joshua asked. "What Star?"

Zyriah took a deep breath while Joshua watched her shift her stance. He felt he just asked the question that was going to open an entire new experience, the question that he did not even know existed until Zyriah had just mentioned that word. He thought there was something in her face that showed she was going to explain the truth of why he was brought there.

"It's one of the relics your mother had collected, Joshua," Zyriah explained. "It's the artifact that is causing the problems that this town is beginning to face. It's the instrument that destroyed that little girl's family just days ago. Its name is Josephine's Star."

Joshua followed along behind Zyriah and Evan on the dead-end road that ended on Morgan's Ridge. He felt some comfort in the warmth of that October day and looked back and forth from the road ahead of him, to the ones he followed, and then back to the town looking at the life it contained. He thought how normal things seemed to be down there, and how abnormal life was in Charleston before he came to Wilcox.

Things were more complicated than what had already been presented, a fact he was already sure of. What was thought of as basic questions that needed answers were suddenly turning into a large mystery but also a total attack to his belief system. The question was how he would continue from this point, and he wondered if the risk of exposing himself to all this mystery was worth having the new assets he acquired. What was surprising him most of all was his willingness to be open to the idea of psychic ability he was being presented. Part of him felt it was easier to listen than to argue. It was not an easy thing for him, but he thought it was necessary.

"What does coming to the Ridge have to do with all of this?" Joshua asked.

"Oh, this is where it all started buddy," Evan turned his head to answer while keeping a steady pace. "This town's got a good bit of history to it. This business with the Star just needs a good starting point."

"A good starting point this is," Zyriah said, stepping off the paved road and into the grassy field, extending her arms outward for a moment to stretch, and turned to face Joshua. "The old Morgan mansion stood right here. Clyde Morgan, his wife, six sons, and one daughter all lived in a grand stone mansion right here back before the Great Depression. Old Clyde made a great deal of money in local West Virginia coal mines and a few businesses down there in the city. His wife, Elise Anne, was a pillar of the community, and the hostess of major social events both in the local women's club but also here in their home. She was often talked about as being the beauty of Wilcox, and when Clyde and she were finally married, many people in the town said he used that business sense in his quest for the perfect bride, and Clyde had succeeded. Soon after, Elise began a long list of pregnancies and deliveries for the large family Clyde always wanted. Most of the births were almost consecutive, year to year, but Elise wanted a daughter. It took all those births, six sons, for Elise to finally get her dream, a baby girl. People said she named her Josephine after her father, Joseph. When the baby grew up, it was said Josephine's beauty rivaled her mother's, and Clyde and Elise became increasing protective. It wasn't long after the girl's eighteenth year that she decided on a beau, but the choice wasn't one her parents would have made. It was a surprise to many."

"Let me guess," Joshua said, "a poor guy from a poor family."

"Quite the contrary," Zyriah smiled, looking pleased that Joshua showed interest. "The Morgan's had some business and societal competition in this town. Another family, after making a fortune in local farming, decided to come to town and own a few of those town businesses themselves. Pretty soon, they bought up those few stores as well as the land that now is called the Knob. That family, Joshua, was yours. The family name was Spiker."

"So, Josephine became interested in someone from my family?" Joshua asked.

"Oh, Anthony Spiker was said to be quite the catch," Zyriah continued. "Well built from working in the farms with his father, James, and having the looks of his mother, Carol, Anthony Spiker became the man every young lady wanted in the town. His father made him a manager for the market that's now Michalski's which they purchased down on Treeclimber Drive, and Anthony's confidence was said to be infectious. He strolled, well dressed, outside on the sidewalk of the store, flirting with the young ladies passing by on a regular basis. One day, he met a young lady named Josephine Morgan, and young Anthony was smitten. However, town gossip was that Anthony was more interested in the status a relationship with Josephine could bring rather than connecting with the girl on more of an emotional level. He was, after all, very desired by women of the town, and rumor had it, even as he pursued Josephine romantically, this did not curb his desire for other types of relations from the pretty girls in town."

"Sex? You're saying my relative was a big player, then?" Joshua asked with a sarcastic laugh.

"Yes, to put more of a direct explanation to it," Zyriah continued. "However, those were times where things were more, how should I say? Hush, hush. It wouldn't look good on a lady at the time to go after a man with a wandering eye for other women. So, the town maintained the quiet for months until news came of a wedding announcement."

"A wedding?" Joshua inquired.

"Oh, it was quite a scandal with battling families. Old Man Morgan was dead-set against his daughter being married to the son of his competitor, with similar objections from James and Carol Spiker. Elise Morgan focused more on the societal aspects of what a grand wedding could bring, so although she didn't approve, she was willing to organize the event."

"A great big wedding," Joshua said, looking back at the town, seeing on one of the side streets a steeple of a church farther back in the network of side streets. "Did they get married in the church down there?"

"Oh no," Zyriah clarified. "That church wasn't even there at the time. They used the old Sunrise Missionary Church for that event. You won't believe where the church was located."

"Where?" Joshua asked.

"You're living in it," Evan laughed. "That's what that building was originally used for."

"A church?" Joshua asked as he looked back at his new home, trying to envision the building for a more religious use. "I can't even imagine that place as a church."

"Oh, your mother did a ton of remodeling to the place when she got her hands on it and her psychology practice was in full force," Evan explained. "In between it being a church and your mother's home, it was actually a hardware and feed store if you can believe it. That place has had a lot of work done on it."

"I guess that explains that sunset window and why a stained-glass window is in the building," Joshua said. He had thought it was strange to have such a large stained-glass window in a residence, and even stranger he never questioned why the window was there earlier. He had liked the artistry of the window more than thinking of why it existed.

"Actually, no," Zyriah explained. "Your mother had the sunset window installed during the remodeling of the building. Another window, a much grander and taller one was on that end of the building. It stretched from the second to third floor, and it was said to be one of the best stained-glass representations of the nativity ever created. The building was quite different then, with the balcony area being on the front of the building, and your wooden staircase was in the front as well and only extended to the balcony area. Your mother decided in her remodel that there were certain elements she wanted to keep. She even went as far to have the same glassmakers create the new sunset window."

"Wait a minute," Joshua said, beginning to lose track of the intended storyline. He admitted he was becoming interested. "What happened to Anthony and Josephine? Did they still get married?"

"Oh, it was to be a grand event," Zyriah continued. "Elise ordered Josephine's dress from Europe and had it custom fitted by local seamstresses. Old Clyde finally gave in, once James Spiker agreed to sell one of his smaller businesses, a woman's apparel store, to Clyde with the proviso that Clyde allowed the wedding to continue as planned. Josephine was said to be rather a braggart, telling stories of how perfect Anthony was and how perfect their marriage will be. Meanwhile, the young ladies that she was bragging to were in some instances the same ones Anthony was physically involved with. Little did Josephine know that one of her own bridesmaids, Ruth Bartlett, was one of those young ladies that not only was sexually involved with Anthony, but she was also intending to marry young Anthony herself."

"So, Ruth broke Anthony and Josephine up?" Joshua said, getting more and more involved in the tale.

"Well, the morning of the wedding came," Zyriah explained. "The bridal party was to use the balcony area for a waiting area prior to the wedding itself. Josephine, Ruth, her maid of honor and another bridesmaid waited for the noon bell to strike and the wedding to begin. Well, the story goes that while Anthony waited at the alter and all the guests were seated and waiting, a wailing cry came from up in the balcony area. The guests grew so concerned that they erupted in conversation, so loud apparently it was difficult to hear the person sitting beside you. Anthony, recognizing that the cry was from Josephine, ran immediately to the balcony area and was confronted by Josephine, just after she was told of Anthony's infidelities by Ruth. The crowd calmed down enough that the conversation between Anthony and Josephine was heard enough so that the guests also became aware of Anthony's sexual escapades. Josephine was apparently furious, striking Anthony hard enough that the slap was heard throughout the church, and then came the sound of breaking glass and a scream that started so loudly but grew slightly distant and abruptly ended. The guests flocked out the church's entry doors and found young Josephine, dead in her own wedding dress and lying on the front grounds. It was said the ones that found her looked up and saw young Anthony standing there looking out of the hole of broken glass down at his future bride panting and sweating in exhaustion from the battle. Your mother has a great deal of paperwork she had collected over the years when she researched this matter as well as other things."

"He killed her?" Joshua was shocked.

"He was convicted for the murder," Zyriah said. "The day of the sentencing was to be a few days after the conviction. Poor Anthony never did make it to his sentencing. He hung himself with a bed sheet in the local jail while he waited for his court appearance."

Joshua grew silent. The story was a bit overwhelming, not only by the drama of it but also due to the murderer being related to him. The more he learned about his biological family, the more he did not want to be associated with them. Still, there was more he wanted to know, more he needed to know.

"Well, what is the Josephine's Star then?" Joshua asked with an inquisitive stare. "Where did it come from?"

"That window," Zyriah answered. "That stained-glass window of the nativity. So much of that window had fallen along with Josephine as she fell, but the piece representing the Star of Bethlehem still hung from the top of the window frame. However, after that tragedy, the Star no longer represented the night Jesus was born. The Star became something different. Your mother discovered exactly what that piece of glass was able to do."

"What did she discover?" Joshua began growing slightly frustrated, feeling Zyriah's answers were becoming vague yet again. "What can this thing do to people? Where is it?"

"The discovery? That this piece of glass contained a certain talent of its own. Whether or not it already possessed the ability prior to the murder remains somewhat of a mystery. However, it's ability has been stretched into something more devious, and more deadly," Zyriah explained.

"I don't understand," Joshua said, growing with frustration. "What can it do and where can we find it?"

Evan, looking at Joshua with calm eyes so that Joshua's fevered pitch dissipated, finally answered the question. "That, my friend, is exactly why you're here."

CHAPTER
SIX

Joshua was halfway back to his new home with a determined stride but an indetermined mind on what to do next. The long stories by Zyriah were more than he expected, but he was more worried about how these two people expected him to act on what they said. Even if he believed the story, even it was true that he had some type of ability, the truth was that he did not know exactly what that ability was or how to use it. The issue of this Star and what it could do also concerned him. If it was true and this piece of glass somehow could hurt people, it could also hurt him. He was not a man that enjoyed putting himself into danger, least of all deliberately.

"I don't know what you expect from me," Joshua said looking towards home, but loud enough that Zyriah and Evan could hear him from their places behind him. "I'm just an artist. You knew that when you met me. You're expecting me to have all these abilities that are going to solve these issues about this Star, whatever it really is, and

I don't know how to help you. You're asking me for way too much here."

"We don't want to pressure you," Zyriah said, slightly winded trying to keep up with Joshua's pace. "I know it's a big burden and it's a bunch of information to take in at once, but I wouldn't have even mentioned it if it wasn't important. I'm just afraid more people will be hurt if we don't act on this."

"More people?" Joshua asked. "How many have been hurt by this? If it is that many, why did you take so long to act on this?"

"We didn't know for sure what was happening, ok?" Evan answered. "I know personally once a little kid gets involved then we have to do something."

"The girl in my dream?" Joshua asked, making a connection with his dream to Evan's comment. "This Sarah Baker girl is part of all this?"

Joshua stopped, turning to Zyriah and Evan for the answer to that question, but their facial expressions were both extremely solemn. Yet, while Zyriah's expression was more one of a respectful calm, Joshua noticed that Evan's face began to build up with a sad frustration. Joshua was just about to turn back toward the direction when Evan's voice erupted.

"She killed her parents!"

Joshua stopped again, turning once again to face the two but mainly looking at Evan, whose eyes began welling with tears and his chest beginning to heave. Joshua had never seen either of them beyond happy or concerned, so this raw emotion he watched Evan express was heartbreaking. The news of another murder in this town was not nearly as important to Joshua as seeing this man in pain. Joshua knew he cared for his friendship. It felt strange how little time had passed.

"Her father was a deputy in the town, a well-known and nice guy. That Star made that little girl kill him and his new wife. That little girl took two pairs of daddy's handcuffs and handcuffed her dad and her new mom to the headboard of their bed, and she burned the house down on them."

Joshua was silent. He listened carefully, but he was silent.

"Do you get it now?" Evan walked up to him to the distance that their faces were a foot apart. "It was just a little kid, and that Star made her do it. I don't know how exactly, and I don't know why, but we got to stop this somehow. I just know in my gut that if we work together we can figure this out, but we got to step up and not waste any more time on this."

"I really don't know what to say," Joshua finally speaking, looking into Evan's reddened watery eyes. "I don't even know where to begin on something like this. I don't know anything about this psychic stuff, but I don't want any little girls involved in something like this. What do I do? I'm completely lost as to what I can do to help this."

"If you want to try," Zyriah, stepping forward, putting her hand on Evan's shoulder in a calming manner, "I can show you how you can possibly help. Evan will be happy to help you as well, I'm sure. We don't want you to feel like we're asking you to do anything by yourself. We're asking you to help us and figure this out together."

"As friends," Evan added.

Joshua looked down to the ground, collecting his

thoughts and attempted to find an answer. The dream entered his mind again, those images of that young girl on that pathway on that dark night, and he thought how scared she must have been. He wondered how anyone or anything could deliberately cause the death of two people in such a way, much less the little girl he dreamed about. He took a breath to collect himself and looked at Evan and Zyriah and committed himself.

"I'll help you to help that girl and to make sure this doesn't happen again, because you're my friends," Joshua agreed.

Zyriah smiled. "Well, it's certainly nice to hear that. Maybe we should make one more stop before you go home Joshua. I think if you met someone, it might help you understand the entire situation."

"Who do you want me to meet?" Joshua asked, not expecting the answer that followed.

"Sarah Baker."

The lettering on the Peaceful Days Senior Center sign was so large that Joshua was surprised he was not able to read it from his front door. The sign stood firmly at the corner of a large parking lot where the building stood, another large, renovated home, but this was a large home that was more ranch style in its appearance with a large wrap around porch with white railing. Joshua admitted to himself the peaceful atmosphere of its location, with its disconnection from the town below.

Most of the residents on the porch were in wheelchairs, conversing with nurses or other patients, but some just stared forward enjoying the overlook view. Joshua noticed a German shepherd resting his head on the knee of one of the wheelchaired men, with a woman holding the man's hand as they both sat looking forward in their wheelchairs overlooking the town. They seemed at ease and comfortable where they were, and Joshua took a moment to appreciate the beauty of the town the couple seemed so focused on.

The walk over to the center was surprising short, but with all the thoughts rushing through Joshua's mind, he was sure his overthinking was the reason why it took such little time to arrive at their destination. He followed Zyriah and Evan once again, still occasionally looking down over the town, but also looking at the center itself and wondering if he had heard correctly who Zyriah had wanted him to meet.

"You did say Sarah Baker, the girl from my dream, right?" Joshua inquired but already knew the answer.

"That's what I said," Zyriah agreed.

"But this is a nursing home. Why would a girl that did those things be here? I thought she'd be in some juvenile facility or a mental institution by now," Joshua said struggling to comprehend the situation.

"Do you really think she belongs in a mental institution?" Evan questioned with a hard sternness. His eyes flared.

"I didn't mean it in a bad way. I just assumed that based on what happened that's probably where she would be," Joshua said in a calm manner, trying not to upset Evan.

"Let me give you a big piece of advice about Wilcox, Joshua. Best thing you can do is not to ever assume anything. Nothing ever is what it seems around here," Evan said, stepping up on the steps of one of the center's multiple entrances. "Sheriff Tucker is very aware of the odd things going on around here. She was a patient of your mother for a long time. Last thing that sheriff wants is having to explain why this little girl did such a thing."

"Why do you think she did though? There has to be more to how this Star works to cause a girl to do this," Joshua exclaimed, trying to unravel the mystery of this piece of broken window.

"You're exactly right about that," Zyriah affirmed as she followed Evan to the front door. She entered in front of Joshua while Evan held the door open and followed them inside. "The more we know we know about Sarah Baker, maybe the more we know how this Star works."

They followed past the general information desk and down a long hall to a door with "Administrator" stamped in gold on the door. Beside the door was a large desk covered with equipment Joshua was not familiar with, as it looked very different than just a computer and telephone he was used to seeing on a secretary's desk. A thin, tan, and bearded man typed extremely quickly, until he turned and saw Zyriah. He immediately stood, crossed to give Zyriah a quick hug, then began speaking in sign language, which Joshua didn't understand. Joshua looked at Zyriah, whose eyes watched the man sign his greeting and she smiled.

"Pleasure to see you too," Zyriah said and signed. "You're right it's been too long. How have you been?"

The man signed another series of words, and Joshua was amazed with the complexity of how quickly he moved his hands and fingers to express himself. He smiled, impressed but also curious as to what the two were saying. The man turned and looked at Evan as if they certainly knew each other, but then he turned to face Joshua with a curious expression and signed more.

"Oh, I'm sorry. I should have done introductions," Zyriah said and signed. "Of course, you know Evan, and this is Joshua Spiker. He just moved into Lenora's home, and he will be staying there. Joshua, this is Noah Wilson, secretary to the administrator."

Noah signed again, politely smirking like he was holding back a laugh. Zyriah, laughing a little out loud, patted him on the shoulder and nodded. Joshua wished he understood sign language at moments like these.

"Oh, I'm sorry. Noah here is the 'administrative assistant'," Zyriah said, explaining the correction Joshua assumed Noah had just given her.

Noah smiled, appreciating the correction, and reached out to shake Joshua's hand. Joshua noticed quickly how strong the grip was and tried to squeeze back to show he also had some strength in his hand. Noah smiled at the effort, nodded and returned to signing his words to Zyriah.

"Actually, we're here to see Kathy, but I wasn't sure if she was in today," Zyriah said without signing at that point.

Joshua noticed Noah focusing on Zyriah's face as she spoke. He assumed Noah was able to read lips. Noah smiled and pointed to the administrator's door. He was certainly a pleasant person, Joshua noted. He was clean cut in appearance, and even as a deaf individual he had little difficulty it seemed to communicate with others. As the first deaf person Joshua had encountered in his life, Joshua found Noah extremely intriguing.

"Any chance she has time to see us?" Zyriah asked.

Noah held up a finger to indicate to wait, walked around his desk, pressing on a separate keyboard from his computer attached to a small screen. Joshua could see within a few moments that words began appearing on the screen, and Noah typing another message into it. He lifted his head, smiling at Zyriah, and signed a response.

"Thank you so much, Noah. We do appreciate it," Zyriah said, then turned to Joshua and Evan. "Kathy will be out in just a minute. Noah asked us to have a seat."

The three sat down into three of the brown leather chairs along the wall near the administrator's door. Joshua continued to watch Noah work as a telephone call came, a light flashed, and Noah turned to type on another computer screen. Joshua then understood that Noah was answering the telephone by communicating through the computer, and he was pretty amazed. However, when Noah turned to write something on a piece of paper, he caught Joshua looking at him, and gave him a little wave. Joshua turned his head down to look at the floor, embarrassed from being so obviously staring. Another light flashed on the desk from the first machine Noah used, and Noah stood, walked around his desk to the door, and waved the three of them into the office.

"Zyriah Flint, what an expected surprise," a lady, grey-bunned hair and catlike grin, sat behind a long desk with two long paned windows behind here. "According to Tucker, I should've expected you here a few days ago."

"Oh, I probably should have been," Zyriah agreed, "but I needed to pick up a friend from down in Charleston. Kathy Ebert? I'd like you to meet Joshua Spiker."

"Spiker?" Kathy exclaimed with wide eyes. "Lenora Spiker's boy? Has it been that long? My goodness, I remember your mother when she was still pregnant with you, and you're already a full-grown man? My word."

"Pleasure to meet you, ma'am," Joshua said politely.

"Ma'am?" Kathy laughed. "I might be a little long in the

tooth, but you can just call me Kathy. Boy, he is a handsome one, isn't he Zyriah?"

"Yes, he's a nice-looking young man," Zyriah said, with a slight emphasis on the word young. "He's moved into Lenora's place, and I thought the two of you should meet."

"You mean I'm going to have a fine-looking man like this as my neighbor?" Kathy said, smiling wider. "My word. Coming to work is going to get better and better for me knowing we have such a fine-looking gentleman right next door. I might have to invite you over for lunch one day real, real soon."

"We're here to see Sarah Baker, Miss Ebert," Evan interjected. "She is upstairs I'm assuming?"

"Oh, she's upstairs and doing just fine," Kathy answered, but still looking Joshua with a slow up and down prowling look. "Still hasn't' woken up, but her aunt has been by her side ever since the other day. I didn't see the harm, with the little girl asleep and all, and Nancy was so concerned. Sheriff Tucker brought her up here to visit the day after. Apparently, she'd driven in from Pittsburgh just to make sure the girl was doing ok."

"Nancy Baker," Zyriah nodded. "Now there's a name from the past."

"Oh, you know Wilcox residents all have rubber bands on their ankles," Kathy jested. "Give them time, and they'll snap back to town for one reason or another. Are you married there, Mr. Spiker?"

"Kathy?" Zyriah said, with a tone indicating the inappropriateness of Kathy's question.

"I may be old Zyriah, but I sure am not dead. Being in a wheelchair just makes me chase a little faster," Kathy said, wheeling her chair around her desk toward the far wall of the room to an elevator door beside a fine grandfather clock. "If I don't jump on the opportunities when they come, how do you ever expect me to find myself a man?"

"Hey, I'm glad Joshua's here now," Evan laughed, as Kathy pressed the elevator button and the door opened. Kathy wheeled herself inside the elevator and turned with a wicked smirk. Joshua felt more and more how much the woman had in common with his former landlord.

"Evan, you weren't ever able to be caught, you know. Your heart has always belonged somewhere else. You wouldn't even give me a chance."

"Oh, I just made room for that dream man to come into your life, Kathy," Evan smiled, as the three of them filed into the elevator.

"Or came into my elevator," Kathy said, as Joshua felt her looking at him, especially taking a more rear view as she arched her neck back. "Today just might be my lucky day."

"So, you said the Baker girl hasn't woken up?" Zyriah said, with a tone she was growing tired of the lady's flirting, which Joshua found funnier as the woman continued.

"No, no, no. Poor thing's been sleeping like a baby all these days," Kathy answered, finally turning her head to Zyriah's stare, with a cocked eyebrow. "Doctor's been monitoring her on a regular basis. She's healthy as can be, but the doctor said it's probably just stress and exhaustion. She should be up in a day or two, he said."

"Well, be sure to let one of us know as soon as she wakes, will you?" Zyriah asked, and Joshua could tell Zyriah was not feeling comfortable talking. "We have a few questions for her."

"Now wait," Kathy asked turning her head looking at Joshua, "are you one of these psychic investigators like your friends here? I did not realize they were recruiting new members."

"Oh, I'm just coming along for the ride right now," Joshua said smiling. "I'm just a beginner, so I've been told."

"Beginner, you say," Kathy replied as the elevator door opened as Zyriah and Evan filed out into the hall. "Well, if you ever need a teacher, you know where to find me."

"Kathy! Honestly!" Zyriah snapped. She appeared to be nearing her wit's end.

"Can't blame a girl for trying," Kathy laughed, as Joshua followed into the hallway, leaving Kathy in the elevator. "Room 202. Come on down the hall elevator whenever your through, alright? Pleasure meeting you Joshua."

"It's been a pleasure as always Miss Ebert," Evan replied for Joshua. "I'm sure we'll see you soon."

"You know where to find me," Kathy exclaimed as the door closed, leaving the three in the hall, just the three of them yet again.

"Now that's a piece of work right there," Joshua laughed.

"Oh, if you think she's bad, you should hear Noah sometime," Zyriah laughed in return.

"Noah? How do you mean?" Joshua questioned.

"Part of the perks of sign language is that not everybody in the room can speak it," Zyriah smiled, looking at Joshua. "First thing Noah said downstairs was 'who's the boy with the cute butt'?"

"What? Meaning me?" Joshua asked.

"They're twins of the wicked souls, those two. Kathy Ebert is just louder about it," Evan laughed, but they all quickly mellowed their tones as they approached the room with the number 202 on the door.

The three of them peeked into the open doorway to see the little girl, lying in a hospital bed. Joshua remembered her in his dream, and for the first time he realized the reality of the situation. The heart monitors, the IV saline tube attached to the girl's arm, and the small sleeping face, now clean and resting.

He thought she looked so peaceful, so tranquil. He wondered how anyone could take a young soul and turn it into a person that could do such an evil thing as that fire. He watched her small chest breathing slowly through her deep sleep, and he hoped she would wake soon. He walked further into the room, seeing a woman sitting near the television with her chair facing the young girl. The woman stood to greet them.

"Zyriah Flint. It has been a real long time since I've seen you. What are you doing here?" the woman asked.

"Just here checking on Sarah. Kathy told us you'd be here. Nancy, this is Evan and Joshua, two friends of mine," Zyriah introduced.

"Please to meet you, Nancy," Joshua said, as she smiled and nodded.

"I certainly wish it would've been under better circumstances. This whole thing has been such a shock to the whole family. My parents are coming down again to finalize a few things for my brother," Nancy said, as Joshua could see the straining wrinkles around her eyes from a lack of proper rest.

"Your brother was her dad?" Joshua asked, feeling awkward with his directness.

"Allan? Sure was. Strange to say Allan in this town. Once he got deputy status in this town, that's all he ever wanted to be called. I'm his sister though, so he said I was allowed," Nancy smiled, with little growing tears in the corners of her eyes.

"Do you have any idea how this would've happened?" Evan inquired.

"Not a clue to be honest with you. I know what the Sheriff told me, but I can't really believe it. It had to be some kind of accident, but she says it was something more deliberate. A fire? Sarah? I'd never believe it," Nancy remarked with confident assertion.

"I can only imagine what has been going on in your mind after something like this," Zyriah said comfortingly.

"She's a fine young lady. Good grades and stays out of trouble. Allen sent her up to Pittsburgh a couple weekends last summer, and she was an angel. Cleaning up after herself. Even cleaning up after me, if I'm going to be completely honest about it," Nancy bragged.

"Did she ever have anything in her history that could've triggered something like this though," Evan asked.

"I mean, Allan did drink his light beer on a regular occasion to wind down from work, but it wasn't an issue on how he raised Sarah. He wasn't abusive by any means. Actually, the only thing I can think of that happened to her would make you think she would be the last person to do something like this. That's why when the Sheriff said it was a fire, I immediately said there was no way that Sarah would have been responsible for something like this. That little girl was deathly afraid of fire of any kind," Nancy explained.

"And why is that?" Evan asked.

"There was a little accident back about three years ago," Nancy continued, whisking her long brown hair over her shoulder. "Ever since, Sarah won't go near an open flame.

In my opinion, its proof positive she didn't set this fire now."

"What kind of accident," Zyriah asked.

"Allan had bought Sarah a little candleholder in the shape of a bluebird, with a little white candle for her nightstand in her bedroom. It was just a little decoration, and Sarah always did love things that fly. There were strict orders in that house about Sarah ever lighting a match. Allan told her she wasn't old enough to light any candles in the house. He told her he was the grown up, and it was his responsibility. Ever since Abby left him and the girl, he was always buying Sarah little things to make her happy. He didn't expect anything terrible to come from it," Nancy explained.

"What did come from it?" Evan questioned.

"It was just a typical Friday night," Nancy continued. "Allan had a long day, so he drank a few too many beers and went to his bedroom. For some reason though, Allan had his bedroom door locked that night, and that left Sarah by herself in her bedroom watching television. Well, she told me she looked over at the candle, and decided to take a matchbox from the kitchen and light the candle. She was going to make sure she blew the candle out before she went to bed. She said she was trying to be so careful. Once the candle was lit, she was afraid it would melt on the nightstand, so she moved that little candleholder over to the window ledge. The way she told me was that she fell asleep, and that the candle was too close to the curtain. The curtain caught on fire."

"Was she hurt?" Evan asked intensively.

"No, but she was awful scared," Nancy explained. "She woke up to a smokey room and ran down the hall to beat on her dad's door. Well, Allan was drunk as a skunk apparently, and he didn't hear the door knocking, so she called 911. Fire department was there within a couple minutes."

"Thank goodness," Joshua said.

"Oh, that just set Allan off," Nancy continued. "He woke up to the fire department beating on his door, and them seeing him in a drunken stupor like that. He immediately was concerned he was going to get into trouble for neglect, and once the firemen left, he told Sarah a thing or two, which just made the whole situation worse. Every day since then, the girl won't go near a fireplace, blow out a birthday candle, or even want to see fireworks on the Fourth of July."

"Did she ever get any counseling?" Zyriah mentioned.

"Oh, I brought it up to Allan that she probably needed to see a professional, but Allan was always dead-set against any of that mind washing he called it. I was able to tell Sarah once that there was always a counselor at school if she ever needed to talk," Nancy replied.

"Did she ever see the counselor?" Joshua questioned.

"That I don't know," Nancy answered. "She never told me one way or another. I always thought it was just a natural thing growing up. Everybody's afraid of something, you know. Something happens to everybody when you're young, and it makes you scared. I saw a boy playing at the park that got bit by a snake when I was a kid, and I've never liked snakes since. I just thought it was more or a less a natural part of growing up."

"So, there's wasn't any animosity towards Sarah and her father or new wife?" Evan wondered.

"Oh, not a bit. Allan and Cheryl both spoiled Sarah

rotten, but they definitely taught her the value of a dollar," Nancy smiled. "Sarah had a white piggy bank she collected the change she earned or found so she could save up for something someday."

"Well, we didn't mean to bother you Nancy," Zyriah smiled, shaking Nancy's hand to leave. "Like I said, if there's any developments in her condition, we'd appreciate hearing from you."

"I live right in the big house at the fork in the road," Joshua added, feeling that Zyriah was ending the conversation too abruptly. "If anything happens and she gets better, go ahead and stop on by."

"I really do appreciate the concern, you all." Nancy returned to her seat by the television.

"Try to have a better day," Evan said saying goodbye, as the three of them left the room, leaving Nancy alone once again with Sarah, deep in her restful sleep.

Joshua followed Zyriah and Evan to the main elevators down the hall, taking the elevator to the main lobby, and exiting the building happy to not run into Miss Ebert on the way out. He felt the talk with Nancy Baker was informative, especially about the young girl's history with her fear of fire. He continued walking forward until something caught his eye enough to make him stop his footsteps. On the porch, Joshua saw the same German shepherd that he viewed when he approached Pleasant Days.

The dog sat there, poised on his front paws while resting on his tail, and Joshua felt the dog was waiting for him. The look in his dark eyes was direct, and although the two had never met, Joshua felt the dog was pleased due to the inquisitive side looks as the dog tilted his head slightly from one side to the other. His coat was brown and black, although the brown had infiltrated the black sections with almost a camouflage pattern of color. Around his front legs and body was a pale green harness like ones Joshua had seen on service dogs, with three silver embroidered stars in a row across his back. His thick black leather collar around his neck had a silver tag dangling underneath. Joshua, almost too curious, slowly approached the animal with the question of whether that tag revealed the animal's name.

"I'm not going to hurt you," Joshua explained, slowly bending down and reaching for the dog tag. "I just want to know your name."

The animal did not advance, and Joshua smiled seeing how cooperative the dog was. His fingers reached the tag, and the dog lifted and turned his head slightly, which Joshua took as an invitation for the reading of his silver tag. Joshua squinted to see the name "Kombat" printed clearly on the silver tag. The dog waited a moment, then stood to walk in the direction of the side of the porch that faced down into Wilcox. Joshua was slightly disappointed, feeling that the dog was rejecting his attention. Instead, once Kombat reached the corner, he turned his body back to Joshua to make eye contact. He, then, returned to turn the corner away from Joshua's viewpoint, so Joshua followed him. He noticed how quiet Zyriah and Evan were behind him, so he turned to see them. They all smiled to one another, then resumed their walk around the porch's corner.

"It's about time you brought him to visit," an elderly woman, sitting in a wheelchair, said as soon as the three turned the corner. Joshua immediately recognized that the woman made eye contact with Zyriah. The woman sat there with an older gentleman, also in a wheelchair, and although the woman was making direct eye contact, the man looked forward towards the town with eyes that appeared in a daze. "We were beginning to wonder if you were expecting us just to come over to the house ourselves."

"Time and a place for everything, Gloria," Zyriah responded. "We had a little bit of work to do first."

"The Baker girl," Gloria said, nodding in agreement. "Certainly, more important than us old folks. Treasure the children, treasure the children. Well, it looks like our friend here isn't much older than a child himself. Step forward so I can get a better look at you, son."

Joshua stepped forward, but he took the time to look at the woman and man. Her hair was blond and raised into a beehive hairstyle, pinned by little copper hair pins in selected places. Although it was not cold outside, she still had a heavy looking woolen black coat with a purple croqueted scarf around her neck. The man, in a brown hunting jacket, had a tag saying "Phillip Underwood" on its left front pocket. In smaller letters, the word "Nute" was printed in quotation marks, although Joshua noticed the letter E appeared as if someone had tried to erase it. He noticed that they had matching silver wedding bands, along with Gloria's diamond engagement ring. Clearly in their seventies or eighties, Joshua assumed they were married.

"You're handsome, son," Gloria said, grinning with the pleasing smile Joshua compared to a kindly grandmother. "Hard to imagine that pair producing such a fine young man."

"Pair?" Joshua questioned, immediately interested in any details about his parents. The woman definitely seemed to have a good deal of information. "You knew my mother and father?"

Gloria sat back, releasing a sighed breath. "I knew them, I knew them. Long history there with that pair. Don't think anybody in this town didn't know them to be honest. They surely made an impact on this place. Even bigger impact once you came along. I never saw you as a baby, though. Damn shame too. I love seeing that spark of life in those early days. Now that I see you though, I don't think you lost much of that spark. It sounds like just the spark this Miss Flint was hoping for. That right, Zyriah?"

"Things are going well," Zyriah said, with the look that they needed to leave. "I don't mean to bother you and your husband today, and we have some things to talk over with Joshua. Nute, it's always a pleasure to see you."

Zyriah walked over to the older man, patting his hand that rested on his wheelchair's arm. She stepped back, and out from the side behind the man's wheelchair appeared Kombat, who rested his head upon the man's knee. Once again, the man never made a motion and continued to stare forward. Zyriah stepped over to Gloria, shaking her hand before returned to Joshua and Evan's side.

"Not even a proper introduction before you go?" Gloria inquired, reaching her hand out to shake Joshua's hand. He felt the coolness in her skin, but her eyes were retaining warmth. "I'm Gloria Underwood, young man. This is my husband Phillip, although most around here just call him Nute."

"Like 'Newt'?" Joshua inquired. "I see it's spelled differently on his name tag."

"Oh, he's been called that ever since he was a little man," Gloria explained. "He had a fondness for living creatures, especially lizards. While some children would sell lemonade from behind cardboard boxes and a lemonade sign, my husband tried to sell any lizard he could find to the neighbor's as possible pets. He never was much of a businessman. The nickname from the neighborhood boys, however, always stuck."

"Well, its nice meeting both of you," Joshua said. "Maybe you can tell me more about my parents someday soon. Since I live right next door, I hope I won't be a bother since we're neighbors."

"Oh, no problem at all," Gloria said with a smile. "Any visitor is a welcome visitor, and if I can help lift that burden, I'll do whatever I can."

"Burden?" Joshua asked quickly.

Gloria, taking another deep sigh before speaking, focused her eyes on Joshua. She brought her shoulders slightly forward, and Joshua noticed that a pendant on a chain slipped out from behind her scarf. It appeared like a cloudy crystal with a silver bail.

It was the same pendant he received when he came to Wilcox, and Joshua felt it draw his eye. Gloria smiled, and Joshua wondered if she caught him staring at the stone.

"Your parent's life ambition has finally become your burden," Gloria explained. "It happens over and over in families. You'll see plenty of that once you reach my age. Parents never thinking their actions could change the futures of their children's lives. Over and over, over and over. The burden just gets passed and passed. You'll need some guidance, Joshua, but there's plenty of help around to be there for you. If the past is any indication, you may need that help more than you realize."

"My name," Joshua said, listening to the woman's voice

and feeling the comfort behind the words. "How did you know my name?"

Gloria turned her head, resting back into her chair and directing her eyes into the town the same as her husband. Her smile dissolved slightly into a grin, and her head began to nod slightly and repeatedly. Joshua wondered if she was reviewing her next statement in her head before she said it.

"See those hills?" Gloria questioned, with a breathy sound in her voice she did not have moments before. "There's one thing about these West Virginia hills. They hold secrets, they sure do. Some secrets I'm sure have been inside them a lot longer than I've been around. They sure do hold secrets, but you know what?"

Gloria smiled, outreaching her hand and pulling Joshua's ear down to her face to whisper something. Joshua felt the mystery in the conversation, and he became more and more intrigued. There was something about this woman, he thought.

"If you catch those hills at the right moment," Gloria explained in a whisper, "those hills love telling stories. Oh, yes they sure do."

She sat back, letting go of Joshua's hand, and let out a hearty laugh. Joshua felt a good energy from Gloria and a good presence. He stepped back to rejoin Zyriah and Evan, but Kombat stepped forward nudging his nose to Joshua's hand. Joshua rubbed behind Kombat's ears which made his tag whip back and forth quickly. The two appeared to have made a friendship.

"Don't worry about Kombat," Gloria said. "He's known to run to a neighbor's house from time to time, but he always finds his way back here. He's a good pup."

"Certainly, appears to be," Joshua said with a grin,

finally stopping the petting of the dog. "We really need to be going."

"I'll see you real soon then, new neighbor," Gloria exclaimed as they began walking away. Joshua followed Zyriah and Evan as they left Pleasant Days, and Joshua felt more like he was getting to know the town and its people. They continued in the direction of his house.

He began thinking of Sarah, laying in the hospital bed in a peaceful rest, and thankful she was calm and relaxed. Still, his mind was complicated with the thoughts of what she had done, and he focused more on the possibility that this Star had contributed to the girl's actions. He just could not believe such a child could commit a double murder intentionally.

"This Star," Joshua said, "What exactly do you think it did to Sarah?"

"Actually," Zyriah explained, walking side by side with Evan with Joshua following closely, "I'm fairly sure that the effect of that Star is causing that child to remain in that state. What I found interesting about what her aunt just said is why the child would commit a crime using a tool she had such an intense fear. It sounds as if the Star somehow forces the individual to not only face the person's greatest fear but also to force that person to utilize the object of the fear against the person that helped create that fear originally. Sarah's father bought her the candle that set her room on fire. Sarah's father didn't help her once the curtain was in flames, and Sarah very well could have blamed him for that."

"I don't understand why an object like that would be helpful to somebody wanting to strengthen their psychic abilities," Joshua wondered.

"First challenge of doing a reading is determining the main reason why the person wants the reading or, even more importantly, needs the reading," Evan said. "Most of the time, the person wants to know something important in their current life or near future they think is vital to know, like who they might marry or will they get a better job. Many times, they can think of some silly question treating the reading like a game asking what they should wear for that date on Saturday or does my boyfriend think I'm fat. What usually happens is that the reading ends up focused on the most important issue, whether the person is aware of it or not."

"So, it's possible that the Star brings that issue to the forefront from the beginning," Zyriah added. "If there's any connection to the Josephine story, it was certainly important that she had known her soon-to-be husband had been having encounters with other women before she married him. She was at the church prepared to marry him that day, and the news of his infidelities led to the confrontation that took her life. Perhaps, the Star is a weapon of revenge against those that created your greatest fear."

"Once again," Joshua pointed out, "I didn't think that psychic readings were only about things people fear. Doesn't that mean the Star is limiting in what it does?"

"The main point," Evan, looking back at Joshua, then back in the direction of Joshua's home, "Is that the Star brings out the most important truth that the reading needs to focus on. It sounds like the person using it is manipulating it somehow, but I'm not sure why they would do that."

"Well, if it is a weapon of truth and revenge," Zyriah

started to conclude, "then perhaps the user of the Star is seeking his or her own revenge against the person he used the Star on."

"In Sarah Baker's case, it might not be Sarah that the user wanted to be the victim," Evan added with speculation but with a certain level of confidence. "Perhaps the intended victim was her father."

"He was a deputy," Joshua said, thinking out loud. "Cops always have somebody down the line of their career that they've made mad at some point. That can be really tough to narrow down."

"Well, that's where your training is going to come into play," Zyriah turned saying, finally reaching Joshua's front door. "I have a feeling if Evan and I teach you a thing or two, we might be able to find out more about the Star's current owner."

"I'll be honest with you," Joshua, finally standing in front of his new home, finally agreed. "I'm willing to give this whole thing a shot, because I don't want that little girl to be hurt anymore. Let's just figure this out and make it stop so that little girl gets better."

Zyriah and Evan smiled at each other, then smiled at Joshua.

"It's nice to hear buddy," Evan said. "You feel the way I do about it. Let's not waste any more time, alright Zyriah? Let's just try it and see what happens."

Zyriah nodded.

"It certainly seems like you've got more interest in what's going on around here," Evan added with a solid smile. "I think this the situation is moving in the right direction. I can feel it. It will all be about doing things the proper way."

"Well, what do we do first?" Joshua asked, with a growing feeling of real interest. He felt like he was really prepared to act on what was happening there, but she was not sure of exactly how much he could contribute. In truth, he was finding the situation more mysterious and more fascinating.

"First thing?" Evan answered, smiling wider. "We're going to take you on a little trip."

CHAPTER
SEVEN

Joshua went inside and up to his bedroom, looking through his closet to find a new shirt to change into, while he heard Zyriah and Evan opening and closing the cabinets and the refrigerator serving themselves a beverage. He finally had a little more excitement and certainly more interest in seeing what Zyriah and Evan had in mind for their training exercise, as he attributed the perspiration in the shirt he was wearing to not only the long walk but also a growing curiosity. Once, he changed his shirt into a clean one, a clean pale green t-shirt, he stepped into the living room, seeing Zyriah and Evan sitting down in the recliners sipping on what looked to be ice water. He wondered where this trip Evan had just mentioned would lead them.

"How many days do I need to pack for?" Joshua asked Evan.

"Pack for?" Evan asked.

"Yeah. I just needed to know how many clothes to bring," Joshua inquired.

"Oh, no. Joshua, you misunderstood," Zyriah laughed,

sitting her drink on the glass coffee table. "We're not going anywhere."

"Oh," Joshua said confused. "But Evan said that we had to go on a trip?"

"Not a trip you need sunscreen for buddy," Evan said, also putting his drink on the table. "This is the cheapest trip you'll ever going to take. It doesn't take any gas, or maps, or even a change of underwear. I say it's still the best way to travel."

"Sit down, please," Zyriah requested. "I can explain it a little better than Evan can apparently."

Joshua walked over and sat on the plush sofa, looked at Zyriah, and wondered what the new twist to this scenario was. He had been bombarded by so much new information, that nothing really surprised him. He was more confused by things, and he was slowly realizing that expecting anything to be what it was at face value was a mistake.

"Part of what we need to do is see what you are able to do already, Joshua," Zyriah began. "I am certain you have some precognitive ability to see the near future as well as some postcognitive ability to see the past. What I am amazed with is what you could see when Sarah Baker was under the influence of the Star. I'm betting once we introduce you to the Shardland, then things will really start to open up for you."

"The Shardland?" Joshua asked.

"It's a place where you mentally go often when you're doing a reading for someone," Evan attempted to explain. "Let's just call it a place of memories and future images."

"The difficult part of it is the interpretation," Zyriah continued. "The memories and images are often fragmented and in pieces. I guess you can say it can be as fractured as a jigsaw puzzle. The tough part is how you put them together and interpret them."

"Best time is just after things happen or just when things are about to," Evan said. "It's when the images are the most whole, before people start twisting memories in their head into the memories they want to have. Everybody remembers things in a prejudice way, often thinking of things in their favor. Ever complete a project with a group and later look back thinking you did most of the work, when in reality you may have done very little? That's how we manipulate our own thoughts."

"Why would people do that?" Joshua wondered, although he could admit to himself he had done it himself before.

"Well, in some cases, just so that people can live with themselves," Evan continued. "If the memory is a bad one and you're the one at fault, it's better for the mind to remember things in a more favorable light sometimes."

"What about the future?" Joshua questioned.

"Things are even more difficult in the looking towards the future," Zyriah said. "The problem there are the random possibilities. It's like having all the different moves in a chess game at your disposal, but each move creates numerous possible outcomes. The truly gifted precognitives are able to not only see each move but also the possibilities that can result. The more training a precognitive has, the more they will be able to gain access and knowledge to what the future holds."

"The problem with the Star is that it has been somehow causing problems in the Shardland, pretty much taking every memory and future image and fragmenting them so extensively that the images are pretty much dust," Evan explained.

"Darkdust we've been calling it," Zyriah added.

"In that dream of yours though, you were able to see some images from that darkdust," Evan said.

"Darkdust that even Evan and I haven't been able to see clearly or interpret correctly," Zyriah explained. "That's why we think, with some guidance, you can be a big help in figuring out what's next for the Star."

"Maybe seeing what the Star is doing before it hurts more people like Deputy Baker," Evan said solemnly.

"One of my biggest concerns is whether all this is safe for me to try," Joshua explained.

"Both of us will be right here with you," Evan said comfortingly. "I'm good enough to help with the hypnotism, and Zyriah knows enough about the Shardland to get you in and out safely. One day, you'll be able to do all this by yourself, you know."

"Until then, just make sure we're with you before you try anything on your own," Zyriah explained. "Just to make sure if there's any problems, we will be here to help."

Joshua took a deep breath, laying back so that his head rested into the back part of the couch. He looked at both Zyriah and Evan, and once again he felt a slight question of whether to trust them. They were friends, and he had already accepted that, but he still wondered if he was too quick to let his kindness overcome his typical suspicion of strangers. He took another sigh, relenting to try this training they were wanting him to attempt so badly, and he made the decision to continue.

"So, how do we get started?" Joshua asked with a slight hesitation.

"First, Evan will need to hypnotize you," Zyriah said. "Just focus on his voice and follow the directions. If it works, then you'll mentally end up in a world that's mostly dark, but you'll see shapes and images like broken photographs on broken glass. Don't worry yet about interpreting anything. We just want to see if we can help you get to the Shardland and back out with no issues."

"But don't I need somebody to focus on?" Joshua asked. "When you do a reading on somebody, don't you need a subject?"

"You have a subject," Evan said. "It's going to be me."

Joshua attempted to relax into the couch, focusing on his breathing, slightly flexing his joints to relieve any tension. Evan and Zyriah had turned off all the lights and curtained the windows, so the only remaining lights was slight sources coming from under the bedroom and bathroom doors. He breathed through the impending test, focused on the silence and the two shadowed figures poised in the recliners, waiting to begin. A willing rat ready to be put into his maze, Joshua thought. Evan pulled his pendant from underneath his shirt and cupped it in the palm of his right hand. Instinctively, Joshua pulled the small chain around his neck upward, releasing the pendant from underneath his shirt, and held it in his right hand. He looked at it quickly, seeing the familiar cloud of grey and white in the stone's coloring before returning his focus on Evan.

"Remember falling asleep last night?" Evan asked. "Look at your stone and remember that feeling. The waiting of each pulsing of the light's reflection as you counted. Your pupils were prepared for that moment, focused and waiting on that flash of light."

Joshua breathed deeply, looking at the pendant in his hand. It was not in motion as it was before, turning back and forth waiting for the light to be caught in a reflective glow from the light in the room. He continued to breathe, feeling himself struggling with a touch of frustration. Yet, the breathing helped him to relax his thoughts, and his focus maintained upon the selenite.

"I want you to calm yourself, Joshua," Evan said in a slow, steady, and calming voice. "Think of a color that you feel represents you. What color comforts you? What color helps you to relax?"

"I've always liked green," Joshua answered in a calm tone similar to the one Evan's voice had been reduced to. "I had a mint green blanket on my bed as a kid. It always felt warm and comforting."

"I want you to see that color, Joshua," Evan instructed. "Focus on the stone as you breathe, waiting for the pulsing of the light's reflection as you did that night. Imagine the flash of light as that color, the color of that warm blanket you remember. Feel your eyes waiting for the color in the stone as you breathe deeper. Focus on the stone and wait for that comforting color, and when you see the color of the stone change, tell me."

Joshua looked intensely at the pendant, his hand feeling the coolness of the selenite in his palm. The cloudy hue of the stone remained steadfast as Joshua continued breathing deeper. He felt something internal, a feeling he could only compare to a radiation from his upper body and mind that felt as if it was pushing itself outward from his skin. His concentration of the stone intensified, and as it did the selenite, from its center began to glow a soft color, that same color of green from his childhood blanket. He felt a peacefulness in it, and he continued to focus more of the energy he felt coming from some place within him into that pendant, which made the stone intensify in its coloration. Finally, through a dazed mind of swimming thoughts, Joshua responded to Evan.

"I see the green," Joshua said in a whisper.

"Look at the green of the light, Joshua," Evan continued. "Feel the warmth of that blanket reflecting and shining from the stone in your hand. Feel that soothing feeling of the blanket against you as your body relaxes in a state of rest. Put all of the feelings into the glow of the stone."

Joshua's muscles relaxed into a liquid feeling of calm.

"Your eyes concentrating on the warm green light," Evan whispering, his voice slowing with a steady decreasing rate. "Your mind collecting your thoughts and releasing them, one by one, steady streams of words and images flowing from your ears and eyes until all those thoughts are one by one gone. Your mind slowly empty, a black empty room with thick walls. Those escaping images emptying the room, and you wanting them to leave. A calm, peaceful, dark space."

Joshua's breathing was deep and slow, his eyelids weighted. His dark room emptying. An empty, relaxing, dark space.

"Can you hear me, Joshua?" Evan said, and even though Joshua could not see him, he could feel the words in the room in a rolling wave.

"Yes," Joshua slowly slurred.

"Are you in your dark room?" Evan whispered, even slower.

"Yes," Joshua slurred, even slower.

"In that room, I want you to think of a name," Evan continued. "One name, that you'll slowly allow to enter that calm, peaceful, dark space. Allow it in slowly, a slow stream slowly filling and filling the room. Allow it to fill the room, slowly, steadily, until the room has no space left within the thick black walls."

"Yes," Joshua said through the deep breaths.

"Evan Scott."

"Evan Scott," Joshua repeatedly breathily.

"Now, only with your mind. Evan Scott." Evan continued repeating his own name.

Joshua, for a few moments, slowly pushed the stream of the name into his dark room. His eyelids drooped and closed, as he allowed the name to fill the room like a flooded ship. His body relaxed to the point of near sleep, looking through his mind at that darkened space. Through the flooded waters, the name appeared and rippled through the dark current of his mind.

Evan Scott.

Joshua looked through the ripples, slowly steadying into a smooth flow so that the room was clear and unobstructed. It was peaceful, a calm space where he felt deeply comfortable. The darkness was soothing, and although he was mostly disconnected from his physical self, Joshua felt no urgency to return to it. It was tranquility to him, and his mental eyes looked slowly left and right for signs of some form to gaze upon.

Slowly, lit images began to flicker throughout the empty space. Color and light joined into forms, objects, and people. The room turned into a hanging gallery of images, with no walls to hang the images like his artwork. They hanged freely in space, oddly shaped like jagged glass, but each image flashing like broken television screens that increased in clarity and form into the images. He began to recognize an image, a face, the curling brown hair, a slight tan, the smile, and the edged jaw. It was himself, not a mirror image, but it was him walking back to his house just earlier from the senior center.

These were images from Evan's eyes, shifting back and forth from Zyriah to Joshua's own image walking back to the house with steady strides. Joshua absorbed the image, the strangeness of seeing himself earlier in the day like a fractured video screen. His eyes turned to find another image, slightly back to the left, showing the conversation from breakfast on the patio. Passing that, he strolled through the dark room like a gallery visitor, seeing himself yet again looking through the apartment for the first time the night before. He continued his mental steps, until seeing a darkened image of Zyriah, standing in a field, holding a lit candle.

Joshua looked through that image, Evan's vision swiping back and forth from Zyriah's candlelit face then down to the line of trees bordering the field. He recognized the area, the field and trees, as part of Morgan's Ridge. However, in one part of the image, he saw something unexpected. Evan had glanced into the town for a moment, seeing what seemed to be a large fire, then back to Zyriah, and although he could not hear the conversation, he could tell by the motion of the image that Evan was feeling a great deal of emotion through the shifting eyes. The eyes went back to that fire. Joshua realized this was a house on fire, and quickly he realized the image was from the night of the Baker fire.

The fire raged, and finally he saw the emergency

vehicles comes to aid, but the image kept dropping into the edge of that tree line. Sarah Baker was coming, he was sure of it. More than that, Joshua was aware that Evan knew ahead of time to look for the girl, and soon the image came, the same image from his own dream of the young face, ash-stained and dirty hair matted around it. It was then that images slowly grew out of focus quickly more and more blurred.

He looked around at the hanging images, and he realized the images were returning to how his view of the room began, simple images of color and light. The images blinked out one by one until the room was dark again. He began to feel his body breathe, his pulse quickened, and his physical being reconnecting to his mind. The dark room vanished, replaced by a warm light, pale and green, and he realized his eyes had reopened. The light pulsed into form and his pendant reemerged in his vision. Back in his living room, Joshua's senses reactivated, and he felt refreshed.

"How do you feel?" Zyriah, having already stepped over to him, her hand on his shoulder.

"Fine. I'm fine," Joshua responded in a sleepy tone that grew more awake.

"Could you see anything?" Evan asked as he eased forward in his chair.

"I saw us walking back here. I saw you and me talking on the patio this morning," Joshua recollected.

Evan and Zyriah looked at each other with a quick glance, then back to Joshua with a pleased smile.

"I saw the Baker fire, too," Joshua continued.

The smile on Evan and Zyriah's faces melted into an expression Joshua thought was either amazement or concern. He looked away for a moment, remembering the images of what he had just seeing and the feeling of the entire experience. Returning his view back to Zyriah and Evan, he recalled Zyriah saying how the images would be pieces of a puzzle, and in his own amateur attempt he tried combining the feelings of what he saw to the actual pictures themselves.

He made a conclusion about the arrival of Sarah Baker that night, and although he was not there himself at that moment, he felt increasingly confident about his resulting opinion and spoke his conclusion out loud. The more syllables were said, the more confident he became.

"I know you were waiting for that little girl to come up on Morgan's Ridge. You knew she was coming."

Joshua watched Zyriah, placing the ham sandwiches she had just made on the kitchen counter onto three plates. She opened a cabinet door, grabbing a bag of potato chips, and placed a handful on each plate. The darkness of the room and been replaced with lamplights throughout the room, and even though the experience had taken what seemed to be a long length of time, Joshua knew it was only dinnertime, and his hunger was welling up inside him.

She handed a plate to Joshua and Evan, and she sat back into her recliner to eat her meal. Joshua collected his thoughts and opinions while he ate, looking at each of them with the assumption that they were doing the same. Once his plate was empty, he placed it onto the table and waited for the others to finish. He looked around the room, once again taking time to get more familiar with his present surroundings. Still, his visit to the Shardland had proven one thing, one thing he had no longer questioned. Joshua had some form of psychic ability.

"We really didn't know much that night," Zyriah said, breaking the quiet. "If we had known more, we would've been able to stop it."

"You were both waiting though," Joshua stated matter of fact. "You knew somebody was coming up there."

"It was a combination of many things, Joshua," Evan said, trying to ease the tension. "Zyriah visited the Shardland herself just moments before. It's very different there when you're dealing with one of these instruments. Those images you saw are so broken it's nearly impossible to interpret anything. What should be lit and visible are not as they usually are."

"My dream wasn't that broken," Joshua added. "My dream was short, but still, I could see images. If you all didn't know that girl was going to come through those trees, then how could I?"

Zyriah, nodded. "It's an excellent point, Joshua. You saw something that night I couldn't, and to be honest I'm not exactly sure why. There's always some variance with these abilities depends on who the person is. I know what I can do and what my limits are. I'm learning more and more about you and your abilities, and in time I'm hoping those gifts will grow and change into even more helpful and useful talents."

"In time?" Joshua, looking with a glare sparked with a piece of anger. "What time do we have here? You got a little girl that can't wake up. You don't know where this Star is or who's using it. All this talking isn't getting us any closer to this thing, and I think we're all just wasting time here. Don't you know a way we can hurry up this whole process?"

"It doesn't work that way," Evan answered, with

disappointment in his voice. He gave Joshua a stare of agreement, but without a plan of attack.

"Well, figure out a way to make it work that way then," Joshua rebutted. "I don't know how, but we got to figure out a way. You figured out a way to know to be on that ridge that night. How did you get out there in the first place?"

"I received a message," Zyriah responded in a odd, mysterious tone.

"Then, figure out a way to get another one," Joshua said determined.

Zyriah nodded, standing and collecting the plates and placing them in the kitchen sink. She walked to the long dining table and sat at the table's end on one of the four chairs surrounding it. Joshua stood, along with Evan, and they walked to opposite sides of the table, taking their own seats and watched Zyriah opening her purse. She retrieved a black felt tipped pen, uncapped it, and turned to speak to Evan.

"Please, can you go to your apartment and bring me some paper?"

"Now?" Evan asked, and Joshua noticed an uneasiness in his eyes.

"It'll be alright. Please, bring me some paper," Zyriah requested.

Evan left into the elevator, leaving Joshua there looking at Zyriah, whose eyes appeared still and fixed forwards and a slightly downward angle. Her thinking appeared deep, and Joshua did not want to interrupt her thinking, so he sat patiently waiting for Evan to return with paper. He thoughts turned to the Shardland yet again and the images he was able to see there. He wanted to go back.

"This going to be enough?" Evan asked, waking Joshua from his daydreaming, as he placed a small stack of paper to the left of Zyriah's writing hand and one piece of paper in front of her. Evan sat down again in the chair opposite Joshua, nodded at Joshua, and they both turned to Zyriah, who turned the paper in an angle to begin writing. Joshua knew this was the first demonstration of Zyriah's automatic writing he had witnessed, and he was slightly eager to see it in real form.

Zyriah remained motionless, her face expressionless, except for her right arm moving as her hand began writing with that felt tipped pen onto the paper. Joshua eased forward to see the markings, which resembled a heart rate monitor with a straight line, occasionally disrupted by a slight lifting and lowering, then returning to a baseline. Once she reached the right edge of the paper, her hand lifted and returned slightly below the previous line, and she began a new line of periodic jaggedness.

She reached the bottom of the paper, then she pushed the written paper forward and moved a clean piece from the left-hand stack in front of her and began the process again. Still, the only part of her that seemed to move was from right shoulder downward, and Joshua wondered what the sensation would feel like within her during this process. He wondered if she aware of her motions. Perhaps, she was envisioning something like the Shardland and her arm was moving involuntarily. Maybe this was an entirely new process that he was unaware of all its components. In time, another piece of paper was filled, and Zyriah began again with a clean piece and continued the writing process. Joshua leaned forward more to see the lines she inked onto the paper. Around three-quarters of the way down that page, the line began changing, dropping below the baseline, twisting and curling into a cursive word and then followed by a second word. Zyriah's hand then ceased moving with a release of the pen, which slightly bounced on the table between her thumb and index finger. Her eyes blinked and she squeezed her lids shut, and Joshua took the paper from underneath her hand. He read the words, not recognizing the handwriting, and looked up to the reopened eyes of Zyriah and the eager glare of Evan's eyes as well, waiting on Joshua's next words.

"It's a name," Joshua said finally. "Who is Donnie Pritchard?"

CHAPTER
EIGHT

The Pritchard home sat on the corner lot of Treeclimber Drive and Ridgeway Avenue, a two-story brick home with white shudders on a spacious grassy lawn with a two stall garage. Evan, after Joshua gave permission to drive his car, had driven Joshua and Zyriah to the home, parking a short distance on the opposite side of the street. Joshua, seeing the driveway empty, seemed skeptical of the location. The house only had an indoor living room light on, as well as the outdoor porch lights that were on once the sun had set. He did not see the flashing reflection of a living room television from the windows or any signs that the curtains were moving from life within the home. Joshua thought they were simply at the wrong place.

"There's nobody even here," Joshua sighed. "Is there any place else he could be?"

"Is there a football game tonight?" Zyriah wondered. "I'm pretty sure he's still playing on the Quiet Tree High team."

"The high school doesn't play until next Friday," Evan said, keeping his focus on the home. "I know my small-town sport's schedules."

"So, it's just a kid?" Joshua exclaimed. Immediately, he thought of Sarah Baker, her small frame and her frailness.

"A fifteen-year-old, six foot four inches, two hundred-and forty-pounds worth of solid muscle, high school football and baseball player's worth of a kid," Evan said with widening eyes. "He's not small by any means. I'm a bit worry about the sheer size of this guy, Zyriah. If he's under the influence of this Star, he's going to be tricky to hold on to."

"You definitely have a point," Zyriah added.

"Well, wait a minute, how do we know that's what the name on the paper meant?" Joshua pointed out. "Couldn't he be the victim of this rather than be the bad guy?"

"You have a point, yourself," Zyriah said, sitting in the passenger seat, turning to Joshua's face peeking between her and Evan. "I just have a feeling the Star has been used on him. If it's in any way related to the Baker case, then the parents would be the victims."

"So, who's this boy's parents then?" Joshua asked.

"Assistant Prosecutor Gordon Pritchard and his wife Melanie," Zyriah answered. "Although Melanie has been in Ohio for the last couple months taking care of things since her father passed away, right Evan?"

"Oh, I heard something about that," Evan responded. "You're better at that small town gossip stuff than I am."

"Well, I heard from Kathy Ebert that she was in Ohio," Zyriah explained.

"If there was ever a queen of local gossip, that Kathy would wear the crown," Evan laughed.

The three grew quiet again, looking at the house and the occasional passing car. The street was mainly empty, except for a couple of SUVs and a blue van parked at random houses along the road. Joshua took a moment to think over the day's events, mainly focusing on the Shardland experience and Zyriah's automatic writing performance. It was a completely new process that he had not been exposed to, and there was one question he continued to ponder.

"Zyriah. This writing ability. The premise of this is that some other entity or spirit is doing the writing, correct?" Joshua asked.

"Correct," Zyriah affirmed.

"My question is, when you are in the middle of doing this or even afterwards, do you know what or who is doing the writing? You said the Shardland and different reading types were dangerous when you left yourself open to just any spirit, so do you know who's writing this boy's name on the paper?" Joshua questioned.

"I think I know, but I'm not ready to say just yet," Zyriah responded as she continued to watch the Pritchard home. "I've been trying to determine this, so you'll have to give me a little time."

"You only think you know? Isn't that a risky thing?" Joshua said with an uncomfortable feeling.

"It can be, but I have a pretty decent idea about who did it." Zyriah nodded. "When I know for sure, I'll tell you. I promise."

"Don't sweat it, Joshua," Evan commented with a faithful tone is his speech. He certainly had a great deal of confidence in her.. "She doesn't take a lot of chances, trust me. She knows what she's doing."

"I just didn't want something going wrong," Joshua admitted. "I still don't understand all these things yet, and sometimes they can be scary and confusing."

"It pays to ask questions," Evan added. "Don't be afraid. If either of us know the answer, we're going to fill you in."

"I hope so," Joshua said.

"I wonder if we should try peeking in the windows," Evan suggested. "Gordon or Donnie could be asleep in there."

"There's nobody in the house," Zyriah said.

"How do you know?" Joshua asked.

Zyriah, turning her head to face Joshua and raising an eyebrow, said, "Trust me, I know."

"So, you said his dad was an attorney?" Joshua asked, attempting to change the subject matter. "A prosecutor?"

"Gordon is assistant prosecutor of this county actually," Evan replied. "I actually sat on a jury last year for a case he tried."

"What kind of case was it?" Joshua inquired. "Let me guess. A murder."

"The assault of a minor," Evan answered. "Not exactly the kind of case I was wanting to think about or still talk about."

"Sorry," Joshua said, looking back at the house. "So, we just wait?"

"We just wait," Zyriah answered.

The three sat in mostly silence after that, with Evan occasionally trying to turn on the radio, and Zyriah turning it off each time. She seemed overly focused on the home. She did not have the same appearance to her eyes as she did when she wrote the name on the paper on the dining room table. There was more life to her eyes, but the focus remained the same. Joshua wondered if she was in the Shardland at that moment. She had said before that a selenite pendant was not necessary once a person was trained well enough. She would not need Evan's hypnosis to make that trip either. Joshua thought how strange it would be to have the ability and also the responsibility it would require using it.

A maroon sedan turned off Treeclimber Drive and onto Ridgeway Avenue after nearly an hour of waiting. It pulled into the driveway, stopped, the lights turned off, and the engine ceased running. The driver, a middle-aged thin man with glasses and a receding hairline holding a briefcase emerged from the car and went to his front door. He juggled his hand in his pants pocket, finally pulling out his keys, unlocked the front door, entered the home, and closed the door behind him.

"Looks like the attorney came home," Joshua said.

"Yeah, that's Gordon," Evan added. "But Donnie didn't come home with him."

"Maybe he's on a date?" Joshua wondered.

"Not old enough to drive yet, but he might be out at a friend's house I suppose," Evan wondered. "What do you all think we should do?"

"We just wait," Zyriah replied.

"This could be all night for all we know," Joshua pointed out.

"We just wait," Zyriah replied again, her eyes alive but unwavering, looking at the Pritchard home.

About twenty minutes later, Evan's curiosity turned overly eager, and Joshua watched as he began getting out the car. He was not exactly sure if Evan felt or saw something, but he knew that Evan was full intent to go into that house. Joshua looked at Zyriah, who looked at him and looked back at Evan bolting from the vehicle, and she got out of the car in a rushed panic. Joshua followed her out of the car, not sure what to expect.

"Where do you think you're going?" Zyriah asked in a panicked whisper. "You can't just barge in there. That's an assistant prosecutor in there. He's liable to call the police or pull a gun on you if you bust through that door. What do you plan on telling the man? That you have a feeling that his son might attempt doing something to him?"

"That's exactly what I plan on doing," Evan said in a full voice, marching across Ridgeway Avenue towards the Pritchard's house.

"Evan, please stop," Joshua said, in a whisper similar to Zyriah. "We don't want to get the attention of all these neighbors. Come back here and let's figure the plan out."

"The plan?" Evan said, turning and facing Joshua with a wide-eyed glare. "There is no plan here. We're just here to stop the boy from possibly killing that man you just saw enter this house."

"Well, there's got to be a way," Joshua whispered.

"Fine. You've supposed to be the one to fix all this. You're the one that Miss Flint here said is supposed to have such great abilities. Fine then. You tell me. What's your plan?" Evan asked demandingly, lowering his voice and walking back to the car.

All at once, both Evan and Zyriah looked at Joshua, and his stress level soared. He went from being a student with some sort of strange ability that he did not even understand to a leader of some sort, and their stares at him seemed to expect him to give some sort of direction, more that they knew themselves. He thought back to Sarah Baker and the few details they had given about what they had experienced that night on Morgan's Ridge.

"The night on the ridge. What happened when you tried to do this psychic thing with Sarah Baker?" Joshua asked Zyriah. He tried to envision the night in his own mind but it was difficult.

"I told you," Zyriah explained. "I couldn't see clearly. The images were pretty much as small as dark dust particles. There was nothing to interpret."

"Then how did you know about the deputy and the stepmother being handcuffed to the bed?"

"I wasn't reading the girl at that time," Zyriah explained, and a sudden awakening lit her face. "I was reading the deputy."

"Read the prosecutor," Joshua demanded. "Can you do that from here?"

Zyriah nodded.

"Quickly, read him now," Joshua demanded again.

Joshua watched as Zyriah clutched her pendant in her right hand. She closed her eyes, and the three grew silent. Joshua felt she needed the quiet to focus. He looked at Evan, watching his body rock back and forth as if he was ready to break the front door of the Pritchard's home down. Joshua put his hands forward quietly pressing into the empty air telling Evan to wait, and Evan stopped rocking. They both continued to look at Zyriah, whose eyes continued to be closed with a slight squint to her eyelids as if she was focusing. Within just a few minutes, she finally spoke.

"He's on his bedroom phone upstairs with his wife," Zyriah finally said.

"No sign of Donnie anywhere?" Evan quickly asked.

"I didn't see him. Gordon went into his bedroom, got undressed, put on a bathrobe, and called his wife. I didn't see any images of the boy at all," Zyriah explained with a slight sigh of relief.

"Then, maybe it's not supposed to happened tonight," Joshua suggested. "Maybe the name was just to give us time to stop all this, a day or two in advance."

"If that were true, then it probably would've happened with the Baker girl," Zyriah explained. "If I was able to write that name, this will all happen soon."

"Let's just get back in the car, ok?" Joshua, stepping over to the passenger car door and opening it. "Let's wait for the son to come home and see what happens then."

Evan burst out a sigh of frustration.

"What else can we do right now?" Joshua said with an annoyed tone in Evan's direction. "Seriously, let's just get back in the car."

Joshua entered the car and returned to the back seat, and Zyriah and Evan followed the example, returning to their seats and quietly closing the car doors. Joshua watched Evan flexing his fingers to crack his knuckles. Zyriah, apparently not liking the sound, looked at him with squinted eyes for a moment then returned her gaze to both the house and then to the corner leading to Treeclimber Drive. Joshua, not sure if he was looking for a car or a boy walking, turned and looked out the rear window. After seeing nothing of interest, Joshua returned to sticking his head over the center console between the two front passengers.

A light appeared in the front left window of the second story. The curtains temporary parted, and the three could see Gordon Pritchard looking for a moment out the window, turning his head both ways looking up and down Ridgeway Avenue, then closing the curtains. The shadow of him in the room shifted from one side of the room to the other, and Joshua could tell the man had removed the bathrobe. The shadow partially lowered for a moment, stood back straight, then slowly lowered so that the shadow disappeared below the windowpane.

"He probably heard us out here yelling like idiots and checked out the street," Evan said, with a calmer tone.

"He heard who yelling like an idiot?" Zyriah asked to Evan, her head turning with that familiar cocked up eyebrow.

"So, he's in the bathtub," Joshua said, proud that his investigative work seemed to be paying off. "We just have to focus on the boy now."

"Want to try to read the boy?" Evan asked, slightly embarrassed by Zyriah's last question. Joshua noticed his cheeks were a little red.

"What would the point be?" Zyriah explained. "If Donnie is under the Star's influence, you couldn't see it anyway."

"Maybe let Joshua try?" Evan asked, and Joshua shifted in his seat with a nervous expectation.

"It's too soon. He's not ready. The whole process would take too long," Zyriah said looking back and Joshua giving her a deliberate disappointing grimace.

Joshua was not sure what the next step should be. He continued looking from car window to car window and seeing very little movement. The occasional turning on and off of lights from nearby houses and a light from one of the parked van windows were the only noticeable things he viewed, but no sign of a boy going into that house. He began to wonder what would happen if he tried to read Donnie Pritchard at that moment. He momentarily grasped at his pendant, then lowered his hand back to his lap. He was too new to this process, and he knew it. He watched Evan and Zyriah continuing to look out of their windows looking for a sign. Suddenly, Evan yelled.

"That window light came on!"

Joshua leaned farther forward and saw that the window on the other end of the house had been lit by lamplight. Evan jumped out the car yet again, and Joshua repeated what happened earlier by following Zyriah out of the car. Immediately, Zyriah closed her eyes and focused. Joshua ran around the car, joining Evan, and they marched toward the front door. Somebody else was in that house, Joshua thought. If the prosecutor was in the bathtub, then he could not also turn on that lamp in that window. Joshua watched as Evan just was about to reach the doorbell, when Zyriah screamed from her stance beside Joshua's car. Joshua faced her direction for a moment, seeing Zyriah once again holding her pendant tightly in her hand and her eyes looking towards the house's second floor.

"The bathroom! Donnie's in there holding Gordon's head under the water!" Zyriah yelled.

Joshua stood back for a moment, watching Evan ram the front wooden door with his shoulder trying to make it open. He joined in, ramming the door with his shoulder along with Evan, and Zyriah ran up to the other side watching them. He felt a sting of pain with his shoulder hitting the hard wood, but they continued. Finally, the door open, with the sound of a metallic popping of the lock, and the three ran inside.

Joshua watched Evan immediately run up the stairs and to the left side of the hallway, and he and Zyriah quickly followed. Once at the top, Joshua turned and tried to figure out where that bathroom light was located since the upstairs hallway did not seem to go that far forward to that corner of the house. Evan and Zyriah looked momentarily perplexed with the same mental question, making little steps in different directions not sure where to go. Joshua ran to the far-left door, opened it, and turned back to his companions.

"It's a master bathroom! This way!" Joshua exclaimed urgently.

The three ran from the hall, through the master bedroom, and into a large master bathroom to find a large muscular boy holding his father into the bathtub water of a large clawfoot tub, like the one in Joshua's bathroom. The man's bare legs flared and kicked into the air as water splashed from the tub onto the white tile floor. Evan wrapped his arm around the boy's neck, trying to pull him away from the tub, and Joshua momentarily stood there witnessing the horror of all of it. He ran to help, seeing the prosecutor's face under the water almost lifeless, with his strength slowly disappears as the legs began to slowly stop kicking. Joshua pulled hard on the boy's hands, trying to remove the hands from the man's neck, but the boy's strength was relentless. Evan struggled with the boy's neck trying to pull back as hard as he could, but the boy was steadfast, and Joshua noticed how cold and unmoving his eyes were, as if in a trance.

Finally, Zyriah, holding the back cover of the toilet with both hands, slammed it into the back of the boy's head. The boy's hands released, and his body fell limp backwards into Evan, and they both collapsed on the bathroom floor. Evan pushed the boy off himself, rolling him onto the tile, and all three stood looking at the scene for a moment. Evan rushed back to the tub, pulling the man out and to the side of his son, the water from him flowing into the blood coming from the boy's head where Zyriah had hit him.

The three stood reunited and once again observed the scene. Joshua looked over to the sink and saw three lit candles, all pink, sitting and burning with an unflinching flame, and then from the center candle, something strange seemed to appear.

"Turn off the light!" Joshua yelled.

"Why?" Zyriah asked, already running to find the light switch.

"Just do it!" Joshua screamed.

Zyriah found the light switch and turned off the overhead light, leaving only the candlelight to light the room. Joshua stepped closer to the sink, his eyes fixated upon that center flame, and he could feel Zyriah and Evan moving closer to see what he saw.

The flame from that center candle was just a bit brighter, then grew in brightness and appeared to change its little form into a four-pointed shape like a compass.

"What is that?" Joshua asked.

Zyriah sighed, looking at the newly form shape, and nodded. "It's the Star."

A drop of water that had splashed across from the bathtub during the quarrel held onto the edge of the candle's rim, and slowly it released itself into the wick. The Star burned for just a few seconds, then was overcome by the droplet. Joshua bent forward blowing the other two candle flames out as well. He stood straight again, and with an exhausted breath he walked over to the light switch turning it back on.

"Call the police," Joshua demanded.

The officer that confronted them had come almost immediately. Joshua, overwhelmed by the attack in the Pritchard's bathroom, had very little else on his mind. He had no desire to pay attention to who this female officer was or the questions that were surely about to be asked.

"Y'all mind telling me what the hell you're doing here?" the officer asked.

Sheriff Monika Tucker was a tall, broad-shouldered, dark-skinned woman that Joshua thought had the qualities of a well-dressed Amazonian, once he decided to redirect his attention. He took a moment to recollect his activities after the Star was extinguished, concerned he made have to give an explanation of what had happened. After Evan had made the call to Emergency Services, the officers and medics reported quickly, and while they were assessing the scene in the upstairs bathroom, Joshua, Evan, and Zyriah sat on the green metal porch furniture outside, saying little and breathing through the shock. It was a minutes before her black luxury sedan showed up, and although the hour was late, she was well-dressed in a suit jacket, black slacks, and nicely placed evening makeup. Joshua watched her enter the house for her initial assessment, but now that she was downstairs and standing in front of him, he could not deny that he felt intimidated.

"That how this is going to be?" she nodded. "Three bumps on a log with nothing to say?"

"It's been a lot to take in, Monika," Zyriah said looking up, her face tear stained. "We're not ignoring you."

The sheriff paced the small length of the front porch, sizing the three of them up with careful measures. She seemed comfortable with Zyriah and Evan, local residents she had already known, but in Joshua's case, she looked down at him like a hungry chicken hawk. Joshua looked back at her, hoping his eyes reflected the shock and emptiness he was feeling.

"This must be Mr. Spiker," Monika nodded. "I heard about you from a few people already. Kathy Ebert for one. What all do you know about what happened upstairs?"

"We were driving by and heard people yelling," Joshua said in a feeble manner. "We could see the fighting through the window once we were driving past the house. Evan and I were just trying to break it up."

"The knock on that young man's head upstairs. Which one of you is responsible for that? I know it wasn't his father," Monika stated very matter-of-fact.

"Actually, Monika," Zyriah said and standing up from her seated position, "I followed my friends in, and I caused the head injury."

"You?" Monika said with a slight laugh. "What did you use to do it?"

"The cover from the toilet tank," Zyriah answered.

"You know I'm going to take a closer look at that cover. You sure that's the story y'all are sticking with?" Monika inquired, stepping across the small porch back to the kicked-in front door.

"It's the truth, Monika. I swear it," Zyriah said with confidence.

"Why don't the three of you come up with me really quick, and then we can take a better look?" Monika said, with a slight grin. "I don't want you three running off, even though I know you're just the innocent bystanders, right?"

"We're willing to walk up with you," Evan stood, and Joshua stood to follow. "Whatever you need."

"Well, in that case Mr. Scott, you can lead," Monika said, and Evan lead the way, Zyriah and Joshua following, with the sheriff trailing behind them.

Going up the stairs, Joshua looked at the spaced family photographs along the wall, showing the growing stages of the Pritchard boy growing up. Joshua did not see anything out of the ordinary, childhood photographs of birthdays and posed pictures of him in football and baseball outfits in his younger years. Evan seemed to instinctively turn left at the top of the stairs, entering the master bedroom, and Joshua followed along then turning to face the sheriff, wondering what the next step in this process would be.

"Why don't the three of you sit down over on that window seat for just a minute," Monika instructed.

Joshua sat on a long bench seat with his friends beside the rear window that overlooked the back yard. Sheriff Tucker walked into the bathroom, and the three waited for her return with the occasional look toward each other just to acknowledge that they were all alright. Monika finally returned, holding the toilet tank cover already zipped in plastic, and Joshua noticed she deliberately had it turned so that he could not see any bloodstain. She told her fellow officers that she needed to close the bathroom and bedroom doors for a few minutes to ask the three a few questions, and she closed the doors. Joshua noticed her strength was apparent, knowing she was handling this toilet cover with one hand and Zyriah had used two hands.

"Last chance, Zyriah," Monika said, calming her voice slightly. "If there's something you need to tell me, if there's something any of y'all need to tell me, now is really the time."

"The boy attacked Mr. Pritchard, and we stopped him," Zyriah responded. "It's the truth."

Monika removed one of her blue gloves that she had on and opened the plastic evidence bag that the toilet cover had been placed in. She opened it up enough for just a corner to be exposed, and she placed one finger on the exposed portion. Joshua immediately worried about fingerprints, and he began questioning the officer's tactics in his mind. It was not until he looked in Monika's eyes and seeing a similar vacant stare that he compared to Zyriah's stare on the street that he realized that the sheriff had some type of ability of her own.

"Are you telling me she can do this too?" Joshua, whispering into Evan's ear. Evan put one finger to his mouth, and Joshua, understanding he was being asked to be quiet, looked back at the Sheriff and waited.

"Looks as if you didn't have much choice in the matter," Monika said, refocusing her eyes to a normal, alert state.

"Are we free to go?" Zyriah asked, standing from her space at the window seat. "If you have any other questions, I'm sure we'll all be happy to answer them after we've had some rest. The entire night has been pretty traumatic on young Joshua here."

"I'm sure it was," Monika noted, addressing Zyriah then stepping over to speak to Joshua. "You did your best here from what I could see. Thank you for trying your best in trying to stop him."

"You're welcome," Joshua said solemnly, not sure exactly how Monika knew what had happened, but he assumed that she was able to visit the Shardland as he had. "I'd really like to just go home now."

"Lenora's old place, right Zyriah?" Monika inquired.

"Yes. We've been spending most of our time moving him in," Zyriah added.

"Well, I'll be popping by tomorrow or the next day to ask a few questions of all of you," Monika said in a professional manner. "I'd appreciate any details from tonight that you have."

"We've be happy to oblige, but we really need to be getting home," Evan said, standing from his seat, and Joshua felt him tugging his arm to do the same. "We all could use a rest."

"Tomorrow or the next day then," Monika said with salutations. "Pleasure meeting you, Mr. Spiker."

"Pleasure meeting you also," Joshua said, as the sheriff reopened the bedroom door and directed the other officers to clear the way for them to leave. Joshua thought they all surely appeared to be more than ready.

Joshua was numb. He momentarily relived the moment in his mind, pulling at the boy's hands, seeing his father's face in the water, and seeing the Star in the candle's flame. He walked quickly to the car, looking around seeing the neighbors already on their respective porches observing the scene, the multiple police cars, and Joshua and his friends preparing to leave. They returned to their previous seat positions in the car, and Evan drove forward. Joshua realized the blue van that was there previous had left, so Evan drove close to the curb, and turned right onto Treeclimber Drive.

The short drive home would have been shorter, but Evan took an additional left turn onto Highland Street to take Zyriah home, pulling into a brick ranch style home's driveway. Once he put the car in park, all of them took a moment of silence, and Joshua wondered if they were rethinking the incident at the Prichard's home or if they were having a moment of prayer. Zyriah took a last look at both Joshua and Evan for the day, and she gave an exhausted smile reaching for the car's door handle, opening it.

"Did the officer have an ability too?" Joshua asked. "She seemed to be pretty confident we did not do anything deliberately."

"Monika has a unique gift, pretty perfect for a police officer," Zyriah explained. "If the death is a recent one, Monika can see how the death occurred using the object that caused the death. When she touched that toilet cover, she was able to see what happened."

Another piece of information for Joshua to add to his list of phenomenal acts in that town. He wiped at his eyes, trying to revive them but failing. He took his own last look at Zyriah before she left.

"It's been a day. A truly long day," Zyriah said with a level of sleepiness in her voice. "I'll be by in the morning, but you two get some rest."

Joshua was surprised Evan did not speak up to say goodnight, and neither did he, as Zyriah left the car, leaving the door open for Joshua to move forward to the front seat. Joshua got out of the car to switch positions, making sure Zyriah unlocked her front door of her home, and got into the house safely, before he sat himself on the front seat and closed the door. He turned, looking at Evan giving a simple nod of the head, and the two were off, pulling out of the driveway and going back to their home. Joshua was tired, overflowed with the day's events. It could be a long night of overthinking and very little rest.

Once they pulled into the driveway facing the garage, they quickly got out of the car, and Evan returned the car key to Joshua. Joshua watched him slowly walking forward toward the garage, and he knew Evan was ready for sleep. He hated asking Evan for one more additional favor. After all he had done for him to that point, Joshua felt a slice of guilt asking for anything else. The day's events were just so overwhelming, and Joshua began to fear something new, something different. He thought for a moment than he might relive those moments at the Pritchard's home in his dreams that night. He was not sure if it was going to happen for certain, but there was enough of a level of concern that he did not want to be alone if it did. For a moment, he was relieved his previous dream of Sarah Baker was limited to the mere walk through the trees leading to Morgan's Ridge and none of the savagery from inside the Baker's home. However, being part of these deaths tonight, he was scared to be alone.

"Evan?" Joshua asked.

Evan turned slowly, making eye contact with sleepy eyes, but he still had a slight smile as if he was aware of what was going to be asked.

"Do you mind sleeping up on the couch tonight?" Joshua pleaded.

CHAPTER
NINE

J oshua's eyes were weighted with the leftover exhaustion
from the day before, and still he managed to crack them
open to get out of bed. Happy to have had a dreamless
sleep, he stretched and strolled around the room getting his
mental bearings. He loved the mornings, the freshness of
them, the clean slate of a new day. So often, within a few
minutes, he bombarded his brain with a list of things to be
accomplished that day, usually one so over extensive that
he knew he would be unable to complete all of them.
Living in a new home with new friends and new
circumstances made making that list more difficult and
more undetermined. He reached for his pendant from its
place near the candles on the nightstand and fumbled to
clasp it around his neck. Once he felt awake to control his
mental and motor functions well enough, he opened the
bedroom door.

"How did you sleep?" Evan, already freshened in new
clothes and combed hair, sat in his usual recliner with a
glass of orange juice.

"Like a brick," Joshua answered, still slightly stretching.

"Want some breakfast?" Evan got up, taking his now half-empty glass to the refrigerator and refilling it.

"A glass of that orange juice will be enough," Joshua said. "Not feeling too hungry yet."

Evan retrieved another glass from the cabinet, and Joshua watched as he filled it for him. His stomach always took a few minutes to get adjusted when he woke up, and sometimes he still forced himself to eat early. Today, however, he was determined to take things a little slower. He sat on the couch, accepting the glass from Evan, and drank it half empty with one gulp.

"I got up a few hours ago and went back to my place and got cleaned up," Evan said. "I just wanted to make it back here before you woke up."

"Wait. What time is it?" Joshua asked, feeling the orange juice waking him up even more so. Vitamin C always did give him a recharged feeling.

"It's almost noon. I figured you needed some extra rest. Zyriah hasn't made it over here yet, so I expect that she's taking a little rest time of her own," Evan said, finishing his orange juice and placing the empty glass on the coffee table.

Joshua finished his juice and placed his glass on the table as well. He eased himself back into the couch, realizing how plush it really was, and almost wanted to doze back off. Instead, he leaned forward again, rubbing his eyes for a few moments, and refocused on Evan and the day at hand.

Mentally, his list began to form with at least a few steps of his own, even though they were mostly questions he felt needing answering again. Still, it was a plan to attack the day, or at least the morning. There were so many things to consider that Joshua felt overwhelmed.

"What do you think the connection is?" Joshua wondered. "The Baker girl. The Pritchard boy. I thought we could try putting some of these things together."

"Connection?" Evan sat back into the recliner, and Joshua watched his eyes squint in thought. "Both children. Both going after their fathers. The girl apparently had a fear of fire over that curtain burning incident, so I'm betting the Pritchard boy had an issue with water somehow."

"Both of the father's had jobs in legal ways," Joshua added. "The Baker dad was a deputy, and the Pritchard dad was an assistant prosecutor. Possibly the person with the Star is somebody at the courthouse, or somebody they got convicted."

"Well, it'd have to be somebody that isn't in jail now either," Evan said. "The tricky part is somebody unrelated to the kids, but still had contact with them."

"Different ages, so the kids went to different schools," Joshua said.

"Different social brackets too," Evan pointed out. "A little girl isn't likely to hang out with the high school football jock clique."

"There's a common thread here somewhere," Joshua wondered.

"But what's the thread?" Evan asked.

"The Star," Zyriah said, emerging from the elevator. "They both were in contact with the Star's owner."

"How did you know what we were talking about?" Joshua asked.

"You said I was psychic, remember?" Zyriah laughed. "I could hear you down the stairwell as I was waiting on the elevator. You both make things so much easier just because you can't turn down your volume."

"Sometimes the obvious is a better answer," Evan said, getting Zyriah a glass of juice and handing it to her. He refilled his one last time and returned to his chair. "You don't need to use the mental powers when you got your ears."

"Ok, I get it," Joshua said, trying to keep the conversation's focus. "So, how then do we find the Star's owner?"

"Well, sitting around trying to figure out who those kids have communicated with the last few days will take an eternity," Evan replied.

Joshua watched as Zyriah sat down, drinking her beverage, and she had a confused look of what the next step should be. Evan, with a similar look, drank his juice almost completely, and he developed that similar empty appearance. Joshua continued to ponder the issue. He knew so little about the piece of glass himself that they were looking for. He thought again of the story of Josephine and Anthony, Josephine landing below in a shower of broken glass. Something in his mind at that point made him think of that sunset painting and his surprise in the window's reality. Another stained-glass window replacing the previous one in the building. He did not think it would be that common for a replacement like that to be made of a stained-glass window.

"Who put the new window in this house?" Joshua asked.

"The new window? Which new window?" Evan inquired.

"The sunset window in my bedroom," Joshua replied.

"Was it made by some place out of state or some local business?"

"Oh, any type of glasswork around here is done by Grewe and Glover's Glassworks, out close to Soccer's where we had hotdogs when you arrived. I'm pretty sure they put that sunset window in. They have a little store up front with a million different glass products they make, but they do the big work in the shop behind the store. That family has been in business for generations. Back to the Civil War, I believe," Zyriah answered.

"Well, if it's been around that long, is there a chance they know what happened to the Star?" Joshua wondered.

"It's a good possibility, and I'd almost bet on it," Evan agreed.

"But we need to make sure of it before we just walk in there asking about something like this," Zyriah noted. "With all the talk that's probably going on about us after what happened last night, walking into the glassworks with crazy questions wouldn't look too good on us, would it?"

"Well, how do we confirm it?" Evan asked.

Joshua took a few moments to think. He refreshed his memory on the story Zyriah and Evan had told him on Morgan's Ridge yet again. He also remembered hearing Zyriah mention his biological mother's interest in these objects to aid in her psychic research. He thought that was the key. Her research.

"Didn't you say my mother kept papers of all these instruments she found? Where's all that paperwork?" Joshua asked urgently.

Zyriah was quiet, looking deeply now into Joshua's eyes for confirmation he was serious, he thought. He felt slightly uneasy in his gut, but he knew his face was steadfast. He wanted that information she had told him about, the research on this Star his mother had collected.

"It's upstairs," Zyriah finally relented. "It's upstairs in your mother's séance room."

"That's what's upstairs? I figured it was an attic or a storage room by now." Joshua said, with a twinge of curiosity. "Let's go check it out."

"Wait, wait, wait. Let me go upstairs and bring it downstairs. There's no reason for all three of us to go rushing upstairs to find that," Zyriah said with a note of concern.

"You don't want me going upstairs? Are you hiding something upstairs we shouldn't see?" Joshua said with a touch of suspicion.

"I didn't say that. I'm just not sure you're ready to go and see that room yet. Your mother did a lot of readings for people in that room, and she brought whatever entities those reading required into that space. My concern is that perhaps the entities decided not to leave just yet and may still be lingering in that room," Zyriah explained.

"Oh, I'm going to sleep so much better tonight now knowing that bit of information," Joshua said sarcastically.

"I'm sorry. I just don't want you to get hurt anymore, like the experience we had last night. That's all I'm saying," Zyriah maintained.

"Let me ask you this," Evan began asking, "do you really believe last night was the first and only time through this whole experience that you think Joshua will be in risk of some type of harm?"

Joshua looked back from Evan's questioning face to Zyriah's expression, slightly wide-eyed and watery. He could see something new in her eyes at that moment, a legitimate caring for him. He felt guilty about pushing the question about why he could not go upstairs into his mother's séance room, but he simply felt it was necessary. He was more concerned at that moment for another traumatic incident to happen, especially if it involved another child.

"Follow me," Zyriah said, standing up and walking towards the elevator, with Joshua and Evan quickly doing as she directed.

The elevator ride was not quick enough for Joshua as the three journeyed upward to the third floor. As the door opened, Zyriah removed her elevator key and began flipping through the keys until she chose a small brass one. The three followed out of the elevator in a straight line, and Joshua looked at the deep green carpet on the floor and the maple hardwood of the double doors that was apparently the entry. Zyriah, taking a deep breath Joshua noticed, used the brass key in the door's lock until the lock clicked and opened both door's wide.

"It's dark in here," Joshua said, almost feeling silly.

"Let me turn on the chandelier," Zyriah said, walking through the blackness as Joshua and Evan waited in the entry. It was a matter of seconds, and a brass chandelier with nearly a dozen bulbs in the shape of candle flames were all lit, reflecting light all around the room. Joshua looked at the bookshelves that lined the right wall, covered in books and stacks of old newspapers. To the left were similar shelves, but these were collections of antiques and objects of all types. Joshua noticed that many of them were clocks of some sort and several were little cat figurines. In the back left corner, he saw a large wooden desk with a high-back chair. A maple grandfather clock stood in the back right corner.

At the center of the room was a large round table, covered in a purple and green cloth patterned with leaves and stars. Six high-back chairs like the one at the left corner desk were evenly positioned around the table so that there was clearly a chair at the head and one at the foot of the large circle. The three walked around the table to the head, where there had been placed some manila file folders, neatly stacked in front of the chair. Joshua noticed that the tabs on each folder all had the name Josephine Morgan written in black ink.

"These are the files on Josephine and the Star," Zyriah said, pulling the head chair away from the table and inviting Joshua to sit. "I had taken the liberty to go through them before I came to Charleston. I left them sitting out of your mother's desk and here on the table."

"Do you remember anything about the glass place you were talking about?" Joshua asked, sitting himself into the chair and scooting it forward.

"To be honest, I was just refreshing myself on Josephine's story and never thought about looking at the window's makers," Zyriah said, opening the top file. "If we took another look, maybe we can find something."

Joshua watched as Zyriah and Evan both took the nearest chair and moved them closer towards Joshua, each taking a file, and the three began reading. Joshua's file was mostly old photographs and a few photocopies of newspaper clippings about the upcoming wedding. He glanced over at Zyriah's file which contained stories about the events of the window crash on the wedding day and the family's reaction. He glanced over to Evan's file which was a collection of photographs of the young couple at various stages of their childhood.

Nothing he could see answered the question of who had replaced that broken window.

"There's got to be more than this," Joshua said frustrated. He knew the situation felt incomplete. "We're missing something."

"These are the only files related to the Star, Joshua. I promise you," Zyriah stated.

Joshua thought more, rethinking some of his earlier thoughts about the previous conversations he had with Zyriah and Evan since he came to Wilcox. Once again, his mind lit with a surprise moment of clarity. He took back the files from Zyriah and Evan, and quickly restacked them neatly in the piles they were originally in.

"This is wrong," Joshua said confidently. "This is all wrong."

"What do you mean?" Evan asked with total confusion in his voice.

"It's the wrong window," Joshua explained. "You said my mother was responsible for the installation of the sunset window, right?"

Zyriah nodded.

"Where's the bill of sale?" Joshua said with an emerging smile.

Joshua watched as Zyriah's smile emerged as well, and he watched her quickly go to the desk in the corner and opening a lower right file drawer filled with addition folders. Using her fingers, he watched her flipping through the tabs on the folders. Finally, pulling a folder out and carrying back to the table in a hurry, she placed it in front of Joshua.

"This one is labeled 'Bedroom window'," Zyriah said happily. "You can have the honors."

Joshua did not take time to thank Zyriah for pleasure of opening the folder, mainly because he was not yet sure he deserved the praise. He opened the file to a series of photographs and flipped through them to see the various stages of the window installation. From an open hole, to partially constructed, to the final product, the photographs took the process through a gradual but precise order of the window's installment. Underneath the stack of photographs was a folded piece of white paper and a folded piece of pink paper. Joshua unfolded both, reading the words and numbers quietly to himself at first, rereading it quickly, then announcing their findings.

"Contract and receipt for completed work of one completed stained-glass bedroom window paid for by Lenora Spiker," Joshua said grinning widely. "The window was installed by Grewe and Glover's Glassworks, 1013 Treeclimber Drive, Wilcox West Virginia."

Zyriah and Evan stood from their chairs and quickly looked over Joshua's shoulders at the finding. Joshua felt a certain amount of accomplishment with the discovery, finally feeling he had made a significant contribution to solve this issue. He watched Zyriah take the files from the table and placed them on the corner desk. The three walked briskly out of the room, Zyriah turning out the lights, and she locked the door behind them. They entered the elevator, and Joshua watched Zyriah press the button for the first floor.

"Where are we going?" Evan asked.

"It's time we pay Grewe and Glover's a visit, don't you think?" Zyriah inquired.

Evan grew silent.

"Makes sense to me," Joshua answered, still reveling in his contribution. "If they made the new window, they might know what happened to the broken parts."

"You two can go over there and find out what you can," Evan said. "There's a few things I need to do around here."

"What sort of things? Aren't you curious about what they know, too?" Joshua asked.

"Oh, I'm curious, but there's a lot of things to do around here," Evan maintained. "The petunias are long overdue to be replaced with some mums. I know it's been warm lately, but that first frost will creep up on you if you don't watch it."

The elevator reached the first floor, and the three walked through towards the front door with an unusual quietness. Joshua watched Zyriah, with the occasional looks towards Evan, and Joshua knew something was not what it should be. Evan had been so direct about his feelings and opinions, and this silence was out of character. His decision about not accompanying Zyriah and Joshua did not feel at all like the man Joshua was beginning to know. Evan opened the front door, the three exited, and Joshua locked the door behind them as they turned toward the car. Evan, however, stepped past Joshua's vehicle looking as if he was going to the rear of the building.

"Evan, stop," Zyriah requested. "What's this all about?"

"You know I was on that jury last year," Evan explained. "The Johnny Glover case about him hitting his son. I know he's out of jail, and the divorce went through. Catherine and the boy are in Pennsylvania with her parents now, and I heard at Soccer's that Johnny is back at his shop."

"What does that have to do with it?" Joshua asked. "That was last year. What if this guy knows something?"

"Would you want to see somebody that was on the jury that took your son away?" Evan asked. His face was one of disappointment, and Joshua felt Evan really wanted to go to the glassworks as much as he did. Evan had really been the protector of this group, especially at the Pritchard's house, and Joshua felt he would feel safer if Evan was along.

"I still think you should go," Joshua said.

"I understand what you mean, Evan," Zyriah agreed. "If Johnny is there, there's a greater chance he will give us more information if you're not with us. There's no point in taking the chance."

"Plus, I can get things caught up around here, so everybody wins," Evan said optimistically.

"Want to meet up for lunch at Soccer's in an hour or so?" Zyriah asked. "I'm buying."

"I'll just grab something from the fridge," Evan replied. "I'll see you two when you get back."

Evan disappeared behind the building, and Joshua got into the car on the passenger side, unlocking Zyriah's door from the inside. Zyriah, sitting in the driver's seat, looked a bit confused to Joshua, as he passed her the car key. He looked out the passenger window for a moment, looking at the flowers with one last look before Evan changed them for autumn.

"Didn't want to drive?" Zyriah asked.

"You'll get us there faster," Joshua recommended.

"To be honest, I like it being just the two of us again. It's how this whole thing started." Zyriah admitted.

Joshua wanted to be honest as well. "Well, if you want

my opinion Zyriah, I'd prefer it if Evan was with us."

"You don't like that we have some private time?" Zyriah questioned with concern.

"It's not that. Evan's just a better fighter than I am. If this Glover guy picks a fight, I'm not much for a battle," Joshua said quietly.

Zyriah pulled the car out of the driveway, turning it to face down Treeclimber Drive, and the traffic appeared to be steady throughout the town. Joshua looked at the car's clock, realizing it was close to one in the afternoon, and most of these drivers were probably returning to work from lunch. Joshua's stomach slightly growled from hunger.

"I'm actually pretty hungry," Joshua admitted. "Can we eat first?"

"Let's swing by to make sure the Glassworks is open," Zyriah said while driving. "If it is, we can't miss the opportunity to ask them a few questions."

"Fair enough," Joshua agreed, with a growling hunger that only continued to intensify.

Grewe and Glover's Glassworks stood on the end of Treeclimber Drive, before the road turned towards Soccer's, and Joshua's first instinct was for a hotdog. However, he did look at the front of the building, a wide remodeled building that looked similar to a barn with large front stained-glass windows. A sidewalk sign stood at its front saying the store was open. Zyriah pulled into the adjacent parking lot, and the two of them left the car to walk towards the entrance.

"This is definitely the place alright," Joshua said, stepping onto the front porch of the establishment, looking at the long window with "Grewe and Glover's Glassworks" in purple glass built into it and the window trimmed in orange and red squares.

Joshua opened the front door using its brass doorhandle and pulled it wide for Zyriah to enter before him. Stores with glassware always made him slightly nervous. Joshua had always been afraid he would walk into something and break something expensive. He rolled his shoulders slightly forward, crossing his arms around the middle of his torso, and walked in hoping nothing breakable would be very close by. He knew he needed to be more aware of his temper but found it difficult under these conditions.

The inside of the store was a room of rainbows, as the display lights from the long glass display cases reflected multiple colors along the walls. Glass shelf displays throughout the center of the room added to the prism effect as the overhead lighting shown down through the shelf panes making colorful patterns on the floor. The products were varied. From a variety of drink glass sets, lamps, and even glass animal figurines, the salesfloor contained a multitude of options. Joshua noticed a baby mobile, with little glass ducks that turned to a little motor at its top. An oddly shaped double-cylindered blue lamp shined blue waves onto a neighboring wall as the two cylinders rotated in opposite directions. Joshua especially liked the other front display window, that had a collection of different colored stained-glass butterflies attached by small suction cups to the main window.

"Just a minute. Somebody will be right with ya," A face quickly looking from a rear doorway peaked and called out. Joshua saw it was a tall, middle-aged man with a short brown beard, before the man vanished into the back room. "That was Paul Grewe," Zyriah whispered. "One of the owners."

Joshua, after taking another look at the butterflies in the front display windows, turned his attention back to Zyriah, and the two walked to the back display counter. Joshua investigated the case, an array of short round glasses that were arranged by color into a rainbow, from red to purple. A short man appeared from the same rear doorway, crossing behind the counter, and greeted them with a smile.

"Roly-poly glasses," the man said politely. "My grandfather started the business off with them. He thought they made good wedding gifts."

"They are lovely as always," Zyriah, looking up from the case, said making eye contact with the man.

"Oh, Miss Flint, I'm sorry. Where is my mind today?" the man chuckled.

"How have you been, Johnny? It's certainly been a long time," Zyriah said smiling.

"Another day, another dollar. Been pretty steady with business lately," Johnny said. "Are you two shopping together today?"

"Let me do an introduction," Zyriah said. "Johnny Glover. This is Joshua Spiker."

"Spiker?" Johnny looked at Joshua, and Joshua felt slightly analyzed. "You're not Lenora's?"

"That he is," Zyriah agreed.

"Man, I never thought I'd ever see you," Johnny said, shaking Joshua's hand. "I remember your mom pregnant with you. Really nice lady, she was."

"Nice meeting you sir," Joshua said.

"My, my, my. Oh, I'm sorry," Johnny apologized. "That

was a bit of a surprise, I keep going on and on. What all can I help you both with today? Some nice glassware or perhaps a decoration or two?

"We thought you might be able to help Joshua here with a few questions," Zyriah said, looking down at the glasses in the case for a moment, then back up at the man.

"Questions? Not sure how much help I can be, but I'll give it a try," Johnny said, pulling a stool from beside the nearby cash register, and positioning himself perched upon it behind the counter.

"I was going through some of my mom's old paperwork and receipts, and I saw that you all did that front sunset window of my bedroom," Joshua began.

"Not me, but my dad and Paul's dad worked on that one," Johnny added. "Paul and I brought up some parts as needed, but the installation was our dad's."

"Well," Joshua said, slightly strolling looking at the merchandise, trying not to sound like he was interrogating, "I was doing a little research on the previous window on that side of the house. Do you know much about it?"

"The nativity window? Sure do. That was our granddaddy's work way back when," Johnny said, with a slightly more serious tone. "Damn shame about that tragedy at the church. Damn shame."

"Do you have any information about any pieces of that window that were spared and saved from that day?" Joshua inquired.

"Are you asking me about the Star?" Johnny asked.

Joshua looked quickly at Zyriah, who leaned in closer placing her hands on the counter. The man knew the Star, and the purpose of them being there intensified. Joshua began to wish that Zyriah would do more of the talking.

"Yes, exactly," Joshua said, trying not to look eager. "My mother had records that she did have the Star part of that window, and I was trying to see what she ever did with it."

"Your mother brought it back down here, of course," Johnny nodded, but grew a bit quieter. "She had the idea of using that piece as something new around the house. A conversation piece she called it. We were talking about a lot of ideas. Lampshades, a glass tabletop, there's a lot of ways to repurpose a piece like that."

"Do you know what it was turned into?" Zyriah finally spoke and asked.

"Sure do," Johnny said, getting off the stool and walking over to the cylinder lamp Joshua has looked at previously. "Pretty similar to this. The Star was part of a large lantern light, that we made three other sides to so the whole thing looked like a Star box. It rolled on its base like spinner. Lenora didn't want a motor or electric installed on it, but those bearings spun that thing for at least a couple dozen revolutions. Put a nice Star effect on the walls. Don't think we ever made another one like it after though. Shame though. Real nice piece when it was all said and done. Lenora sure was happy with it. Paul hand delivered it. I remember that."

"Do you know what happened to it after my mother passed away?" Joshua said, slightly even more eager.

"Oh, what do you need an old lantern for?" Johnny said, and Joshua began to grow wary. "That old thing was lit by a candle for goodness sake. Now this wave lamp plugs right in the wall...."

"I really want the one that belonged to my mother," Joshua said with a bit of sternness. "It belonged to her."

Johnny Glover looked down momentarily, then looked around the store, and Joshua felt as if he was going to try to find another object to try to sell him instead. The man's eyes, however, looked a little more stressed. He grew quiet, and his eyes became slightly watered and moved with swift jerks, until he blinked a few times, then returned to look at Joshua.

"That lantern was sold," Glover said with a certain coldness. "There was an estate sale soon after your mom's passing, and Paul and I went up to see what all that lawyer had up for purchase. The lantern wasn't listed, and Paul found out by word of mouth that your mom sold it prior to her passing. Damn shame too. Would've been a nice display piece in here."

"It sure would have been by the way you described it," Zyriah added. "Is there anything else you know about it? Joshua here really has his heart set on it."

"I don't know anything," Johnny answered somewhat coldly, then changed his expression to that of a smiling salesman. "Now, I'm sure if you all look around here, you'll find something that catches the eye."

"Actually," Joshua replied, walking over to the front display windows, "I have been looking at these butterflies."

"Well, pick yourself out one there fella. All the colors of the rainbow in here. Which takes your fancy?" Johnny said, having followed Joshua to the window. Joshua pointed to one in particular, a butterfly with a stained-glass mint green wing and a red wing outlined in metal Joshua thought looked similar to pewter. Johnny removed the suction cup from the window, and he took the butterfly over to the cash register. After placing it in a small white gift box, he placed the box in a small orange and red plastic sack.

"Well wait," Joshua said, after watching Johnny bag the merchandise. "You didn't tell me a price for it."

"No charge, son," Johnny Glover said smiling politely. "I ain't charging somebody with a mom as good as yours was."

CHAPTER
TEN

Joshua followed Zyriah walking from the Glassworks to Soccer's for lunch, and as he walked he thought about the man he just met. Johnny Glover was a polite man, but Joshua could tell there was a clear difference between his customer service skill's, personality, and his normal manner. He was well-kept, in a nice plaid button up shirt and parted brown hair, but still there was something about his personality that struck Joshua as odd. He was forthcoming to Joshua's questions about the Star, but only to a degree. Joshua began to wonder what else he knew. Even more, Joshua wondered if Johnny Glover had the Star himself.

"What are you thinking about?" Zyriah inquired while leading him forward with her footsteps. "You're awful quiet."

"I'm just thinking about that Glover guy," Joshua admitted. "Did that talk strike you as a little strange?"

"I think it's the beginning of the truth," Zyriah replied. "He's had a pretty tough history lately with his family, according to Evan. That could have explained part of his demeanor."

"How do you mean?" Joshua asked.

"Well, if he is up to something or knows anything about the Star, he's not going to readily admit it. People that were formally incarcerated normally know the penalties of the crime as far as what it's like to serve the jail time. I doubt Mr. Glover wants to repeat his time behind bars," Zyriah explained.

"True," Joshua agreed. "Still, how would you bring charges against somebody for something like this? Let's say he does have the Star, and he was using it against the Baker's and the Pritchard's. I don't think there's any laws in the law books that's going to cover psychic phenomena like this."

"Well, you and I can focus on the Star," Zyriah said, walking into Soccer's turning her head back to look at Joshua. "Let Sheriff Tucker handle the rest."

"What do you need me to handle?" a voice questioned.

Joshua followed Zyriah into Soccer's and hearing the familiar voice of Monika Tucker, sitting at a counter stool finishing her late lunch. Joshua watched as Zyriah was a bit startled by the sudden response to her statement, as she whipped her head back seeing the sheriff sitting there holding her last bits of a hot dog. Zyriah began to sit down in the first booth, and Joshua sat opposite her with his back facing the door.

"You scared me there for a second Monika," Zyriah said, finally sitting in the booth and getting comfortable on the hard seat. "I didn't expect you to be sitting there."

"Well, y'all still aren't answering the question," Monika said, putting the last of the hotdog on her plate and pushing it back unwanted towards the waitress. Joshua could feel she was dissatisfied. "What was it that y'all needed handled?"

"Oh, we were just discussing last night and wondering how things were progressing," Zyriah explained.

"Last night, huh?" a voice asked, and Joshua turned his gaze to Russell, behind the counter wiping breadcrumbs from the countertop. "The word's gotten out plenty. It's been the talk of this place. Another Spiker stirring the pot like his mother, I'm guessing."

"What's your problem, sir?" Joshua said in a defiant manner.

"My problem?" Russell exclaimed, throwing his rag down on the counter. "My problem is I don't want your kind of problems brought into my establishment. Keep it outside. You may own that big house on the hill, but you certainly don't own me, young man, and neither did your mother."

Joshua grew quiet, feeling the conversation intensifying so quickly that he was afraid of a fight. He reminded himself that he was new to Wilcox, and he needed to keep himself under control until he knew more about what had happened there. Russell had just confirmed that his mother had an opponent in that little hot dog diner, and he could not afford aggravating the situation and giving himself a bad reputation.

He took a deep breath, closing his eyes for a short moment, then returned his attention to Sheriff Tucker, hoping the tension with Russell Lloyd would ease as the man turned back to cleaning his workspace.

"I spent the morning with Melanie Pritchard," Monika informed them. "She's back from her father's in Ohio. She got a phone call to come back early. That's one upset lady."

"Well, with all she's been through, I'm sure she's really devastated," Zyriah said solemnly.

"Very true. She gave me a bit of a back story, trying to explain all this. She kept insisting the boy was a good kid. Never gave her or her husband a bit of trouble," Monika said, standing from the stool and walking over to the table, lowering her voice volume the closer she came for privacy. "The one thing that interested me is how strange she thought something like that would happen in a bathtub, considering the boy had such an issue with water."

"Water?" Joshua asked.

"Well, not water exactly," Monika said correcting her previous statement. "Donnie Pritchard had a fear of drowning. So, anything water related, the boy was always a bit nervous about. She said many didn't know it, and Donnie didn't want many to know it. He thought it ruined his tough guy image."

"Any explanation of why he was afraid of drowning?" Zyriah asked.

"Well, I guess many years ago, the family was upstream a fair ways from Rock Falls, enjoying the day having a picnic. Gordon apparently was out in the water with Donnie trying to teach the boy to swim, but the current got him. It took some effort, but Gordon was able to reach him before Donnie got caught going too far downstream and over the falls. The boy had a fear of swimming ever since," Monika explained, taking a moment to look at all of them as if she was making sure they were listening.

"He probably blamed his dad for that fear," Joshua theorized.

"Certainly possible," Monika agreed, repeating herself

as she looked to be considering Joshua's idea. Joshua liked that she was open-minded. She nodded as she thought. "Certainly possible."

Nikki came over to take their order, and Joshua allowed Zyriah to order his food yet again. Monika remained quiet about the issue until the Nikki had the order written completely on her order pad and left the table. Joshua looked up at the sheriff, who then had a very serious expression.

"If you two hear anything more about the situation at the Pritchard's or the Baker's, I'm truly expecting more information as you get it," Monika informed them. "I can tell what kind of case this is going to be, but I can't work with it unless I get all the information I need, understand?"

"We understand," Zyriah replied as Monika's cell phone began to ring.

"I gotta take this," Monika said, looking down at the phone's screen and quickly exiting out the front door. It was then that Zyriah noticed that rain was falling.

"Looks like the rain finally came," Zyriah said. "There's a couple tote umbrellas in the car if we need them."

"Great. I'm glad we have umbrellas...in...the...car," Joshua giggled, diverting his intense thinking to break his own tension. "I wonder what the rush was for the Sheriff's phone call. I don't have a problem with cops or anything, but I still find it strange she can do those things by touching objects. Do many people know about her?"

"Those who know typically are those who already have something similar," she replied.

The food came, hotdogs again, two a piece, on separate places with a chocolate milk for each. Joshua had forgotten the hunger pains he was feeling earlier, but once the food was in reach, he ate the first hot dog quickly. The sauce was a bit hotter today, so he drank some of his milk to wash down the burn. He heard Soccer's front door open behind him, but he paid no attention, until two hands reached around and covered his eyes.

"Guess who?"

Joshua thought when this game is normally played, the person placing their hands over your eyes would whisper those two words somewhere from behind or next to your ear for you to guess who the stranger was. There was something odd about how this game was being played this time. The voice did not come from behind. The voice was Zyriah's sitting in front of him.

"I'm completely confused actually," Joshua admitted.

The hands released from covering his eyes, and in front of him was Zyriah looking behind Joshua, to the owner of the hands. Once again, he first assumed it was Evan, deciding to give up on mum planting to join them for lunch, so Joshua turned around in his booth seat expecting to see him. Instead, there was another familiar face, thin, tan, and bearded with a childish grin. It was Noah Wilson.

Joshua finished his lunch, sharing his booth seat with Noah, while Zyriah focused more on the outside rain from a window close to Soccer's cash register. Distant thunder was rolling forward, slowly increasing in volume, and Joshua watched Zyriah's eyes squint slightly with each sound. Noah was eating quietly, a pepperoni roll with cheese and drinking from a plastic cup of soda, and he occasionally looked around the table from Zyriah, to Joshua, and back to his meal. Joshua was pretty sure Noah winked at him deliberately at one point, but he took it as a sign of friendliness. A brisk, wet breeze of air rolled in behind him as the front door opened, and Evan rushed in from the rain, hair wet and a bit matted. He shook the excess off with a headshake and stood over the table, looking at the remnants of their lunch.

"Looks like I didn't make it on time after all," Evan said, scooting himself in beside Zyriah. "So much for planting today with rain like that."

Noah signed his words in Evan's direction, and Zyriah helped to interpret.

"Noah's asking how bad the roads are?" Zyriah translated

"Nothing on the roads yet. Few crazy drivers out though driving a few miles over the speed limit, but there's nothing too bad going on," Evan said in Noah's direction, careful to speak slow enough so Noah could read his lips and understand the reply.

"What can I get you?" Nikki asked Evan as she approached the table, her order pad in hand.

"Couple dogs. Hot sauce with everything and a chocolate," Evan ordered.

Nikki walked away, and Joshua tried to remember the manner how Zyriah and Evan ordered at Soccer's. He wanted to fit in, considering he was planning on living in Wilcox, so he tried remembering the wording of how to order each time they ordered for themselves. He assumed he would catch on to the wording eventually.

"So, how did things go at the Glassworks?" Evan asked.

"Good, I think," Joshua answered. "Mr. Glover didn't know who owned the Star now, but he did say it was used in a new lantern built by their company."

"What kind of lantern?" Evan asked curiously.

"Well," Zyriah responded, "it's a four-sided glass lantern with stained-glass on all sides, the Star being one of the sides. The sides swivel on bearings on a circular track, so if you light the candle in the center and spin it, stars should appear on the wall."

"Whose idea was it to use it like that?" Evan asked. "The Star, I mean."

"Perhaps it was Lenora," Zyriah answered. "Mr. Glover said he and Paul Grewe went up for the estate sale after Lenora's death, but they were told, probably by Enoch Burke, that it was already sold prior to Lenora's passing. They weren't able to buy it."

"Johnny Glover," Evan said shaking his head slightly, as Nikki placed his order in front of him. "I hope he got his act together."

"How do you mean?" Zyriah inquired.

"I'm sorry," Evan explained, "but any man that hurt his kid like that deserves what he gets. I can deal with a lot of things some parents do to punish their children, but anybody who is just a flat-out abuser deserves what he got. That wife and child is safer now that he's not in the picture."

"Wait, wait. Explain this to me," Joshua requested, wanting to make sure the story was complete. "What kind of abuse?"

"He hit the boy on the back with a baseball bat. The boy's friends all saw it happen. The medical report showed a broken rib. The boy ran to his mother in the house after it happened in the back yard, where Johnny and the boys were playing ball. Johnny got mad at Paulie for talking back to him," Evan explained.

"Paulie?" Joshua asked.

"Paulie Glover," Zyriah answered. "Johnny and Catherine named him after Paul Grewe."

"So, Mr. Glover got arrested for it then," Joshua responded.

"Arrested, convicted, and served his jail time," Zyriah stated, first speaking in a direct manner but becoming more intrigued. "I'm betting he's got a lot of resentment against those that put him in there, too. Evan, was Deputy Baker one of the witnesses?"

"Sure was," Evan explained, in between bites of his hot dog. "He was the responding officer that day of the baseball bat incident. He arrested Glover on the spot."

"Who was the prosecutor?" Joshua asked, his suspicions growing.

Evan sat down his hotdog dog, and Joshua could see in his eyes there was a eureka thought behind them but also a bit of anger. Evan had been such a mixture of emotions when it came to discussing that court case, and Joshua was not sure which emotion would be vocalized next. Still, Joshua knew the answer to the question before Evan said it, based solely on his expression.

"Gordon Pritchard," Evan said, pushing the remainder of his food on a plate to the side of the table for Nikki to pick it up. "You think that case is what's causing all these Star issues?"

"Well, there is a connection between Baker and Pritchard. Plus, Glover's business is responsible for making the lantern the Star is currently a part of," Zyriah rationalized. "The question is where is the Star, and if it is Glover, who will he use it on next?"

"Glover said it was sold before he could even buy it," Joshua said. "Could we ask Mr. Burke if he remembers the lantern as part of the estate sale? Maybe he has a bill of sale from the estate auction, or he remembers Glover asking about it. I'm just betting that lantern is in that shop somewhere."

Noah signed something in Joshua's direction, and Zyriah, reading Noah's words, let her eyes grow wide.

"Noah says you win your bet, because he's seen it in the shop," Zyriah said in an urgent voice.

"What?" Joshua asked, forgetting Noah was even still sitting at the table. He was so consumed with Evan's story of Glover, the boy, and the lantern that he forgot the three had an additional person at the table. Noah seemed to have some necessary information that could be helpful, and Joshua knew it was needed.

"Noah says the Star lantern that spins? Sure, he's seen Paul Grewe working on it in the showroom before. The Star that spins. Paul said he was working on it for Johnny," Zyriah translated as Noah explained.

"How did you even know what this was about?" Joshua inquired, Zyriah continuing to sign his words for Noah.

"He says he didn't," Zyriah said vocalizing for Noah, changing the point of view from explaining his words in third person to as if Noah was speaking out himself. "You just asked about the Glassworks' Star lantern, and I'd seen it. Good thing you guys were talking about it while I was here. Lip reading does come in handy when people don't think you're listening."

"Now it's a question of getting it back from Johnny," Evan said. "I told you that guy was bad. Anybody that hits his son is dangerous man deep down."

"Oh, he didn't do that either," Noah continued. "Catherine had been trying to leave Johnny for a while before that whole thing. Paulie's friends on the t-ball team were making fun of him because Johnny didn't show up for the dad/son game that summer. Paulie got into a fight with that Brad Henson that broke into the high school last year. Brad hit Paulie with the ball bat, and Catherine blamed Johnny for it."

"How do you know all this?" Zyriah asked.

"I work at the Senior Center, otherwise known as 'gossip central'," Noah laughed, as Zyriah continued speaking for him. "Brad Henson's grandmother, Phyllis told Kathy Ebert shortly after the Glover trial was over. Big scandal in Wilcox, and those old folks love it."

"So, if Johnny Glover was innocent the entire time..." Zyriah began.

"...he's getting his revenge on the people that took his son away," Joshua concluded.

"We need to find Johnny," Evan said, standing up and with Zyriah moving across the booth seat to stand up as well. Noah stood up to let Joshua out of his seat. Joshua looked back at the booth seat and realized he had brought his bag with his purchase from Grewe and Glover's in with him, grabbing it to take it with him.

"You've a good man for helping us," Zyriah said, giving Noah a quick hug.

Noah said something to Zyriah and she laughed.

"I'll do my best," she said jovially.

The front door of Soccer's opened as an older man rushed in from the rain with a young girl. Both had matted hair from the rain soaking, and the man shook his body with hopes the droplets remaining on his coat would shake themselves free before soaking into the material. Noah approached the man, signing something to him quickly.

"I'm not going to get sick," the man said, combing his greying hair back with his fingers. "Audrey wanted something to take home to eat and I thought this would be a quick trip. I thought it'd cheer her up."

Joshua looked at the young girl, her eyes with a warmth that could evaporate rain with that look of sincerity. Nikki, calling from the other side of the counter, asked what they needed. The man, acknowledging Nikki by name, ordered six hot dogs with mild sauce to go. Joshua looked again at the girl, who looked to be a little frightened.

"Ronald, it's nice to see you," Zyriah greeted. "Still keeping all these grandchildren in line?"

The man patted Noah on the shoulder and grinned. "I need to keep a better eye on this one, but the girls are doing fine. Audrey got scared by a cat she saw outside of Michalski's store. I had to pick up some milk, and I almost dropped it when she hollered out. I still blame Noah for all this."

"You don't like cats?" Joshua asked the young girl, now assuming the man was Noah's grandfather and the girl was his sister. "How did you brother make you scared of cats?"

Zyriah had apparently been signing the conversation to Noah out of Joshua's view. In response to his question, Noah bent down, putting his weight on his hands, and arched his back almost unnaturally. Joshua could imagine what Noah was trying to accomplish, appearing to imitate a scared cat with a high-arched back like the drawings Joshua had seen of black cats around Halloween.

Noah's attempt at frightening the girl was an effective one, making the young girl curl up and grabbing for her grandfather. Ronald, on the other hand, looked far more annoyed than scared as he smacked Noah on his rear, making Noah stand up straight again and smiling.

"Keep it up and you're going to give your sister a complex," Ronald scolded.

Noah, Joshua could see in his eyes and manner, suddenly felt the guilt of the situation. He sat himself down on one knee, placing his hand over the center of his chest in a fist, and made a movement like a small circle over his heart. The girl looking more scared from Noah's cat impersonation now looked less bothered by her brother's action, calming her eyes and face from their frantic expression. Noah opened his arms, and the girl slowly walked over returning the hug to her brother.

"Kids," Ronald said to Zyriah. "Will they ever grow up?"

Noah stood again, doing the same motion with his fist circling over his chest as he had done for the girl. Joshua interpreted the sign as "I'm sorry" and smiled as the grandfather patted Noah on the shoulder again. Nikki, placing two paper bags of food on the counter, called out to Ronald that his order was ready. The man, pulling cash from his pocket, gave the money to Nikki and collected his food and granddaughter's hand.

"We got to get home before this food gets cold," Ronald explained. "Zyriah, pleasure to see you. Noah, I'll see you when you get home."

The two left quickly out the front door, and Joshua noticed the hard falling rain outside before the door closed behind them. He turned looking at Noah, who had a guilty smirk on his lips for his actions against his sister. Joshua knew it was just teasing, but he did not like seeing the little girl scared as she was.

Evan reopened the front door to Soccer's and all but

Noah exited. Joshua expected to be pelted by the raindrops, but the three were spared under the awning over the front window. The water was collecting on the sides of the streets in small pools that flowed down into the random drains along the sidewalk. Joshua watched the passing cars creating waves when their tires ripped through the water, splashing the waves onto the sidewalks. Zyriah dug into her purse, retrieving the key to the Joshua's car, and gave it to Evan.

"There should be two or three tote umbrellas in the trunk," Zyriah requested. "My word, is she still out here?"

Joshua looked in the direction that Zyriah was facing, and Sheriff Tucker was in her police car talking on a cell phone. It had been a decent length of time since she left Soccer's, but apparently the phone call had lasted longer than he expected. Evan ran next to the police cruiser, splashing his feet into the running water on the parking lot towards Joshua's car still parked in the Glasswork's parking spaces. He opened the truck, retrieving three black tote umbrellas, and he opened one to protect him from the rainfall. Joshua watched him as he walked back, but when he was close to the cruiser Sheriff Tucker lowered her window slightly, and Evan bent his ear close to hear her say something. Putting the two spare umbrellas under the arm holding his open umbrella, Evan reached into his front pocket and pulled out what appeared to be a cigarette lighter. He passed it through the crack in the window to the Sheriff, and in a few moments she returned the lighter and closed the window. Evan waved, shifting the two umbrellas back to his free hand, and walked back to Joshua and Zyriah under the awning.

"I didn't know you smoked," Joshua pointed out.

"Huh? Oh no, I don't. I just keep a lighter handy. Dad always told me to keep a lighter and a pin knife with me. He always kept one of each in his pocket, and I guess I continued the tradition," Evan explained, pulling out a red cigarette lighter and a small pin knife with wooden sides. "Actually, this pin knife belonged to my pap, and my dad gave it to me when pap passed away."

"That explains it then," Joshua said. "I figured if you did, I would've seen you smoke one by now."

"So, what's the plan?" Evan asked, giving an umbrella to Joshua and Zyriah.

"Well, I thought we could go over and talk to Mr. Glover again," Zyriah suggested. "I figured if you two kept him talking I could check his Shardland and see what information I could get."

"Why can't I do it?" Joshua asked, with a bit of determination. "How am I ever going to get better at this if I don't try to do it more often?"

"This is important, Joshua," Zyriah replied. "You can have plenty of practice reading Evan or me another time. We're under a big-time constraint here if we're going to try to retrieve that Star before Glover uses it again."

"Well, we can't exactly just ask him for it, can we?" Joshua said sarcastically. "Let me try to read him, even if it's just to show where he put the Star. It's got to be around that shop somewhere."

Joshua was feeling the ambition to help more, even if it meant trying to understand this new ability as fast as he could. He did not have a full grip on feeling comfortable enough to go into the Shardland, and he certainly needed their help to get there. He remembered the first night and the dream that resulted from falling asleep using the pendant, and he did not feel comfortable going into the Shardland on his own. He wanted the teamwork, but he also wanted the challenge.

He watched Zyriah and Evan looking at each other for a few moments, debating on his participation, when Noah exited Soccer's front door and put up his own umbrella waving goodbye to the three of them. Joshua waved back, watching him walk away into the rain, as he noticed Sheriff Tucker putting her window down again, passing a piece of paper to Noah once his umbrella shielded the paper from getting wet. Noah read the paper, shaking his head to express a "no", and Sheriff Tucker looking down again. Joshua figured she was probably writing another message to Noah, when he heard the distant sound of a CB radio. Joshua watched the sheriff talking into the microphone, her car window still cracked open, and Noah standing their patiently. Within a few moments, she said something to Noah, waving goodbye, and put her cruiser into reverse. Slipping it into drive, she turned on the police sirens and cruiser lights, flashing red and white, and passing in front of Soccer's at a fast rate.

Joshua, feeling the splash of the wave as the water from the street splashed upon him, stepped back from the sidewalk's edge closer to the window and farther under the awning. He turned back to Zyriah and Evan, who apparently had been whispering about what they had been talking about before Noah left Soccer's. Joshua, feeling left out of the conversation, kicked at the wet puddle that formed on the sidewalk. He wanted to do more.

"Joshua?" Zyriah turned to face him, slightly monotone in her voice.

"I just want to try more and help with this alright? Give

me a chance here," Joshua said defending himself. He noticed there was not much of a rebuttal and looked up to see Zyriah's eyes growing slowly vacant in expression.

"Are you alright?" Joshua asked, holding her shoulder. She turned looking at Evan with the same vacation expression.

"I need to sit down," Zyriah said with deep breaths. "Evan, I need a piece of paper."

Zyriah began scrolling with pen in hand, using the paper provided by Nikki and using a pen Evan retrieved from Zyriah's purse. The line Zyriah wrote with alternating jaggedness reminded Joshua of when she had written the name Donnie Pritchard back on his dining room table. Her body was still like before, except the free-flowing motion of her right arm gliding the pen over the paper that looked much more comfortable with her automatic writing process. Joshua sat in the same seat he had eaten his lunch at, while Evan and Zyriah returned to sit across from him. Business within Soccer's continued as usual with people eating behind Evan and Zyriah, and Joshua was, for a moment, amazed how unaware the rest of the clientele was to what was happening at their table.

"What do you think this is?" Joshua asked Evan. "Another name?"

"Very well might be," Evan replied.

Zyriah continued scrolling, and Joshua suddenly felt the rush of wet wind rush in behind him as the front door opened. Noah, rushing in and sitting back beside Joshua, closing his umbrella, and slightly gasping for breath. Joshua could tell the rain had intensified somewhat, and the thunder he had been ignoring had intensified.

"Raining harder than you expected," Evan said to Noah.

Noah gave a thumbs up and smiled, as he took a deep breath to gain his composure, and Joshua watched him looking at Zyriah. Zyriah, still moving her pen over the paper line after line, was still vacant in expression, and Noah looked over at Joshua raising his hands in an expression of "why?" Joshua realized that if Zyriah was continuing her automatic writing, he had lost his sign language interpreter.

"She's…got…a…headache," Joshua said slowly, deliberately over exaggerating the shape of his mouth.

Noah looked at him, with a look of slight humor and sarcasm mixed with irritation. He looked into Joshua's eyes, then down, then up again, somewhat scanning over him as if he was doing some type of physical examination. Noah pointed at his chest, and Joshua attempted to try to understand Noah himself. Luckily, Joshua knew Noah could read his lips no matter what, but Joshua noticed a sly smile forming on Noah's lips.

"You," Joshua said, trying to translate.

Noah took both hand, brushing them outwards palms down in opposite directions.

"You're not?" Joshua attempted.

Noah pointed to the side of his head, moving the pointed finger at his temple in a circular motion. He stuck out his tongue and tried to cross his eyes.

"I never said you were crazy," Joshua said, understanding his words and finding a certain amount of humor in it. Joshua thought Noah had a great and colorful personality. It was definitely something Joshua needed. "What did the sheriff want?"

Noah moved his hands as if operating a steering wheel and pointed to his chest.

"She asked if you needed a ride?" Joshua guessed.

Noah smiled, blinking one eye at Joshua, and gave a thumbs up.

"Well, it looks like she had to leave anyway," Joshua began talking at a normal rate. "We can give you a ride home or back to work, whichever you need to go. We came back in because Zyriah said her head was hurting, and she wanted to sit down a minute."

Noah, looking down at the paper that Zyriah was filling with penned lines, looked back at Joshua, shrugging his shoulders and making circular motions with one hand as if he was holding a pen. Joshua was trying to be patient for the message Zyriah was writing, but he felt himself tapping his right foot with impatience. The situation had become more intriguing. Noah appeared to have been confused by Zyriah writing when she was supposed to have head pain, so Joshua offered a poor explanation.

"Why is she writing?" Joshua said, getting proud of himself for figuring out how to communicate so quickly. "She says it helps relieve the pain by focusing on something else."

Noah tilted his head slightly, and Joshua could tell he did not believe him. He moved only his doubtful eyes over to Evan, who nodded and smiled back at Noah, and Noah moved those eyes back to Joshua. He shrugged his shoulders and shook his head. Joshua knew he was not being believed. Joshua took one hand and put it up beside his mouth, blocking Noah's view in an unobvious way that he was sure was not working.

"Did she write anything?" Joshua asked.

Noah sighed with an annoyed breath as if Joshua was being rude. Evan just shook his head "no". Noah, pulling out a small spiral notebook and a short pencil from his pocket, wrote his own message on his paper. He ripped it from the spiral binding, passing the written message to Joshua. Joshua read it and turned facing Noah so he could read his lips clearly.

"Everybody gets a little privacy ya know," Joshua responded to the note saying, "that was rude".

"Did the Sheriff say where she was going in a hurry?" Evan asked Noah. Noah refocused his attention on his notebook, scribbling his words on the paper, and passing the note to Evan. Evan, after reading the message Noah had written, looked back at Joshua with a wide stare.

"He lipread the Sheriff talking on the car radio. She said something about a kidnapping, Judge Echols, and a shovel," Evan said stunned.

"Was that the judge?" Joshua asked.

"In the Glover court case? Yes," Evan replied.

"I just wish we knew where the Sheriff drove off to," Joshua said with frustration.

Zyriah lowered her head and dropped her pen to the table from her hand. Joshua had been so involved in communicating with Noah that he had not been paying close attention to what Zyriah had been writing. Evan collected the paper from under Zyriah's hand and read the words she had written. Zyriah's head rose, looking from Joshua to Noah and back, with a growing smile.

Evan turned the paper to face Joshua and pushed the paper across the table so Joshua could read it. Looking down, Joshua scanned over the page until the straight and jagged lines finally formed into a properly written cursive pair of words, which made Joshua immediately asked a question.

"Where is Westview Cemetery?"

CHAPTER
ELEVEN

Joshua felt his car wanting to hydroplane on the wet pavement as night began to fall as hard as the rain was falling. The passengers in the car were all quiet, and Joshua was more focused on Evan's driving ability in that weather more that he was about their destination. Joshua had insisted Noah come along, mainly for all the help with the information he provided at Soccer's, but also because he did not want to leave him stranded in the storm. They had a name, Judge Echols, and a location, Westview Cemetery, but neither was providing the events that were happening or were going to happen at the location. Joshua was fearful of that unknown factor, so he sat in the backseat with Noah, clutching onto his bag from the Glassworks containing the butterfly he purchased. He prayed that all four of them would get to their destination safely.

"Is it far?" Joshua broke the silence.

"It's about ten minutes," Evan yelled back, trying to look

through the windshield covered in spattered rainfall frequently wiped away by the windshield wipers. "We're going to get there."

Joshua leaned back and took a sigh, looking over momentarily at Noah, who was looking out his window at the darkening land and sky as nightfall surrounded them. The car's interior grew so dark it was nearly impossible to see, and it began to dawn on Joshua that he had an opportunity. They were getting closer to Judge Echols, and he wondered if he would be able to see the Shardland from that distance. He had never tried it before, but any information he could find would be helpful. He removed his pendant, cupping it in his hand, and tried to remember the moment he had last used the stone. He raised his eyes, looking at all of them. Noah, Evan, and Zyriah were more focused on the events outside the vehicle as far as the storm went than what he was attempting in the back right seat.

He remembered more of his earlier attempt with Evan in his living room, focusing on his breathing and focusing on the comforting green light he wanted to see from the selenite cupped in his hands. He remembered the dark room, and how he needed to empty the thoughts and images in his mind. Finally, he knew that he needed to focus on the name, but not Evan's this time. Now he must think of Judge Echols, a man he never met, and he felt the amount of risk in this endeavor.

He breathed deeply, concentrating on seeing the light. The steady, steady blinks. His breathing in and out slower as he focused to bring the stone it's desired color. The pendant was dark in the car, but he could still see the outlines of its cylindrical form once the familiar pale green color began to be visible. The color grew strong, and Joshua, proud of his efforts, continued to focus on his relaxation. His eyelids grew heavy, and once he felt relaxed enough, he closed them and envisioned the dark room. The leftover images of thoughts and ideas in his mind. The conversation at Soccer's became less of a focus. The meeting of Johnny Glover disappeared momentarily as his concentration moved in the correct direction. The emptiness washed through his mind until the room was empty.

Judge Echols.

The ripples of the Shardland were strong, a black shimmering through the dark space, and Joshua continued to scan through it. He told himself to be strong, to be patient. The ripples bounced little points of light and color, and Joshua held his mind's eyes steady until those points of light began to glow and grow. The ripples slowly began to stabilize as the images grew into shards with a huge size difference.

The flickering images before him were his size, edged like broken glass fragments pulsing blurred images that clarified by the moment. However, behind them were large, building size fragments with the same distorted images trying to clarify. He knew somehow there was a connection, these smaller shards with the larger ones, so he focused back and forth between them. Finally, the larger shard closest to him was clear, two boys in a basement wrestling.

The clothing was very old in style, ripped jeans and checkered button up shirts on each boy. He felt they were related, perhaps brothers, wrestling in their parents' basement. For a moment, he saw the reflection of the eyes he was looking out of, a young boy, dark parted hair smiling to his reflection in a full-length mirror hanging from a basement door. The boy was playing with his brother, and Joshua could not understand how this led to fear. It seemed normal for two brothers.

Joshua scanned the image, seeing now that the eyes were focused around the basement looking for something, something in particular. In the rear corner, opened with folded quilts inside, was a large black trunk, and as the boys wrestled, the boy that he assumed was Judge Echols as a child, continued to pull his brother closer to that trunk. The other boy was struggling and continued to fight back. Upon reaching the trunk, the brother twisted back and forth as the Judge's younger self held him with a locked arm around his neck, pulling the quilts out of the trunk and discarding them onto the concrete floor.

The Judge twisted his brother around, picking him up with his other arm under his knees, and putting him into that truck very quickly, closing the lid and latching the front latch of the trunk closed. The Judge's image bounced, and Joshua was not sure if it was due to laughter or the brother kicking the roof of the trunk from the inside, as Joshua realized that the Judge's younger self was sitting on top of the trunk.

Joshua regained focus from the large image and began focusing on the smaller one at the forefront of the Shardland, seeing a man exiting a vehicle on a driveway of a nice grey two-story home with white pillars. The man, well dressed in slacks, a white button up shirt, and green tie, walking to the rear of the vehicle and opened the trunk of the car preparing to collect boxes of filed paperwork. This was not an image from a long ago past from the Judge's childhood. This was recent. Very recent. The Judge's eyes turned to see the approach of another man, rocking an object back and forth from hand to hand past his line of sight. Joshua knew the object had a handle of some sort. It was not until immediately before the person reached the Judge and struck him on the back of the head, knocking the Judge to the concrete of the driveway did Joshua realize what the object was. It was a shovel.

Joshua began to evaluate the images. He focused on another shard with a gazed view as the Judge was being pulled down the driveway by the assaulter, dragged by his ankles. His head turned to face a parked brown station wagon along the street's curb, with an open rear door. Once the man pulled the Judge past the door and around to the back of the car, Joshua saw the white rope along with a hammer, nails, and a long white candlestick. To the left in the back on the wagon was a long wooden box, and Joshua realized it was long enough to put a person inside.

Joshua pulled back from the smaller image and took both into his line of vision, mentally stepping back to take in the full view of the shards. The childhood trunk, the boy trapped, the new box in the man's car that would serve as a reminder to the Judge of what he had inflicted upon his brother all those years ago.

A word began entering his mind, and although he knew what the word was somewhere inside his head, it was too difficult to verbalize. He focused and thought. The more he did, the more his mind stepped back from the

Shardland, and the images blurred again and rippled into the dark room they were once in. He felt his breathing again, and the word entered his mind with a painful force that pushed him to yell it out loud.

"Claustrophobia!" Joshua yelled.

Joshua's true eyes opened, and he reclasped his necklace around his neck, only to find that Noah and Zyriah were looking at him sitting in the corner. The sweat began to form on his brow, and he could feel the pain in his head. He took the pendant back into his hand and placed it back into his shirt. He looked up at Zyriah, whose glare even in the dark was making him fearful.

"You went there? Now? Why did you do that?" Zyriah yelled, and Joshua opened his eyes wide. It was the first time he had really seen Zyriah's anger.

"He went where? To the Shardland?" Evan said, quickly turning his head back to give Joshua an angry look of his own before returning his eyes to the wet roads ahead. "Why would you do that? We told you not to do that without us."

"I had to know what we were driving into," Joshua tried to explain with a louder voice than he normally used. "I didn't want to go in there blind."

"Oh, c'mon man," Evan spoke out, angry and disappointed. "Use your brain."

"I thought I was," Joshua said defiantly, but with hopes the sarcasm might lighten Evan's anger.

"That's not being funny at all," Zyriah explained. "You going there unprepared is a risk we're not willing to take. We need you right now, don't you understand? I know you want to help, but now is not the time."

Noah began signing something to Zyriah, and Joshua

hoped for a moment that Noah was somehow defending his actions. He quickly realized that Noah was completely innocent in the conversation and unaware of what Joshua had done by going to the Shardland. The fact that Zyriah and Evan were so upset was probably confusing to Noah, and Joshua felt guilt over the man's confusion. Zyriah, shaking her head in response to him, made Noah slump back in his seat and cross his arms in frustration.

"I can't explain all this right now," Zyriah said clearly so Noah could read her words from her lips. "Joshua just did something we asked him not to do. That's all."

Noah looked at her with a very questioning look as if he could not fathom what Joshua could have done just by sitting in a vehicle that would cause that much turmoil. Noah turned his head back to look out the window at the rainbands streaming the windows. Joshua, realizing that Noah was defending his actions in some unknown way, felt a quick kinship. He was glad to have somebody on his side at that moment.

"So, why do you think it had something to do with claustrophobia?" Zyriah asked, calming her voice. "What did you see?"

Joshua detailed the shards and what they showed, both the smaller and the larger, noting the size difference he was unfamiliar with. He tried to help them visualize the scene in the basement, and the frustrated boy locked in the trunk by his brother. He went into detail describing the scene on the driveway, the shovel, and the contents inside the rear of the station wagon. He was happy that at least they were listening, taking in all the information he was providing for them. In a way, he knew he was wrong disobeying their instructions not to use the Shardland without them. However, he could feel that they valued the information's usefulness.

"Do you know this brother?" Evan said quickly asking Zyriah.

"Carl Echols. He works in the circuit clerk's office at the courthouse. Frank got him the job, or should I say Judge Echols," Zyriah explained, turning back to face the front windshield.

"So, the Star is making him get revenge on the brother for putting him in that trunk," Joshua said, trying to contribute to the thought process. "What about the nails and the hammer in the station wagon?"

"That's what I'm afraid of," Evan said, pressing the gas pedal down harder.

The rain stopped shortly before they reached the cemetery, but already the warmth of the afternoon had begun to evaporate the rain into a low-riding fog, beginning as what looked like ground-ridden cirrus clouds then uniting into a wet grey blanket. The sight reminded Joshua of one of his favorite stories of a schoolteacher being chased on horseback.

Near the cemetery's entrance was a large stone building with a lit sign on the street's edge saying "Goff's Funeral Home" in large pine-green letters. Joshua liked the floodlights illuminating the property as well as a floral shop directly beside it. It had its own sign dangling close to the front door saying "Floors by Telena" in fuchsia cursive writing. Evan, slowing down looking at the property, was intensive in his stare.

"I hope Brier and his mom don't catch us out here," Evan said, focused out the window but directing the words at Zyriah, his head turning back and forth hoping for privacy.

"Oh, I think we should be fine," Zyriah affirmed. Joshua felt she had a good sense of people's behaviors. "The Goff's have always been early risers. I'm sure Telena and Brier are in for the evening."

Joshua had recognized the name Brier as being the redheaded man talking to Evan at Soccer's when he first arrived. He looked out his own window trying to see any signs of people or movement, but he could see nothing noticeable. He redirected his focus back to looking out the windshield towards the main road. He thought a minute about the last name of Goff and wondered why it sounded so familiar to him.

The headlights of the car squinted though the clouded street, seeing only the yellow road lines marking the forward direction of the car. Joshua peeked over the center console as he did previously, looking for any signs of the eventual destination. The location did increase in its creepiness the further the vehicle travelled.

"Are you sure they'll be out here?" Joshua asked, still focusing on any sign or tombstones. "The men from the shards?"

"I'm sure," Zyriah said, now completely calm and focused. "Try and sit back."

Joshua returned to the comfort of his seat, stretching his back slightly, and looked over to Noah, already looking back at him with concerned eyes. Joshua smiled at him, appreciating whatever Noah said to Zyriah earlier in his defense, and nodded his head slightly. Noah, with the same concerned looked, pointed at Joshua with one finger then made a circle with his index and thumb, outstretching his other fingers.

"Yeah, I'm ok," Joshua answered, understanding Noah's concern.

Noah's face changed into a smile, and he patted Joshua on the knee before returning his look out the window. Joshua thought for a moment how he was not used to having so much friendship, certainly not so much in such an enclosed space, and now within a few days, he felt these individuals had become his friends. It was a strange feeling, but a satisfying one, and he sighed turning his head to the window.

The grass outside was still layered in a small layer of fog, but through the fog appeared a stone, and then another. Joshua looked at the gravestones, appearing like side-by-side dominoes standing in the mist, and he shifted his position back to looking over the center console. Evan had slowed the speed to the car rather quickly to a creeping pace as they approached an entryway with two bricked walls lining the road and curving inward to a gravel road.

High above was a metal archway, with the name "Westview Cemetery" spelled in solid metal letters, and they drove the car underneath and forward. The car bounced over the gravel with short, quick, occasional bounces, and Joshua looked back and forth from his vantage point looking at all the gravestones, varying in shape and color.

Everyone in the car was looking for something, some form of actual life in this space, and Evan turned the steering wheel to follow the road's left-handed curve. Joshua felt Noah shifting in the back seat and moving forward, peeking up beside Joshua looking for someone or something out of the ordinary. Joshua noticed that on the right of the gravel road, the hill dipped into a small valley that looked like a pond, once the light from the now-visible moon had shown down upon it after the storm clouds had retreated. He looked back to the left-hand side for the stones close to the driver's door passing by.

He was about to return his view to the right-hand side and back to the pond, when Noah, looking forward, began slapping Joshua on his back, then extending his hand forward to the windshield. Joshua saw the light beam, a long stretch in the distance that seemed to be the low beams of a car's headlights.

The four all began to focus on those two light beams growing as the car got closer to the headlight's source. The light seemed to deliberately shine on an area of the cemetery, and Joshua could see the stones, standing dark and black as the light shined in front of them. He focused more on the light's source, a long dark outline of a vehicle in the distance. The closer they got to the vehicle, the more the type of vehicle became easier to identify.

"It's a station wagon," Joshua said, pointing ahead to the car in a similar manner that Noah previously had. "That's what the brother was driving."

"Everybody be on guard out here, alright?" Evan said. "Zyriah, you and Noah need to stay in the car. Joshua can come with me."

"In the car?" Zyriah asked, almost with a tone of feeling insulted. "I'm going out there with you."

"With a crazy guy with a shovel?" Evan rebutted, not seeming to Joshua that the idea of Zyriah and Noah staying in the car was even a questionable concept. "You two can stay in here, alright? I don't want to see you getting hurt."

"What do you two think you'll get accomplished together then?" Zyriah asked.

"Hopefully save a judge and not get killed," Joshua said, mocking the tone.

The station wagon was getting closer as Evan continued driving forward, and Joshua prepared himself for exiting the car. He passed the bag with his butterfly to Noah, who looked down at the bag when it was passed. He looked back up to Joshua with the familiar questioning look. Joshua looked at him, hoping his confident appearance looked calm and not frightened.

"Hold on to this for me," Joshua explained, mouthing the words with a slight over exaggeration. "Evan and I are going to check these headlights out. You and Zyriah stay in the car, please."

Noah nodded then taking a downward glance at Joshua's bag in his hand. His eyes rose back to Joshua, and he gave a small yet concerned smile. Joshua felt the car stop as Evan pressed into the brake pedal and placing the car in park. Joshua looked in the current direction of the light, seeing something in the distance appearing long sticking out of the ground. Evan looked back at Joshua, nodded that it was time, and got out of the vehicle. Zyriah opened the door, getting out of the car to allow Joshua out of the back seat, then took Joshua's back seat beside Noah. Joshua shut the door, looked toward Evan, and walked around the car to meet him.

"You ready?" Evan asked.

"Let's go," Joshua replied. "I thought I saw something sticking out of the ground over here."

They walked, slightly twisting their feet on the rolling gravel, until they reached the grass of the cemetery that wrapped around the stones. They soon reached the low beams of the car stretching a good length of the grassy area between the stones. Joshua felt Evan's hand outstretched and pushing back against his chest to stop his movement, and they both peered forward to see the object Joshua had seen from the car.

It was a shovel, stuck in a tall pile of dug-up earth, the head of the shovel barely visible as it was deep into the muddy dirt. Joshua noted the length of the disturbed area and realized it was too late. Collecting his thoughts and grasping a fast conclusion, he grabbed the shovel and quickly began digging frantically.

"He's already in here!" Joshua said in a panic. "The judge is already buried!"

Joshua watched as Evan dropped to his knees, using his hands to shovel back the dirt and mud, while Joshua used the shovel as fast as he could to move the dirt himself. The box had been buried in an extremely shallow spot, only inches from the main lay of the land, so the removal of the dirt and mud did not take much time. Joshua watched finally as Evan used his hands, pulling and brushing back the last of the dirt cover to see the top of a long nailed-shut box.

"Judge, can you hear me?" Evan yelled in the direction of the box's lid. Joshua was sure the yell was loud enough that the Judge could have heard Evan.

There was no response.

Joshua felt it as Evan grabbed the shovel from his hands, trying to pry the lid of the box open. The nails were haphazardly nailed into the edges and corners, with most of the nails sticking out half-exposed. Joshua scanned around the site, looking for something he could use. He realized a hammer, a long piece of rope, and the candlestick were laid out neatly in front of a nearby stone. He grabbed the hammer, returned to the sight, and began prying out the nails sitting on his knees as Evan tried pushing the shovel into the edges underneath the box's lid and trying to get enough leverage to open it. The process only lasted a minute, when Joshua heard what seemed to be Zyriah's muffled yell from inside the car, followed by a long honking of his car's horn.

Joshua felt the foot kick him under his head, kicking him headfirst into the nearby ground and landing on his side. The jolt to his throat drove the air from his lungs, and he gasped to breathe looking sideways at a balding, older man struggling with Evan over the shovel's handle.

The two rotated positions so that the low beams from the headlights illuminated the man's form, and Joshua saw the muddy shoes and pants, the sweat covered buttoned up shirt, and the blank stare he had not seen since the face of Donnie Pritchard. He knew this was Carl Echols, struggling with great strength over the shovel, and his manner was completely unrelenting.

Carl had far greater strength that a man of his age and size should have had in Joshua's opinion. He gasped for more air, rolling over and realizing he was close to the extra rope and the candlestick he had seen earlier when he picked up the hammer. He heard a car door opening and closing and quick rushing footsteps, just as Carl knocked Evan to the ground, freeing the shovel in his hands. He stood over the two of them with that blank stare, raising the shovel high, the low beams lighting his face, when an arm quickly wrapped around his neck pulling him slightly off balance. It was Noah, struggling to restrain the man as hard as he could. Joshua watched as Evan, who apparently had seen the rope scurrying over Joshua to retrieve it.

"No," Joshua said, finally catching his breath. "Give me your lighter."

"What?" Evan asked loudly, looking exhausted and confused, began digging into his pocket. "Why?"

Joshua, ignoring the white rope, grabbed the long white candlestick laying in the grass. He opened his hand, retrieving the lighter once Evan had pulled it out of his pocket, and began to light the candle. He held the lighter's flame to the wick waiting for the wick to light while hearing Noah struggling with Carl behind him, and the wick would not burn.

"It's not working," Joshua said frustrated. "It's wet from the rain."

"Give it to me," Evan said alarmingly. Joshua passed the candle to Evan, as he pulled something else out of his pocket. It was his pin knife in his hand, and he cut into the wax about two inches down the candle's length and cutting off the small section pulling it off the wick. He took the long string of wick, bending it over the blade of the knife, and cutting it down short enough so that Joshua could light it. Joshua was amazed in the speed of Evan's quick actions. In only seconds, Evan had the candle ready to light.

"Here, its dry," Evan said, passing the new candle back to Joshua, who held the candle upright, lighting the lighter, and pressing the flame to the new wick, lighting it instantly.

Joshua stood up slowly turning to see Noah struggling with both arms now trying to hold Carl back. He cupped the burning flame and walked forward until he was arm's length from the struggle. Looking up, he could see Carl's vacant stare directed straight at him in the light of the low beams. Joshua dropped his cupped hand, raising the candle forward with one outstretched arm and taking one step forward into a fighting stance. He shown the light into Carl's blank stare, and the flame from the candle, flicker in the little movement of the air, began to change.

The flame shifted, pulling itself to two side points as well as a high and low point, and Joshua knew that the Star had returned, the same star in the flame he saw in the Pritchard's bathroom in the candle flame on the bathroom sink. Joshua watched Carl Echols' eyes begin to widen, blink frantically, then finally look into that flame. He became motionless.

Noah, realizing that his adversary had stopped moving, turned his head to face Joshua. Joshua realized Noah was too afraid to loosen his grip, and he looked at Joshua's face with that same questioning look as to why Carl was not fighting back. Joshua looked into his eyes and mouthed the words so that Noah could see.

"Let him go," Joshua commanded, feeling the sternness in his tone that he hoped translated into his facial expression.

Noah released Carl, whose eyes were still transfixed upon the flame, but Joshua's stance did not move. Joshua stood there solidly, holding the candlestick in his hand, and looking into Carl's face that slowly began changing as his mouth began to open wide. He screamed, a deep wailing scream pushed from deep down into a long shriek of a sound, and once it was completed, he collapsed into the pile of dirt and mud that he had piled on the ground.

Joshua moved the candle back to his face and relaxed his stance. The flame was now a normal burning flame, and Joshua blew it out into a wisp of smoke from a charred wick dropping the candlestick to his side. Noah approached him, exhausted and sweating, and put his arms around him in a tight hug, which Joshua returned. They both turned back to see Evan, now slightly bent over holding his knees to regain his composure, stand back up erect. Zyriah approached from out of the dark and into the light of the low beams. The four looked at one another, and Joshua felt that everyone was alright.

"How did you know that would work?" Evan said, still trying to catch his breath.

"I didn't," Joshua replied, slightly smiling, while walking over to give his friend a quick hug.

"Are the three of you alright?" Zyriah asked, shuffling through the wet grass.

"I think we're all alright, right?" Joshua agreed, looking at his friends and seeing Evan and Noah both nodding in agreement.

"Looks like we have a visitor." Zyriah said, looking past the men towards the red and white rotating lights slowly bouncing a short distance away.

"Looks like Monika finally came to the rescue," Evan added.

Joshua laughed, shaking his head and bending over to fully catch his breath. He began rolling his shoulders with hopes of stretching his back. He looked in the opposite direction of the sheriff's cruiser, over the station wagon, to a shape in the far distance. It looked like another car on the main road close to a nearby streetlight. Instantly, he could hear the distant sound of an engine, and he saw the headlights of the vehicle turned on. It blazed forward as it pulled away. It moved at a fast pace, but still Joshua was able to see more of the vehicle once it passed underneath that distant streetlight. He could feel his friends coming closer to him, and a hand on his shoulder.

"What is it?" Evan asked, removing his hand from Joshua's shoulder.

"That van," Joshua said, almost in shock, pointing his hand in the direction of that moving car, "That's the blue van I saw parked across the street from the Pritchard's house that night."

CHAPTER
TWELVE

Joshua slept in late the next morning, not due to any unexpected dreams or visions, but just due to the shear exhaustion of the night before. Once Sheriff Tucker got to the area of the cemetery the four of them were standing on, they immediately began once again prying on nails and the lid of the unearthed box, hoping to find an unconscious Judge Echols inside that their nail pulling or yelling could not awaken. Once it was open, they realized their vain effort, as the man was gone from life, blood dried and welled into the box around his head. Joshua felt the agony of not doing more or being able to stop the tragedy from happening, and he struggled with that as he finally arose from his bed, putting on the same pants from the day before, and pulling a fresh green shirt from his closet. He put on his necklace, grabbing the selenite pendant tight for a moment, and left to enter his bathroom.

He combed his hair and brushed his teeth, not feeling any hunger for breakfast, but he did feel thirst. He walked through to the kitchen cabinet, retrieving a glass, and grabbing the orange juice container from the refrigerator and filled his glass. He reviewed the previous night again in his mind, drinking the juice, and trying to wake himself up for another day ahead. For once, he was dreading the day to come and he much preferred going back to his bedroom and resting a few more hours. Truthfully, he was surprised that neither Evan nor Zyriah was already in his living room waiting for him once he opened the bedroom door, but he expected they felt the exhaustion as much as he did.

He thought a great deal about Noah and how he struggled with Carl Echols. He felt a certain amount of shame, thinking that Noah's deafness would make him more vulnerable in a situation like that, but Noah had fought and fought well. He appreciated that friendship more and more, and he remembered how much help Noah had really provided that day, all that information at Soccer's and what he had done at the cemetery. Joshua had considered the group of Zyriah, Evan, and him to be a team of three. Now, it almost seemed just as fitting that Noah should make the team a group of four.

Once the juice was finished, Joshua rinsed the glass and left it sitting in the kitchen sink. He approached the elevator, checking his pockets to see if his keys were still in one of them, and pulled out his key ring after pressing the elevator button. When it arrived, he entered, inserting his key, and lowered himself to the downstairs floor. Stepping off the elevator, he turned left to go to the back door, past the bend of the spiral staircase. He stopped at the back door, turning his head to press it against the door itself, and heard voices from outside on the patio.

"I swear. Do these people ever sleep?" he whispered to himself and opened the door.

Zyriah and Evan both were outside, sitting on the patio, very much awake and quiet as soon as Joshua stepped outside. He scanned over their faces, slightly concerned probably over his tired appearance, as he gave them a quick smile. He walked around Evan to an empty chair, pulled the chair out, and joined them.

"I didn't check the clock," Joshua admitted. "How long have I slept in today?"

"It's almost one," Zyriah replied. "We didn't see the need to wake you. I'm sure you needed the rest."

"The rest?" Joshua said with his typical sarcasm. "If I rested enough to recover from another night like that, I could sleep in until tomorrow morning."

"There's no harm in going back to bed, you know," Evan responded in a sensitive manner. "If you need sleep, we aren't going to stop you."

"Well, if I sleep more now, then I won't sleep tonight. I better stay up," Joshua relented. "So, what's on today's agenda?"

"Maybe you really do need a day away from all this," Zyriah replied. "I don't want this to end up being too much for you."

"What I really need is for all this to be over with," Joshua answered firmly. "I don't want anybody else getting hurt because of all of this. I've seen too much in the last few days to want to see any more days like those. What happened to Carl Echols after we left?"

"Monika would have taken him to Pleasant Days, like she had with Sarah Baker," Zyriah responded. "I'm sure that's where he is."

Joshua did not have time to think about a new resident next door. He had enough of thinking about the events of the prior evening, and he wanted to finally bring this problem to some sort of satisfying conclusion. He was not sure exactly what the next step should be.

"What do we need to do to make this stop?" Joshua asked.

"Confront Johnny Glover," Evan recommended sternly. "Go down to the Glassworks and see if it was him driving that van last night."

"How do you want to do that?" Zyriah said in a seriously focused tone. "Just walk into the Glassworks and demand that lantern? We still don't know for sure where it is."

"Then, we go and demand it from him," Joshua replied. "We demand it or tell him he's going back to jail for it if he doesn't give it to us."

"That could make him desperate, and he'd be in his own place of business," Zyriah explained. "We don't know if he has any weapons hidden behind that counter, and I can only imagine what tools he could use against us in the shop behind the building."

"Fine, then how do we do it?" Joshua asked, expecting Zyriah to answer.

Zyriah took a deep breath, and Joshua could see she was straining for the right response, but she was empty of thoughts. He thought perhaps she was more tired than she appeared to be, her mind dry of new ideas and new insights on how to proceed. He waited, struggling to be patient, until she finally leaned forward to speak.

"I'm not entirely sure," Zyriah admitted. "I suppose we could use the Shardland for Johnny or Paul to see what all they have as far as weapons are concerned. If we focus long enough, we might actually find where he would have hidden it. Could save us from another dangerous situation like last night."

"Waste of time," Joshua said firmly. "We go in. We get it. We leave."

"You could get shot in the process," Zyriah responded.

"Then, I'll die trying," Joshua snapped back.

Zyriah sat back again, looking at him with a look more questioning than Noah had given him in the back of the car the night before. She shook her head side to side, and Joshua could see her disapproval in his brute force tactic, but he felt it was the right thing to do.

Evan, finally showing signs that he too was feeling tired, held his heads and closed his eyes for a few moments to relax and to think. Joshua, looking at him, felt Evan needed more rest as much as he did. His eyes were stressed and darkening on their lower lids.

"You've only been here a few days, and now I want you listening to yourself," Zyriah said. "Only a few days, and you're sitting there talking about putting yourself into harm's way yet again, just like you did with going to the Shardland last night on the way to the cemetery. When are you going to learn how important you are in all this? I'm not going to deliberately put you at risk with this instrument when there's more we still have to find."

"Well, if something happens to me, then you two can step up and find the remaining ones on your own," Joshua said stubbornly. "I want that Star."

"Why?" Zyriah said, looking into his eyes more closely. "Why is finding this Star so important to you all of the sudden?"

"Because I'm tired of people getting hurt," Joshua explained. "Families getting hurt. People dying. Kids dying.

We must make it stop. We have to get that Star in order to do that, right?"

"That's right," Zyriah agreed. "I just wanted to find a way to do that without anybody at this table getting hurt the same way the Baker's, the Pritchard's, or the Echols' did. Can you understand that?"

Joshua took a deep, long breath. He knew his irritation with the situation had grown, but it was also being fed by sleepiness and exhaustion. He felt he was right about retrieving the Star and making the problem cease, but he also had to be concerned about his own welfare. More had happened that week than just the situations involving the Star. Joshua now had a home, a car to drive, and new friends. His life was increasing in value more and more, and it somewhat shamed him that he was so willing to be thoughtless and give that good fortune away. He was not used to the idea of having something to lose.

"I understand," Joshua replied with a much clearer view. "Now, can we please figure out a way to approach Glover about that lantern?"

The three of them heard a car horn blowing from the front of the building, interrupting the conversation. They all stood, looking at each other with confused expressions as to who would be honking their horn in such a manner. Joshua had a gut feeling, as they walked to turn the corner into the driveway, that the car would be a police cruiser with Sheriff Tucker behind the wheel, ready with a fresh list of questions about the previous night's activities at Westview Cemetery. Instead, parked perpendicularly in the driveway was a silver SUV with a woman behind the wheel with long straight brown hair. The driver whisked her hair over her shoulder and turned to face them. Since her window was already lowered, Joshua could recognize the face of Nancy Baker, Sarah Baker's aunt.

"Please, tell us there's some good news today," Zyriah asked approaching the car, as Joshua and Evan followed up behind her until they were all just feet from the door. "Sarah getting any better?"

"No change, unfortunately," Nancy reported. She shook her head with a disappointed stare down to the floor. "Her vitals are still stable, but she hasn't woken up yet. We're being patient."

"I'm really sorry," Evan said disappointedly. "We were all hoping for that to change."

"I hope you all don't mind me stopping by like this," Nancy said apologetically. "I just knew you all had said if there was any information I could provide that I should stop by."

"You said Sarah wasn't awake yet, though," Joshua said curiously.

"Oh, no. Not about that. It's just that Sarah had a visitor this morning, one of her friends from school. The little girl is Ashley Newcome, and she lives a couple doors down from my brother's old house. Ashley brought Sarah some flowers this morning, and she asked how she was doing."

"Did she say anything else?" Zyriah questioned. Joshua could feel that Nancy had more to say about the unexpected visitor.

"Apparently, that night Sarah was supposed to spend the night at the Newcome's, but Ashley's mom said Sarah wasn't feeling well and wanted to go home. Ashley walked her down to the front door of the old house, but Ashley remembered Sarah saying something strange before she went into the house."

"What did she say?" Joshua asked, completely awakened with interest.

"Ashley said Sarah didn't look well, especially her eyes like nothing was behind them, because she was so sick. Sarah looked at her and said, 'I only wanted to buy a butterfly'. Does that help or make sense to you?" Nancy asked.

"What a strange thing to say," Zyriah replied, quickly enough so that she would speak before Joshua or Evan could have the opportunity. "After all, if she wasn't feeling well, it's hard to tell what she was thinking or feeling at that moment. We just hope she gets better really soon."

"So do I," Nancy said, looking slightly disappointed that the information did not yield a better response. "Well, I'm off to grab a late lunch, so I better let you go."

"Thanks so much for dropping by, and wish Sarah our best," Zyriah said smiling.

"Oh, and one more thing. Do you all know the administrator's secretary? Noah Wilson?" Nancy asked.

Immediately, Joshua stepped forward with an energized face full of concern for his new friend. A great number of questions flooded his head as soon as those questions were asked. He feared the possibility that Noah was in danger, and he quickly replied.

"Noah? Yes, we're all friends of Noah's. What about him?" Joshua asked quickly.

"Well, Miss Ebert told me to keep an eye out for him when I left to go to lunch," Nancy explained. "She thought he might be walking home. She said he didn't look very well this morning."

"Well, I know that Noah had a long night last night and probably needed the rest," Zyriah responded.

"That's what Kathy said too," Nancy said with concern, "but when I was leaving, she was asking some of the residents if they saw him leave. The Underwood's were sitting on the porch and said Noah left the building, and a man they didn't recognize helped him into the passenger seat of a blue van."

"A blue van?" Joshua asked, just to make sure he heard Nancy correctly.

"That's what they said," Nancy responded. "Know anybody that drives one?"

Evan pulled out of the driveway quickly once Nancy Baker had left for her lunch, and the three were back in Joshua's car driving down Treeclimber Drive. The road was unusually busy with traffic, and Joshua kept shifting from looking forward through the windshield wanting the traffic to move to looking out of the side windows hoping to see the van parked along the road somewhere. He really hoped to see Noah, walking on the sidewalk in the direction of home with a simple case of exhaustion. He knew better.

"How long does it take to get to where he lives? Do you remember how to get there?" Joshua asked with a certain amount of panic.

"It was dark, but I remember where I dropped him off last night," Evan replied. "He lives about five minutes off the end of the Treeclimber out on his grandfather's farm."

"His grandfather's farm?" Joshua questioned.

"Yeah, he said he and his sisters have lived out there all their lives," Evan explained. "Noah has a single mom, but she works for the bank and does a lot of traveling. So, his grandparents took them all in."

Joshua focused forward, seeing that the traffic was

breaking loose, and their drive on Treeclimber Drive had quickened pace. He was nervous, desperately nervous, worrying if Noah was hurt. He hoped Evan would go faster, even if it meant breaking the speed limit.

"Why Noah?" Zyriah asked, rationalizing the situation. "If it's the same van from the Pritchard's and the cemetery, then we have to assume Noah is involved in that court case somehow."

"Or his gossip got the better of him, and somebody thought he knew too much," Evan responded, eyes focused on the road as he reached the end of Treeclimber Drive and turned left.

"He did say that he saw that Grewe guy working on the lantern for Johnny Glover," Joshua said, recalling the conversation with Noah at Soccer's the day before, sure that was the memory.

"You were there in the jury box, Evan," Zyriah inquired. "Was Noah a jury member? Was he in the courtroom?"

Joshua looked at Evan, whose eyes remained forward but his eyes were widening as he began shaking his head.

"Noah wasn't a jury member." Evan replied, the daze affecting his tone.

"What?" Joshua immediately asked. "You know something? What is it?"

"Noah wasn't there," Evan responded, and Joshua could tell he could hardly focus to drive. "His grandfather, Ronald Wilson, was the jury foreman."

The farmhouse was settled in between two large sections of land, with scattered round bails of straw, freshly cut, sitting in random spots throughout both fields. Joshua saw how a stream traced the front edge of the property as Evan pulled into the driveway, crossing a small bridge over the stream, then back on the remainder of the driveway that lead to a garage separated from the home. The house itself was redwood, two stories, with a long wrap around porch with white railing that reminded Joshua of Pleasant Days Senior Center next door to him. Two girls appeared to be playing until they crossed the bridge. The girls saw the car approach and ran back inside the home, shutting the screen door behind them. The three filed out of the car and walked towards the porch. They were greeted by a tall woman, grey-curled hair pinned back on the sides, with large, framed glasses in a floral-printed housedress.

"May I help you?" the woman asked.

"This is the Wilson's farm isn't it?" Evan asked in returned.

"Well, yes. I'm Maddie Wilson. What can I do for you?" she asked, very polite and disconcerting.

"We're friends of Noah's," Joshua replied. "Is he home today?"

"Noah's up at work at the Senior Center today. What is this all about?" Mrs. Wilson asked, growing more inquisitive.

"We don't mean to bother you ma'am," Zyriah replied. "By chance is your husband home?"

"Ronald just left, but he should be back soon," Maddie answered.

"Do you happen to know where he went?" Joshua asked, with a certain level of concern.

"He got a phone call and went into town. Like I said, he told me he'd be back soon," Maddie replied, turning to go back into the house. Joshua could see the girls standing behind the screen door, similar in height and appearance with long curled locks of brown hair draped at their sides. He realized the girls were twins, and he remembered meeting one of them at Soccer's when Noah had imitated a scared cat. He just was not sure at that moment which of the girl's he had seen.

"We just had a question for him ma'am," Zyriah said calmly. Joshua could tell Zyriah was not trying to be alarming. "We're heading back that way back onto the Treeclimber as soon as we leave here."

"Then, stop by the Glassworks. That's where he is," Maddie responded.

"The Glassworks?" Evan said with a certain eagerness.

"Yes. He said they called and got something in he wanted. Probably an early birthday present for himself. He always said the best presents are the ones you buy yourself," Maddie chuckled. "Now if you'll excuse me, I need to finish up dinner and get Abby and Audrey to get themselves cleaned up."

"Thank you," Joshua said finally remembering the girl from Soccer's was named Audrey. "We didn't mean to bother you."

"It's not a bother," Maddie said, now from behind the screen door.

"Can I ask you a strange question before we go?" Zyriah continued asking in a polite way.

"What question is that?" Maddie inquired.

"I thought you could help me. Noah and I had played a little game over at the Senior Center a couple days ago with a couple of the patients, and he made me a bet that I couldn't figure out what he's afraid of. Do you know what it might be?" Zyriah asked indirectly.

"Oh, Noah is scared to death of heights," Maddie said nodding, still behind the screen door. "It's a long story. We had done some travelling and were on the way home. It was a windy day, and Ronald had decided to drive across the High-Level Gorge Bridge. Well, Noah was a young boy at the time, and when the wind hit the side of the car, he was convinced the car was going to get pushed off the side of the bridge. I can't get the man to even go up a step ladder nowadays. He always did blame his grandfather for taking him across the bridge that day."

"Ah," Zyriah exclaimed. "A fear of heights. I never would've thought of that. Thanks again for the information."

The three quickly returned to the car as Maddie went back inside the house. Evan turned the car around, driving back over the small bridge, and made it out to the main road. Joshua felt he was certainly driving over the speed limit. Evan was just as determined to get to the Glassworks as Evan was. Noah's grandmother said that Ronald had just left for the Glassworks. There was still time to make sure Noah was safe.

The road was twisting, but Evan straightened it out yet again by driving more in a straight line, ignoring the lines in the road. No oncoming cars came the other way, so the drive moved quickly back towards town. Evan slowed down slightly the closer they came to Treeclimber Drive, and once the car made it to the corner for his right turn, Evan was within the speed limit. Not much longer after that, the Glassworks was on the left-hand side, and Joshua watched Evan turning the steering wheel to drive the car into an adjacent parking spot. He placed the car in park, and the three got out to run to the front of the building.

Joshua ran faster than Zyriah or Evan, seeing the sidewalk sign signaling they were open, and turning up the front steps to the store front. Zyriah quickly caught up to him, grabbing his shoulder to slow him down.

"Remember, take it slow," Zyriah said, trying to slow down Joshua's movements. "If they're here, it'll be soon enough that we stopped all this."

"I'll be slow, I promise," Joshua said sarcastically, smiling while Zyriah moved her hand from his shoulder. "I'm perfectly calm."

Joshua pushed open the left-hand door of the store so hard it knocked nearly a dozen of the butterflies off the front display window once the door hit the windowpane. He stomped in, seeing the shop was void of any people, and marched his way past the glass shelves toward the back corner doorway to the shop area. He paused, not sure exactly what he was going to find back there, but he was determined to control this situation.

"Glover! Where are you?!" Joshua yelled.

The three waited, Joshua's chest heaving with adrenalin as he looked back to Zyriah and Evan, who both looked annoyed and disappointed with his behavior. Joshua thought he surely had yelled loud enough that anybody, even in the back of the shop, could have heard him. When nobody appeared, he yelled again.

"Glover!"

From the back room, Johnny Glover emerged with an extremely concerned expression on his face. Joshua glared at him nastily, thinking of Noah and his grandfather somewhere on the premises and determined to find them. Johnny Glover, on the other hand, looked oblivious to the situation. Joshua could see that his foe was truly surprised.

"What's all the yelling about out here?" Johnny asked. "You're the Spiker boy from the other day. What in the world is going on?"

"Where's Noah and Ronald Wilson," Joshua demanded. "We know they're around here."

"The Wilson's? They're not here," Johnny responded. "They left just a couple minutes ago with Paul, but they didn't tell me where they were off to."

"So, you're trying to tell me you don't know anything?" Joshua asked forcefully. His thoughts were so focused on Noah that it was hard breathing. "You don't know where they are. You didn't buy that lantern we asked about. You're completely innocent in this."

"I told you we didn't buy that lantern," Johnny contended. "I don't understand what that has to do with the Wilson's though."

Zyriah stepped closer to Joshua, holding his hand for a moment. The gesture eased his tension and changed his focus. His anger eased momentarily, and his concern over Noah and his grandfather lessened for a second by the feeling of his hand being held. He turned, facing Zyriah, whose face had a look of honesty and sincerity.

"He's telling us the truth, Joshua," Zyriah admitted. "It's not him."

Joshua relaxed for a moment, taking in the truth he had just overreacted to a man who possible was not responsible for this. The theory had long been Johnny Glover was at fault for all of this, all the people hurt, and Joshua still was not completely convinced Johnny had not hurt his own son. There was something in Zyriah's look at that moment that made Joshua reconsider.

"The van," Evan spoke up. "Who drives the blue van?"

"That's the work van for the shop," Johnny answered. "Paul drives it most days, even on his off times."

"Paul didn't say where they were going?" Zyriah asked, in a calmer more respectful way than her male companions.

"He just said he'd be out the rest of the day," Johnny explained. "I know he said Noah was in the van, and he took Ronald out back once he arrived. Paul called him down here to show him something."

Joshua slowly came to realize that Johnny Glover was telling the truth, as Zyriah had told him. His anger grew to concern over Noah and his grandfather yet again, but now that neither of them were at the Glassworks, a feeling of hopelessness began to consume him. He watched Zyriah, grabbing some paper from a notepad left on top of the back counter and placing it in her purse. Joshua realized there was another way possibly they could learn the location.

"I'm really sorry about the butterflies I knocked down," Joshua said apologetically. "If you write up a bill, I'll come in and pay you tomorrow. I promise."

"It's fine, son," Johnny said, as Joshua noticed his face was getting more and more worried about their presence there. "I need to lock up though, if you all don't mind. I have some work to do in the shop."

"Thank you for your help, Johnny," Zyriah replied, and the three walked across the sales floor and exited the building.

Joshua was sad and frustrated, more so than ever. He went down the front stairs of the store and to the car, with little tears he could feel welling in the corners of his eyes. He knew what Zyriah intended to do with that paper, but he could feel the entirety of the drama beginning again, the way it had all the other times the Star had influenced someone. He placed his hands on the car's hood and started crying.

"This isn't over yet, Joshua," Zyriah said, with a comforting hand rubbing his back. "Let me see if I can find the destination like I did with the cemetery."

Zyriah removed a black pen from her purse and after placing the loose paper from the notepad she obtained from the glassworks, she began the familiar process. Joshua watched those forming lines eagerly, from the first page to the second page, and hoped something would help them in this situation. By the midpoint of the third page, Joshua began to feel doubt overcome him, until the line began to curl and curve into a string of letters. He read them as she wrote them, still amazed by her ability, but in shock over what he finally read. Zyriah, once refocused, looked upon the paper, and Joshua knew his concern by her reaction was warranted.

"Oh, my lord. High-Level Gorge Bridge," Zyriah said in a panic.

CHAPTER
THIRTEEN

Evan said the drive would be nearly forty-five minutes to reach the bridge, but for Joshua the time and the distance melted in his thoughts into the pool of stress of worry his mind was consumed in. He knew Evan was driving fast, and he hoped with a van that size that Paul, Noah, and Ronald would not be driving nearly as fast as they were. Most of the drive was back on Interstate-79, but Evan said the last part was off the main road. Driving on the interstate would be a good opportunity for a faster rate of speed, but Joshua's concern grew. He realized it was close to four in the afternoon, and by the time they reached the bridge, it might be heavy with after-work traffic. They had already driven several minutes in actuality, but Joshua had lost all sense of time.

The three were quiet, focused. Joshua usually relished the idea of conversation to make a car trip go by faster, but he wanted the quiet to remain. He looked out his window, watching the passing trees and the clouds darkening overhead. He felt a level of energy that he felt inside the vehicle that he assumed was outside the vehicle as well. He felt that energy before, with bad weather as well as stressful events in his life. He kept his eyes upward for a few minutes, looked at the clouds accumulate and hoping that it would not lead to another storm. In a way, however, he knew they were driving into a storm of a different sort named Paul Grewe. He had only seen for a moment in the Glassworks prior to Grewe sending Johnny Glover out to greet them. It made his concern grow more, this unknown individual, whose exact motivation in all this was completely unknown.

He shifted to put his head over the center console, watching the interstate traffic as Evan sped by passing drivers. Zyriah, for a moment, looked over to him, and although her look was one he had seen before of a motherly concern, he did not really want to hear a comforting word from her at that moment. He stared forward, looking out the windshield at the lined road as Evan weaved back and forth continuing to push them forward and away from the other cars.

Noah. He hoped his deafness would not become an issue in this circumstance. He thought of Noah walking on the bridge and not hearing an approaching car. He thought of him not hearing someone approaching him from behind and pushing him too far forward close to the bridge's edge. Noah was his friend, and he had to get there. He momentarily wished he knew the directions to the bridge himself, so he was solely responsible for the rate that the car was moving. He would know for sure that the car was going as fast as it could go, and they would reach Noah and Ronald as fast as they possible could. He felt the repetition of his thoughts making him more and more stressed. He sat back into the back seat, still in the center of the bench seat, looking forward out the windshield, but trying to rest his eyes.

He was so full of a tremendous energy, but his body felt lagging. He knew the adrenaline would be back in him once they reached the bridge, the same adrenaline he had walking into the Glassworks and yelling Glover's name. He called upon that strength involuntarily, and he hoped he would have that same amount of drive once they reached the destination. Finally, Evan slowed down enough to exit the interstate, stopped at the initial stop sign, then turned left and increased his speed.

Road signs began to appear within just a few miles of getting off the interstate exit, large orange signs flagging drivers to watch for road construction ahead. Farther down the road, a sign flashed that there was construction on the bridge from seven at night until seven in the morning. The sign, however, failed to say if the bridge was still drivable during the day, so Joshua assumed that the bridge would be open for vehicles. The next set of signs clearly instructed drivers to take an upcoming detour.

"What's the detour for?" Joshua, finally speaking, said to Evan.

"Just wait. Let's see what happens," Evan said continuing driving and looking for the next set of orange signs.

Within a couple more miles, the detour signs were very direct, telling people to turn two miles away and follow the signs after the turn. Joshua grew in frustration. The bridge had to be open. The words Zyriah had written previously, whether it was Donnie Pritchard's name or Westview Cemetery, had always been correct and taken them to the right place. He worried something happened wrong this time with her ability, and he looked out the side windows again, urgently waiting for the next of the detour signs to approach them.

"It's West Virginia," Evan said confidently. "There's nothing but road construction around here on any given day. We'll get on the bridge."

"What if it's closed?" Joshua asked with pain in his throat. "What if we can't get the car on it?"

"Closed to cars, maybe, but not closed to people," Evan said, reaffirming they were going in the proper direction. "If we have to run, we run."

Joshua shook his head, unsure of the way things were going now. It did not feel right, the signs with all the roadwork up ahead and signs directing them to avoid the bridge. The clouds in the sky were overcasting with darkness, and Joshua felt it was some type of warning. The signs and the weather were almost directing him to rethink the entire process, the direction they were going, and the bridge they were traveling to. He did not want to question Zyriah and her abilities, but the concern for Noah forced his words.

"Zyriah, I have to ask you something," Joshua said, really trying to not offend her, "are you completely sure that we're going to the right place?"

"It's the bridge, Joshua. I promise," Zyriah confirmed. "I don't understand these signs just like you don't understand them, but I'm sure we're supposed to go to the bridge."

Joshua did not choose to respond. He was afraid of his frustration boiling into anger and turning the car drive into a conflict. He admitted to himself that he was inexperienced. He had never attempted something like Zyriah's writing ability before. He had barely attempted any ability, except going to the Shardland on those two occasions. He wanted to do so much more, and he thought again about being in that same seat the night before and deciding to look at his pendant. He admitted something could have gone wrong. He was trying so hard to help that he was using an ability he did not have complete knowledge of. Zyriah and Evan cared about him, and their concern after he did go to the Shardland for the second time proved that. He genuinely knew they cared about him.

The "bridge closed" signs grew in frequency, with more detour signs alternating between them. Evan ignored the detour when it finally arrived, and continued to go forward, although slowing down the car. Joshua could tell he was concerned about their safety, and the bridge was soon approaching. The tree line had changed, and Joshua viewed from the window that he could see more trees at a greater distance. There was definitely a break between the pines and maples that were close by to the far-off trees that were way too far to determine what they were. Joshua knew they were approaching the gorge.

Ahead of them was a barricade, long wooden beams crossing in an X formation on both sides of a large sign that read "BRIDGE CLOSED" in large black letters. The beams were wrapped with thick orange plastic, and the sign itself was bordered in the same reflective color. Joshua could see the concrete structure behind the sign, stretched over a vast deep space he could only imagine the depth of. Evan slowed the car as he approached the sign and turned slightly onto a small side road on the left-hand side. There, sitting there, was the blue van.

Evan immediately got out of the car, leaving the driver's door open, and Joshua, not willing to wait for Zyriah to get out of the car, moved across the back bench seat, and got out on the driver's side. He ran, following Evan over to the van, and they immediately went to opposite sides. Joshua looked into the driver's door window and Evan looked into the passenger window. Once realizing the front of the van was empty, they raced to the rear doors, Evan pulling a large silver handle and turning it to open the back.

There was nobody inside, no Noah, no Ronald, and no Paul Grewe. Joshua saw some familiar objects, hammer and nails like the ones that Carl Echols used in the cemetery, as well as rope and boxes of long white candlesticks. Joshua, knowing how the candle had helped them at the cemetery the night before, grabbed two of the candlesticks from the box and shoved them awkwardly in his back pocket. There were a couple deer knives unsheathed, and Joshua was relieved that the blades were blood-free. He saw three large toolboxes as well, but he was more concerned about where his friend was. Once Evan stepped back from peering into the back of the van himself, Joshua grabbed the silver door handle that Evan used to open the rear and slammed the door shut.

"There's nobody here," Joshua called out, as Zyriah began to catch up to them at the van. "They have to be on the bridge somewhere."

Immediately, Joshua and Evan began running, running as hard as they could towards the barricade. Joshua felt the awkward candlesticks sticking out of his back pocket and pulled them out, gripping them in his right hand as his feet sprinted towards the orange plastic wrapped crossed beams. He sat on the lowest point of the crossing, flipping his legs over the wooden beams and reached out to offer Evan a hand as he flipped his own legs in the same matter. Zyriah, lagging far behind, was close to the beams when both Joshua and Evan were on the other side.

"Go! Go!" Zyriah yelled, urging them to move forward and not wait for her. Joshua knew as well as she did how urgent the situation was.

They ran, crossing the vast bridge, and Joshua quickly realized its length, looking across and not able to see the bridge's end with the naked eye. The farther they ran, wind began to flow up from the gorge and over the bridge, pushing them back and forth an inch or more with their steps. Joshua continued to self-correct his footsteps, trying to stay in a constant forward motion and ignoring the wind's effects.

The adrenalin he had been concerned about in the car had come to his aid, and his speed was good and fast. He was so in tune with running, he did not even try to mentally hold the candlesticks in his right hand, but they remained in a firm grip during the sprint. Evan was nearly always running directly on his right side, as the two pushed forward looking for what they had come to do.

It took a few minutes and Joshua worried that something had already happened when he did not see anyone, but eventually figures began to form along the roadside. From a distance, they looked like images from the Shardland, blurred and unrecognizable, but the closer Joshua came, the images were clarified like the shards and finally he could see who was there. Noah holding an older man by the neck, and a tall, bearded man close by with a strange object next to his feet. The closer he got, Joshua realized it was Paul Grewe that was the tall, bearded man, and to his side on the bridge was a lantern. Joshua knew for certain that object was Josephine's Star. He looked back up in Grewe's hand and realized he had something else, a pistol.

"Well, well, well," Grewe yelled, raising the pistol and pointing it in the direction of Joshua and Evan. Joshua could see the gun was pointed more towards Evan than it was to him. "Looks like we have a couple visitors, Ronald."

"Help me!" Ronald yelled, struggling to call out as Noah's arm apparently wrapped tighter around his throat.

"Oh, you don't need help today my friend. Least of all from these two. What a surprise. Another lying juror and the son of the woman who started it all," Paul laughed.

"I didn't lie, Paul," Evan affirmed. "We made the decision about Paulie on the evidence we received in the courtroom."

"Yeah, lying evidence from a lying prosecutor. I wonder how well Gordon enjoyed his bath a couple nights ago. What do you think?" Paul said, continuing to laugh at the seriousness around them, his hand on the gun unwavering.

"Why are you doing this?" Joshua demanded. "Noah and his grandfather did nothing to you."

"Did nothing?" Paul explained. "Ronald here destroyed my family. Johnny went to jail, Catherine and Paulie left town and aren't coming back. All because this man stood up in that courtroom in front of Judge Echols that day and convicted a man who's like my brother for something he didn't do. Anybody that knows Johnny knows he'd never do something like that. He wouldn't hit a full-sized man much less his very own son. This man drove my brother and my family away from me. I got Johnny back, but it's never going to be the same. Paulie, the son my brother named after me, is never coming back to either of us. It's all your fault."

"We know Johnny didn't do it," Evan said, Joshua looking how focused his eyes were on that pistol. "We know Brad Henson hit Paulie with the baseball bat and they all blamed Johnny for it. The truth is out now."

"Now?" Paul grew in anger. "What does the truth matter now? You all should've realized all this in the jury room. You should've realized those boys were just being boys and lying to cover their own asses. Instead, you threw Johnny into jail. Don't you know what that does to a person? Don't you know what it does to him, once he's out of jail and can't see his own son? I live with that man and those tears every day I see him. You blamed the wrong person for this."

"You're right," Evan agreed, and began slowly moving to the right and widening the space between Joshua and himself. "We just need to go to Sheriff Tucker and explain all this. She can talk to Johnny and Paulie, and everything that happened will be reversed."

Joshua looked at Paul, pointing the gun at Evan as he slowly moved away, and his eyes went back to Noah, still strong holding his grandfather in his strong grip. Noah's back was to Joshua, so Joshua wasn't even sure Noah knew what was happening around him, or that people were even behind them. Joshua hoped he would turn around, enough to at least see his face, just enough so that Joshua could at least try talking to him so that Noah could read his lips. Noah remained looking away towards Paul, as Paul reached down to grab the lantern. Joshua realized that somehow the lantern was lit, even with the occasional winds blowing across the bridge from the gorge. Paul gripped the lantern, angling it down slightly, and Joshua could see the flame begin to flicker.

"Paul don't do this," Zyriah said, approaching the group and placing herself in between Joshua and Evan, Evan continuing to slowly move farther away to the right. "Nobody here is responsible for what happened to Johnny. You have to understand that."

"Nobody?" Paul stepped forward, beside Noah and his grandfather who continued to turn and twist in Noah's arm grip. "This is Ronald's fault, Deputy Baker's fault, Gordon Pritchard's fault, Judge Echols, and now Evan Scott's fault. It's time somebody pays for me losing my family."

Paul continued angling the lantern lower and lower, keeping his eyes and pistol on Evan, and Joshua saw that the wind had blown out the candle inside the lantern. Noah, turning himself and his grandfather around to see Paul, turned also to face Joshua, and Joshua could see that vacant stare on his friend's face he had seen before, bewitched by the lantern in Paul's hand that no longer burned with light. Noah, still appearing hypnotized by the effects of the Star, stared in the forward direction facing Joshua. Paul turned in Evan's direction, keeping the pistol pointed at him.

"So, what do you say juror?" Paul said wildly with a shaking-gun hand. "Got anything to confess?"

Joshua felt into his pocket of his pants and realized they were the same pants as the night before, and something familiar was in it. He moved slowly, retrieving the object from his pocket, and looked down into the palm of his hand. It was what he had been thinking. It was Evan's lighter, still in his pocket from the cemetery, and he had not returned it. He looked hard at Paul, so focused in on

Evan that his slow motions were unnoticed. Joshua felt the wind over the bridge die down and took the risk of lighting one of the candles in his hand. He held it up slowly, seeing the Star forming in the flame, and directed his arm in Noah's direction. Noah's eyes widened, blinking, and his mouth began to open. Joshua lowered his arm and lowered the flame, and Noah looked at Joshua's face and the mouth closed before screaming. Noah had returned to himself, slowly trying to figure out what was happening. Joshua, once Noah was focused back on his face, began mouthing the words he wanted to say.

"Grab the lantern."

Noah released his grandfather, and he looked down at the lantern in Paul's hand. He looked back for confirmation, and Joshua nodded enough so that Noah could see. Noah took a deep, chest moving breath.

"Paul, the only person that needs to confess anything around here is you," Evan said, rushing forward to grab the gun, as Noah grabbed at the lantern, trying to release it from Paul's grip. The three struggled, but Paul elbowed Noah in the throat, causing Noah to fall to the ground, with the lantern in his hand pulling it away from Paul. Paul pushed Evan back with his forearm and pulled the pistol back up in direct aim of Evan's head.

"No no no, my friend," Paul laughed. "It's not going to be that easy. I've worked too hard to make the wrong move right now."

Joshua looked down at Noah, on the ground holding himself up on all fours trying to catch his breath. Joshua could see him struggling, seeing his chest heave and his head rise and lower with the deepness of his breathing. Noah finally let his face rise to meet Joshua's who watched as Evan stepped slowly forward and Paul stepping slowly backwards toward Noah's crouched position. Joshua had a risky thought, but he felt the need to try it. In his mind, there was no other way out of the situation. With Noah looking at him, he began saying words under his breath, hoping his mouth was still able to be read correctly.

"Scaredy cat," Joshua mouthed the words, remembering the scene with Noah and his sister.

Noah, seeming to understand what Joshua had said, looked confused and frightened.

"When I say, arch your back as high as you can. Do it like you did to scare Audrey," Joshua explained.

Noah looked at him with that familiar confused face then shaking his head in a negative way. Joshua could see how upset he was, and the tear wetting his eyes. He did not want to push Noah any farther, but he knew he had to do it.

"You can do this," Joshua continued saying the words, watching Paul stepping farther and farther back. "On three."

"By the end of today..." Paul called out.

"One," Joshua whispered.

"I'm going home to tell my brother..." Paul continued calling.

"Two," Joshua whispered, crossing the fingers on his left hand.

"His family is coming home." Paul continued, stepping far enough his calves were right at Noah's side.

"Three," Joshua whispered.

Paul took another step, and Noah rolled his shoulders forward, pushing on his hands planted on the bridge, and raised his back and hips as high as he could. Paul rolled back, over Noah and plunged over the bridge with a loud scream that echoed down through the gorge into an empty sound of nothingness. Paul Grewe was gone.

Noah fell back to the ground, after feeling the weight of Paul on his back, and Joshua rushed to him to make sure he was alright. He squinted his eyes in pain and breathed in short shallow breaths. Joshua rubbed his back as Zyriah came over to them, squatting down. Joshua looked over at Ronald being helped up by Evan, his hand rising to the back of his head apparently feeling pain in the location. Joshua looked back to Noah, opening his watery eyes to look back at him. Joshua and Zyriah helped Noah roll to his back, and Joshua saw him wince in pain but relax quickly. Joshua stood, extending his hands to Noah, and helped pull him up with Zyriah helping to support his back. Noah lifted his face forward once he was standing, and he smiled.

Ronald came over to Noah, and Joshua saw Noah break into tears as the two embraced. Ronald held him tight, patting him on the back, then pulling back so they could smile at each other. Evan stepped over with Joshua and Zyriah as they watched the grandfather and grandson reunite. Ronald rubbed Noah's head messing up his hair, and Joshua laughing thinking what grandfather does not do that to their grandchild.

The two spoke in sign language for a few moments, then Noah looked back at Joshua, Zyriah, and Evan standing together. He walked over to them, and the four embraced. Joshua felt the unity. That previous feeling that Noah should be part of the team was reinforced by everything that had happened those couple days. They released the embrace, and Joshua looked at Noah, continuing to smile.

"You ready?" Joshua said out loud.

Noah gave that curious look again, raising his hands palms up and shrugging his shoulders.

"What do you mean 'what'?" Joshua laughed, feeling the need to overexaggerate his mouth were never necessary.

Noah laughed out loud, his laughter followed by Zyriah and Evan's own laughter of relief.

Joshua, looking at Noah sincerely, said, "Let's go home."

CHAPTER
FOURTEEN

Joshua awoke the next morning feeling a sensation of refreshment and vigor. The drive home was long, having Noah and his grandfather in the car as well. Zyriah insisted Ronald sit in the passenger seat, which forced Joshua over in the center of the bench seat, uncomfortable and wedged between Zyriah and Noah. It did not take long for Noah to fall asleep, and even though he dropped his head to Joshua's shoulder and fell asleep there, Joshua did not want to wake him. The past few days were finally behind them, the lantern with Josephine's Star was safely in the trunk, and they were driving home. Zyriah said she would notify Sheriff Tucker about what had happened on the bridge, that Paul Grewe had jumped into the gorge, leaving the blue van along a side road. Joshua felt a relief, knowing the lantern was behind him, secure and safe, and it could no longer bring harm to anyone.

He got out of bed with a great amount of energy and left the bedroom to go into the bathroom to comb his morning hair down to something manageable. Looking into the mirror, he even admitted to himself that he looked more alive and rested. He turned around and faced the clawfoot tub, and even though it was morning, he decided on doing something to satisfy his mind, a nice bubble bath. He took a bottle of bubble bath from the linen closet, a washcloth, and a towel, and turned the water on, checking periodically to make sure it was warm enough. He watched the tub fill and the bubble emerge, rise, and fill the wide bathtub. He realized there was no longer anything to fear since the night at the Pritchard's in that water. He saw his bathtub, the type he always wanted, and he quickly undressed and slipped into the water under the bubbles.

After nearly an hour, he regretfully stepped out of the tub, dried himself off, and wrapped the towel around himself. He went back into the bedroom to pick an outfit for the day. He chose a mint green button up shirt, his favorite color, and a pair of jeans that were hanging neatly hung in his closet. While he dressed, he looked around the room, from the sunset window to the bed, to the nightstand, and to the dresser. The room truly felt like his bedroom, and in his mind it made him feel comfort. He walked to the nightstand, grabbing his selenite pendant, and placed it around his neck. He smiled, buttoning up the last of the buttons he wanted fastened on his shirt, and left the room in the direction of the elevator.

He went on the elevator down to the first floor, and once again, pressed his ear to the back door listening for any conversation outside. Even that morning, he heard familiar voices outside, and he turned his head back facing the door shaking his head. However, he shook his head laughing under his breath at how predictable his new friends had become.

"Do you people ever sleep?" Joshua said laughing, opening the door to see Zyriah and Evan sitting on the patio with a nice breakfast of eggs, bacon, toast, and orange juice on the table.

"Actually, we were wondering if you ever wake up," Evan said, laughing at Zyriah as she nodded while eating a fork full of scrambled eggs. "I know you said you could have slept an extra day you were so tired, but we didn't think you really meant it."

"An extra day? What do you mean?" Joshua said confused.

"You slept all day yesterday, Joshua. Do you even realize it?" Zyriah finally said with a slight giggle. "The bridge was night before last."

"Are you kidding me?" Joshua exclaimed, then began laughing at himself. "I knew I felt some energy this morning and I wasn't sure why."

The three laughed as Joshua walked behind Evan to a waiting breakfast on the table that he was so hungry for. The three enjoyed their meal together, occasionally looking and smiling at each other between bites. Joshua did not feel the need to be modest with the fact he was hungry, gobbling up the meal in a short amount of time. He drank half his orange juice and lowered the glass back to the table. He sighed.

"It's a beautiful day today too. So warm. I hope it never gets cold," Joshua said grinning.

"It's autumn in West Virginia," Evan reaffirmed. "Guaranteed it's going to frost when we least expect it."

"Well, why not enjoy it while we have it, I always say," Zyriah said, raising her orange glass for a toast.

"Here, here," Joshua agreed, as he and Evan both

raised their glasses to Zyriah's clinking their glasses together.

Joshua finished his juice and sat back to relax. The stress of that week had been lifted, and he found himself thinking of what the day could bring. Life would become simpler, without the need for chasing down Josephine's Star or any more tragedy coming from the instrument. He felt the relief, and he relished in it. Still, he had one question about the lantern.

"Where is the Star now?" Joshua inquired of Zyriah.

"Locked upstairs on the third floor," Zyriah replied. "It'll be safe there, I promise."

"Are you sure about that?" Joshua said with his usual cockiness.

"Who's sure about anything bud?" Evan asked, following the comment by his last drink of juice. "I'm sure though that with the three of us around here all the time, there's no way that lantern is going to leave that room."

"The three of us," Joshua questioned the remark. "It doesn't feel like that to me anymore. After all, Noah did provide us with information that helped us find the Star. He certainly contributed on how we dealt with Paul Grewe. He feels part of the group now."

Zyriah began to look a bit grim. "I went and saw Noah yesterday at the farm," she explained. "It was a long afternoon, but now he knows what happened on that bridge."

"She also told him about our abilities too," Evan added.

"How did he react to all that?" Joshua asked, feeling concerned.

"It wasn't the main issue he's having difficulty with, Joshua," Zyriah continued. "He's a young man with a lot on his plate right now, with his job, the farm, and his family. He's constantly working to the point that he rarely gets any breaks. Now, he's really focused on trying to understand what happened on that bridge. It's a heavy load on anyone's mind."

"You said he wouldn't remember it if he was under the lantern's influence," Joshua said, trying to figure out Noah's difficulty.

"He doesn't remember that part of it, but he knows what happened," Zyriah explained. "That man really loves his grandfather, and to do what he did has really had an effect on him."

"We thought we should let you know before we head over there later today," Evan said.

"Over where? The Wilson's farm? Why are we all going there today?" Joshua asked.

"It's Ronald's birthday today. The big seventy-sixth birthday according to Maddie," Zyriah smiled. "She invited us all out for the party today."

"To be honest," Joshua admitted, "a party is long overdue for me. I'm actually looking forward to it since you mentioned it."

"See if you can talk to Noah," Zyriah urged. "See if you can help him."

"I already planned on it," Joshua smiled.

The driveway and the area around the garage of the Wilson's farm was crowded with cars, as Joshua crossed the bridge trying to find a place to park his car. He followed the other car's example and parked in the yard near the front of the house. The three of them exited the vehicle, and after hearing noise in the back yard they followed the blue and yellow streamers intertwined that led from the garage to the rear yard of the home. Several picnic tables covered in blue table clothes were covered in food. From hamburgers to pasta salad, the tables set up in a buffet styled manner. It was certainly a party atmosphere, and Joshua could not wait.

"So, how did it feel driving your own car?" Zyriah asked.

"Long overdue," Joshua laughed. "Now it's just a question of keeping the keys away from Evan. Although I think he drives a lot better than I do. The shear amount of close calls we've had lately with his speeding, I'm surprised I'm still living."

"What's that I hear about a speeding driver?" a voice from behind Joshua called out. Joshua turned to see the sheriff was among the people he still had not realized were present.

"Oh, I was talking about this police cruiser I saw the other day," Joshua joked. "Nearly ran me down cornering the curb at Soccer's going at least sixty miles an hour."

"Uh huh. Y'all know I got the badge," Monika said confidently. "Just doing my job. Just stay out of the way." She began laughing, and the three joined her.

"How are you doing, Sheriff?" Evan asked.

"Well, I think I have all your escapades the last few days covered," Monika answered. "I'm still working on the reports of what happened here in Wilcox and down at High-Level Gorge, but that's not why I'm here."

"Is there something else?" Zyriah inquired.

"Sarah Baker," Monika continued. "The little girl woke up night before last. She doesn't remember what happened that night."

"Well, that's a good thing isn't it? That she didn't have to remember?" Joshua asked, thinking how he would not have wanted to remember.

"True, but the little girl still lost her parents. Nancy Baker is going to try to get custody and make sure the girl gets the help she'll need," Monika said with a solemn smile.

"Well, I'm glad she has an aunt that cares for her that much," Zyriah responded.

"What about Carl Echols?" Evan asked.

"I tried getting him to the Senior Center, but he passed away on the way there," Monika explained. "Doctor said it was a massive heart attack."

The three took a moment of silence. The night at the cemetery was traumatic, but still Joshua knew it was a death that should never have happened. He took a quick look at the beautiful sky before the sheriff began to speak again.

"Y'all go ahead and enjoy the festivities," Monika said with a new happier grin. "I don't turn down Maddie's pasta salad anytime I can get my hands on it."

Sheriff Tucker walked away towards the pasta salad bowl, and Joshua sighed with peace knowing that the legal matters had been handled. He admitted Monika was a unique lady and a fine officer. He continued watching her spoon herself a plate of food until he heard a car door slam.

"One of you kids going to help me with this or do you just enjoy watching the old man work," Russell Lloyd yelled, opening the passenger side of his brown pickup truck and taking out a platter covered in plastic. Evan hurriedly ran to collect the platter, and the two approached Joshua. Joshua felt hesitant, remembering the last conversation with Russell was not a pleasant one.

"Heard you did some good with Ronald and his

grandson," Russell said to Joshua as he approached, his eyes holding firm as he spoke. "I might had misjudged you. It's not right of me to judge people for other people's mistakes."

"I can be just as guilty of that sometimes, I have to admit," Joshua said, feeling slightly intimidated even by the small, stern man.

"You did good, Spiker," Russell admitted, extending his hand for Joshua to shake.

"Thank you, sir. I appreciate it," Joshua said while returning the handshake.

"Now, if you can only do one more thing, everything will be fine," Russell said with a disappointment in his voice.

"Sure! What else can I do, sir?" Joshua asked.

"Learn to stop ordering ketchup!" Russell demanded, and Joshua could see the man was completely serious.

"You got it, sir," Joshua relented. "No ketchup."

Russell smiled, leaving the group to speak to Ronald. Joshua felt better now, looking at Russell and glad the two had made amends. He tried to think of all the people he had met in Wilcox in just a few days, and he did not want any animosity from any of his new neighbors if he could help it. Even a small moment like he just had with Russell gave him a large feeling of relief. Plus, with all the photographs Russell displayed on his wall above his booths, Joshua hoped that maybe his own photograph might be included one day.

Joshua began walking forward with Evan and Zyriah, smiling at the onlookers, and Joshua felt slightly out of place not knowing the people he was seeing. Finally, sitting at a table with his twin granddaughters, there was Ronald, looking back and forth at the twins as they laughed, turning his "6" candle upside down to make it look like a "9" and placing it before the "7" candle.

"You think I look I look ninety-seven, huh," Ronald laughed. "Don't worry. Your pap is planning on living to one hundred years old one day."

"Why not one hundred and one?" Joshua laughed.

"Hey, you all came," Ronald acknowledging them all, Joshua pleased to see him looking so happy. "This here is Abby on my right and you know Audrey here on my left. I still can't tell them apart without the hospital toe tags, but eventually I'll get their names right. Girls, this is Joshua, Zyriah, and Evan."

"Hi," the young twins said together quietly, brown curled hair slightly blocking their views.

"Nice to see you both," Zyriah said, stepping forward and greeting them. "I've been looking for Noah. Is he inside?"

"Noah's actually on the gazebo around the corner of the house over there," Ronald turned his head, tilting it to the left for a moment to point the direction. "He's still not in a very talkative mood. Maybe you all can talk to him more."

"I'd like to try," Joshua said stepping forward. "Nice seeing you again."

Joshua walked to the side of the house, quickly realizing that Zyriah and Evan were giving him privacy by not following him. He followed the flower bed and streamers to the corner of the house, and as he walked around the corner he saw a small wooden structure, like a mini pavilion he thought, where Noah sat in a chair overlooking the field of straw bales. A strong wind had developed into the valley, and Joshua felt the moving air push him forward into the gazebo. Noah, seeing Joshua's feet, looked up and smiled for a moment, but the smile resolved into a sad expression.

Joshua sat down in a chair beside him, looking out over the field for a moment, enjoying the beauty of it, then back to Noah, who's face showed signs of tear-stained sadness. Joshua hunted for the words, the right words, to help his new friend. They eventually came out a little easier than he expected.

"I hear somebody's not been so happy the last couple days," Joshua said, turning his face to look at Noah so he could read his lips with no interference.

Noah gave a slight smirk, shrugged his shoulders, and returned his eyes to Joshua's face.

"You're not even happy to see me?" Joshua said, with a growing smile.

Noah shrugged his shoulders and gave a momentary grin before returning to his saddened expression. Joshua was him dropping his head with a slight embarrassment, and he looked back.

"Just to be honest with you? I think what you did on that bridge the other day was really brave," Joshua admitted.

Noah lowered his face, his smile gone, and reached into his pants pocket. He pulled out his spiral notebook and his little pencil. He wrote a message on the first page of paper, ripped it from the notebook, and gave Joshua the paper.

"I hurt my family. I hurt my pap," Noah had written.

"It wasn't you doing that. Zyriah told you yesterday, she said. You're a good person, and I know you'd never do something like that on purpose unless you had to," Joshua said, feeling sadness growing within him.

Noah took the paper with the message back and wrote another message below the first. Joshua looked closer and realized Noah had begun crying again. He passed the paper to Joshua for Joshua to read.

The paper read, "But my pap knows what I did. What if he's scared of me now? What if he's scared I'll hurt Abby and Audrey?"

Joshua looked back at those tearful eyes, and he felt such immense sorrow for his friend. He put his arms around Noah, feeling him sob and cry into his shoulders, Noah's hands pressing into Joshua's back. When the sobs seemed to stop, Noah pulled back, and Joshua lifted his hands to the sides of Noah's head, so that he was unwavering and focused on what he was going to say.

"Anybody that truly knows you and cares about you knows that's not the person you are. I've only known you a few days, and I can tell that's not the person you are deep down. I'm sure your family loves you. Every one of them. No matter what you do, they're going to be there for you and love you. Always," Joshua explained.

Noah smiled, and Joshua felt he had understood every word. Joshua wiped away the last of the tears, and Noah nodded in appreciation. Joshua felt Noah would take time to understand that he was telling the truth. He felt deep down that it would not take long for Noah to realize the love and support he had around him.

Noah did something that Joshua did not expect at that moment. He took Joshua's right hand, manipulating his fingers so that it looked as if Joshua was pointing. Then, taking his own second finger on his own right hand, Noah grabbed Joshua's finger, locking the two fingers together. Noah raised his eyes to Joshua's and smiled.

"He's saying you two are friends," Abby voice came as she approached the two from around the corner, or at least Joshua thought it was Abby.

"Well, he's right," Joshua agreed smiling. "We are definitely friends."

Noah smiled happily.

Abby was excited and immediately changed the topic of the conversation, "Audrey and I have an idea? Want to help us?"

"Sure, what do you two have in mind?" Joshua asked.

Audrey seemed to come around the corner on cue, holding several kites as well as her hands could. The two girls laughed at Audrey's carrying skills, and they turned back facing Joshua and Noah sitting on the gazebo. Joshua turned his head to see Noah's reaction, that questioning look Joshua had attributed to Noah's character. Joshua laughed. He watched Noah smile and stand from his seated position, maintaining the look on his face so that the girls could see it clearer. Joshua tapped Noah's arm to get his attention.

"C'mon," Joshua said smiling. "This'll be fun."

The wind grew strong and constant as Evan and Zyriah joined the kite flying attempt. Joshua and Zyriah got the string and kite ready for the green kite as well as the purple one, Noah and Audrey worked on the blue kite as well as an orange one, while Evan and Abby wrestled with the yellow. The boys held the spools of string, unraveled a few feet from the girls who held their respective kites upward and waited for a strong wind.

"You all know it isn't April. It's October," Ronald Wilson yelled from his standing position beside Maddie, as the rest of the guests stood behind them as a crowd of spectators to this unseasonal spectacle, which Joshua thought made it even more fun.

"Just you wait, birthday boy. This one's for you," Joshua yelled back laughing, and the boys turned around with their backs facing the girls, holding their spools in their right hands. Joshua could feel the wind picking up speed.

"On the count of three," Joshua continued to call out loud, facing Noah so he could see. "One...two...THREE!"

Joshua, Noah and Evan all began running as the girl's released the kites, and wind began to carry them upward. They each released more and more string as they ran across the rear field, and Abby and Audrey cheered for the kites rising quickly into the sky. Joshua watched as his kite rocked back and forth with the wind, letting more and more string out to let the kites fly higher. He looked over at Noah, letting out more string, and then to Evan as he did the same. The men passed the kites to the three ladies, then Noah and Joshua took the two remaining kites and began running until they were also airborne.

The five kites were high and almost appeared to keep themselves in a straight line. Joshua thought for a moment, looking at the kites in the sky and remembering the painting Zyriah had bought at the auction. Once again, another of his paintings had come true, with five kites in flight over the West Virginia trees. He thought for a moment how the lady in the yellow dress must be at Rock Falls seeing their kites in flight, and he wondered who the woman could be. Joshua looked back at Noah, who was smiling and laughing at how high his kite was, and his interest in who the woman was erased by something much more important. Noah was not sad anymore.

Joshua had insisted Noah join the three at his house after the party, so they waited until the appropriate amounts of Ronald's birthday guests had left so that Noah could ask if he could go. Joshua found it funny for a moment, that a grown man would ask his grandfather for permission. Still, under the circumstances, Joshua felt it was the right thing to do. It warmed him inside to see the grandson and grandfather smiling and hugging yet again before their departure.

Back at the house, Joshua walked to his front door then turned to look down at the town of Wilcox, and his three friends joined him in enjoying the view. Joshua really had not taken enough time to notice the beauty of the landscape, but he already remembered how the town unfolded and mirrored itself down the middle on Treeclimber Drive. He thought there was something about the symmetry of the town that made it beautiful, besides the buildings and the maples outlining the area. Really he knew it was not just the symmetry. It was the overall impression the town was continuing to make on him the more he looked at it. It was becoming home. It was a feeling he had always hoped for and it had taken a long time to absorb it.

"Wait, wait, wait," Evan stepped forward, as Joshua turned to the front door trying to retrieve his key ring from his pocket. "Zyriah, you didn't tell him about a couple other surprises, did you?"

"Well, that's why we call them a surprise," Zyriah said smiling.

"What did you all do?" Joshua said, questioning what was about to come.

"Well, we finally thought it was time to make you feel a little more at home," Evan said, taking the keys from Joshua's hand, and selecting the proper key for the front door. He opened the door, with Noah's hands on Joshua's eyes like he had done days ago at Soccer's, and the group filed into the front room of the downstairs' floor. Joshua could feel a hand on each arm guiding him while Noah covered his eyes, until Joshua was positioned for the reveal. Within a moment, all hands were lifted, and Joshua, whose eyes were already closed behind Noah's hands, opened his eyes in wonder.

His sunrise painting and the painting he sold to Zyriah in Charleston were both framed and mounted into place on two of the front white walls in the entry room, behind the leather sofa he had seen his first time entering the building. The track lighting was angled towards both works, and Joshua looked at them, seeing a new value to them. He looked closely at Zyriah's purchase and confirmed what he had thought at the Wilson's about the kites in the distance being the same colors as the ones they had just used, and for a moment he wanted to question how it was possible. He kept quiet, just enjoying the beauty of seeing those paintings in his home, and he felt a welling pride looking at them. He thanked each of the others for their work, giving each a hug showing the amount of gratitude he was feeling for all they had done for him since arriving at Wilcox.

"You know," Evan mentioned, "This floor could make a nice little gallery with a little work."

Joshua saw Noah get excited, nodding his head and patting Joshua on the back, encouraging the idea. Joshua knew the truth, that he had considered that idea at one point, and at that moment he visualized paintings on all the walls, with people filing around looking at each one by one and appreciating their artistry. It was an idea he was more than willing to consider.

"Well, before you all get sidetracked with a new gallery, he might want to check out the garage," Zyriah added.

"The garage?" Joshua said with an inquisitive look, then getting a feeling of excitement building within him. He ran out the front door, leaving it open, around the corner, past the cars to the garage door. He reached for his keys in his pocket and grimaced in disappointment. Evan still had them.

"I think you'll need these," Evan said as he, Zyriah and Noah strolled out laughing at Joshua and each other. He held the keys in his hand, already having the key apparently for the garage separated from the others. Joshua felt a bit of embarrassment.

"Well thank you very much, sir," Joshua said, taking the key ring by that singular key and looking back and forth trying to figure out which door to open.

"It's the left one," Zyriah said, and Joshua quickly went over to the door handle. He inserted the key, turning it and the door handle, and pushed the door upwards. He hoped it was another car. He thought how great it would be for a surprise to have been sitting in the garage waiting for him that entire week.

Boxes. Boxes and boxes. That side of the garage was half full of boxes and furniture, and once he saw the bed he realized where it all had come from. He turned to Zyriah, who had a strange smirk on her face, and he knew she had been responsible for what was in that garage.

"Well, I called your old landlord, Miss Amos, and she

had all your things moved up here so you wouldn't have to go back to Charleston to get them. All delivery fees are paid," Zyriah said, smiling. "She also would like to inform you that upon her inspection, all bills she currently has for you gives you a current balance of..."

Joshua cringed, thinking all bills had been paid, but imagining that Miss Amos had uncovered a bill or two in his absence.

"Zero," Zyriah laughed.

"When did you call her to move all this though?" Joshua wondered. "It takes time to pack all these boxes."

"Oh, I called the first day you were here," Zyriah smiled. "I had a feeling you would want to stay."

Joshua looked back at the boxes, imagining the life he had in Charleston and all the changes that had been made. These were boxes of his old life, but so many of the things from then were still part of him. He could look upon those things from the past and remember where he came from. Also, he wanted to appreciate the things he had now.

"I just have a couple questions," Joshua said, as he turned back to face his team, "How many more of these instruments do we need to track down?"

"Well, a few," Evan said nodding. "Still, you know we're going to work together. We'll find them."

Joshua smiled. He looked at each face, Noah's, Zyriah's, and Evan's. He felt so much genuine caring from them that he knew he was in the place he wanted to be. Wilcox had become his town, and this place had become his home.

Noah signed something to Zyriah, and she vocalized for him. "Noah's asking what the second question is?"

"Well, which one of you wants to help me unpack?" Joshua laughed.

Noah raised his hand, stepping forward with Zyriah and Evan raising their hands volunteering. They walked into the garage, each grabbing a box, and turned for Joshua's instructions on where to go with them.

"I didn't mean now, you guys," Joshua laughed. "It's nice though to see the team effort."

"Three has officially become four," Evan said, rubbing Noah's head messing up his hair in a similar fashion like Ronald had done. Joshua thought there was a charm to Noah's willingness.

Joshua finally sighed, taking in the effort of how quickly his friends were so willing to help him, and he smiled widely.

"It's the team of friends I always wished I had," Joshua admitted.

The remainder of the day was spent talking, laughing, and telling stories. Joshua felt more at ease with his new living situation with the people he now considered friends, and he thought to himself how different things had been just a few days ago. The struggle with money and constant worry about keeping a home were no longer issues. Those problems were now gone, and the release of those fears certainly lightened his stress.

Things were feeling better, and as the group disbanded towards the end of the day he felt the need for a long night's rest free of dreams and images. As he retired into his home, he looked at the increased cloudiness of the sky as a chilly night air drew its breath and pushed across the hillside. He thought that there was a chance of a storm, so by going up to his second floor living area, he thought he would avoid the change in temperature and staying dry. He began to prepare for bed.

CHAPTER
FIFTEEN

Changing into a shirt and a pair of shorts helped him feel more comfortable, but still Joshua debated about taking another bath. Walking into the bathroom, he looked at the bathtub wondering if perhaps he might fall asleep in the water due to sleepiness. A quick image into his mind at what happened at the Pritchard's home made the deciding vote, so he turned to brush his teeth. He was disappointed with himself, remember how his last bath did not bother him, but for some reason it did not feel like the right time to be in that tub. His eyelids were heavy, so after brushing his teeth he took a wet washcloth to wipe his face which gave him a slight feeling of waking up. Still, it took only a few moments for his eyes to renew their weighted feel. He took another moment to look into the mirror.

He pulled his pendant that had been under his shirt out to hang on his chest and focused on the stone. So much of the events and what he had been able to do was due to that object. There was the thought of removing it and keeping from wearing it, but he knew there was more that needed to be done using it in the future. The remaining instruments were still in the world somewhere, so any advantage Joshua could have in the future would be worth wild.

The pendant looked so simple to him, a simple crystalline object that could do so much and still be such a small object. He continued to focus on it, his eyes feeling more strained and his eyelids slightly lowering and lowering. His breathing felt clean and heavy, his chest rising and dropping that made the pendant move slightly from its position then returned with each exhale.

Joshua's arms, which were at his sides, suddenly felt a tension and unwillingness to move. He began struggling to move them and realized his entire body felt immobile. He refocused in the mirror while attempting to shift even an inch in body position, when the view of the pendant began to change.

The white cloud of the stone began changing as if a prism deciding through a rainbow's palette, until finally deciding on a deep dark purple that Joshua could only compare to an amethyst. His stone had never been anything but pale green in color, so the change began to alarm him. His arms and legs did nothing to aid him, unwilling in his struggle to cooperate.

The pendant began from its center point opening a white glow like it had not done before, but the brightness of the point was more brilliant and brighter than Joshua had seen. He was feeling consumed by the sight of it, and although previous uses of it brought him into the Shardland, he did not feel in control of what was happening. His forehead began to sweat with small droplets, and he lowered his jaw taking in large breaths of air in attempts to release himself from the bind.

Joshua could feel a heat from the stone, and although nothing was burning, it felt as if it was making the contact spot on his shirt that began to increase in temperature. His heart quickened more, his lungs felt strained, and his mind began to panic into a heightened state of terror. Although his eyes were focused upon the selenite, his mind focused only on his right arm, wanting his hand to move and release itself from the immobility.

The brightness of the white section of the stone had become so overwhelming that only a small part at each end still maintained the amethyst color he had first seen. Finally, he focused every aspect of his thoughts into his right hand, no longer feeling any other part of his body, and with one full push he drove all his body's energy into that arm, driving a surge from his chest to his shoulder and down into his palm and fingers. The arm bent, and Joshua grabbed the pendant in his fist. His body immediately collapsed onto the bathroom floor.

The howling outside awakened Joshua, but only enough to initially open his eyes. He closed them again as if it was a nap interrupted, but when the howl came again, he opened his eyes with slowly increasing awareness. His body was heavy, and the feeling of complete exhaustion overwhelmed him. Still, the howling coming from outside persisted, so he forced himself up from the bathroom floor.

The stone remained bright, and Joshua through a hazy attempt at thought did not chose to remove it. Something was happening, and like all things he had experienced since arriving at Wilcox, he chose to continue to discover the meaning behind this event. The howling, although not increasing in volume, did begin to make him feel drawn to its source. The sound was urgent, he felt, so he journeyed into his bedroom to put on his shoes and to retrieve his set of keys. The sound was steady, and the entire act of moving from room to room, using the keys to operate the elevator to the bottom floor, and exiting the house seemed to be automatic movements which Joshua had limited control.

He felt the temperature of the night air being cool on his skin, except in the location of the stone on his chest. That area remained hot on his sternum, but although he could feel the sensation, he no longer had any concern for how it made him feel. From the back door, he walked around towards the driveway. The howling had continued the entire time, and only walking around the outside of the house did the sound increase in volume as Joshua approached its source.

Even in the limited amount of light, Joshua recognized the German shepherd he had seen at Pleasant Days when he met Gloria and Nute Underwood. The animal looked at him, and Joshua felt the friendliness of the dog as it changed positions from sitting to being on all fours and approaching him. His tail wagged like a short whip with excitement, and Joshua, even in a state of partial exhaustion and clouded thinking, bent over to talk to the animal friend he had recently made.

"You're making a lot of noise out here, you know that Kombat?" Joshua said in a mumbled but definite tone. "Wanted to get my attention, did you?"

Kombat rubbed against Joshua's leg, and Joshua stroked his fur down his back avoiding the pale green harness with three stars he remembered Kombat wearing on the day they met. Joshua loved the affection from the dog, and he continued rubbing the animal's back while trying to gain more awareness of the moment. His breathing was deep and labored, and he tried to awaken his mind into a more alert state. He took a quick glance at his pendant and realized that it had continued to be glowing. Feeling he could not change what the pendant was doing, Joshua focused more on Kombat, petting him and seeing the dog grow more and more excited. Feeling around the top of the dog's harness, Joshua noticed something unexpected. Although he did not see it clearly when Kombat first approached, Joshua realized that a slender leash had been wrapped around the dog's neck with the looped end being placed under the harness itself. Joshua quickly unwrapped the leash from Kombat's neck, quickly realizing it was not placed there tightly so that the dog was comfortable.

"Do you always keep you leash wrapped around like that?" Joshua asked. "Did you sneak away before somebody had the chance to walk you? I bet that's it, isn't it?"

As he continued holding the end of lease in his hand, Joshua continued stroking the fur and thinking. He was not sure of the time anymore. How long he had been on the bathroom floor remained unknown, so he looked around the night sky to estimate what time it could be. It was late, and with lack of movement in the town below, he estimated the time was leaning more towards sunrise rather than sunset. The sounds from birds confirmed his thinking, as he could hear chirps coming from the neighboring trees.

Joshua stood with the looped handle from the leash in

hand, looking over into the direction of Pleasant Days and seeing a few scattered lights on, including the porch light. He was not desiring to walk the dog home, but he did not want the dog to be lost either. Kombat was already considered to be a good dog, and Joshua felt temporarily responsible.

"Well, Kombat, let's get you home," Joshua said, with a breathy soft voice. "Are you ready?"

Joshua waited seconds to see if the dog understood his command, and Kombat did begin moving, but in the direction of going down Treeclimber Drive and into the town. Joshua tugged back on the leash to make the dog stop, and he watched Kombat turn his head back to him and making eye contact. Joshua watched Kombat turn his head back to the direction of going down into the town, and the animal surged forward enough to jerk Joshua forward.

The motion had caused his pendant to bounce back and forth, so with his remaining hand Joshua grabbed the stone to prevent it from moving. With Kombat charging forward and Joshua's footsteps following the animal's path, he felt the stone make his thoughts begin to dissipate, putting him into a sleeplike state. The warmth from the stone had travelled up his left arm, through his neck, and into his skull. His sight, once full and complete showing all surroundings, closed like a camera's lens bringing him into the familiar darkness of the Shardland.

At first, it was difficult to focus on the darkness. Joshua felt the exhaustion wrap his mind so much that his attention to detail was becoming increasing absent. The blackness, if anything, was making him want to concentrate less so that he could fall into a deep slumber. The strain on his brain was becoming a throbbing sensation that only rest could help to resolve, but what slight awareness he had to the situation was forcing him to work with what remaining energy he had. The situation felt more deliberate in its presentation, so he did what he could to make sense of the experience.

The shards emerged with a directness that Joshua could only compare to walked into a gallery of art. They appeared with an immediate presence, crisp and clean in their images and Joshua immediately recognized the shards as memories he had created in the past few days. The auction at the Austin's gallery, the first time at Soccer's, and seeing his home that initial day were all present in the photographic images in front of him. The images of going into the Pritchard's house, the fight at the cemetery, as well as Paul Grewe tumbling over Noah's arched back and off the High-Level Gorge Bridge were all present as well. Through his exhausted glare, he was overcome by the amount of endurance he felt he had gone through in just a few days times. The images hanged as a reminder of those moments, and Joshua strained to relive them by viewing.

While he continued to view those days of memories, the shards began to tremble, making the images difficult to see clearly. Something was wrong, and Joshua felt his own concentration due to his sleepiness was a possible issue. He focused more intently, but the images continued to shake with an uncontrollable movement. At the bottom of each image, Joshua could see the shards beginning to crack with small breaks of split glass. He did not understand what was happening. If the images were to shatter completely, he grew increasing concerned he could lose those memories.

As the number of hairline splits continued to grow, Joshua focused harder to keep them united. However, from the pendant on his chest, there came a growing glow.

From the bottom of every shard, a growing of translucent purple energy enveloped the images. The energy stretched like a thin skin from bottom to the top of each shard, surrounding each in a purple glow. Joshua focused on the cracks that had begun to form at the lowest part of each shard and realized that fractures had resealed themselves so that no split in the images remained. From shard to shard, he looked to confirm that all the images were whole once again. All the shards began to pulse with the energy skinned around them, then the images began to shift.

As if they were swiveling on a centered bottom turning point, the images began to turn in front of him, and Joshua realized that what he was seeing was no longer his viewpoint of the events. While some of the shards turned left, the remaining images turned right to reveal someone else was in each location which Joshua was unaware. At each moment, either walking by, hiding in trees, or standing nearby was a woman, red-haired and often in floral attire.

He thought of Brier Goff, and the brightness of his hair when he saw him at Soccer's that first day. The hair was familiar to him, he knew that. Then, seeing the shard from the auction, he remembered why the name Goff was familiar to him. The redheaded woman that was bidding was called Mrs. Goff by Oregon Pyles. The shard showing the view from the car approaching Westview Cemetery turned and focused on the fuchsia lettering above the neighboring florist shop. "Flowers by Telena", the sign had read, and upon seeing the refreshed shard, Joshua remembered the woman and realized her name.

He realized he was being shown that Telena Goff had seen him and was present in all those moments. Each shard showed her, hiding behind trees and cars watching his moves. He was being followed. As his focus intensified, he felt himself falling forward, and the images moved back from his descent. His mind returned to blackness as he fell, and he once again could feel his eyelids again, strained from being held so tightly together. With relief, he opened his eyes.

He had fallen into a cold dewed grassy area, and even in the darkness he could see things surrounding him. Trees, small bunches of flowers, and a sporadic collection of tombstones were encircling him. He had returned to Westview Cemetery. He forced himself to stand, feeling his legs strain underneath him. He had walked all this way and was so focused on the Shardland he did not realize the distance he had travelled. His mind reflected upon the images he had just seen, and he grew in fear of why that woman had been following him.

He looked at his right hand and realized Kombat's leash was still in his hand, with the dog at the leash's opposite end looking up at him intensely. While Joshua took a second to realize how far he had walked and how sore he felt, it appeared to him that the dog seemed unbothered by the long journey. Kombat charged to Joshua's left, and Joshua felt himself being pulled yet again.

The time of night was still unknown to him, but he could see from the sky that things were slightly lighter than a night's blackness. Dawn was beginning to approach, as Joshua was led farther into Westview Cemetery to a small corner. The tall pines almost entirely encircled a single tall monolith of a stone, and once Kombat and he reached it, Joshua released the leash. His eyes were focused on the name on the stone, a familiar name. He had found the grave of Lenora Spiker.

CHAPTER SIXTEEN

Her gravestone was unique, a tall monolith of black marble veined with what appeared to be copper, giving the stone a strange appearance of being spiderwebbed with shiny metal. The letters were carved deeply and done with copper themselves, spelling only her name. The stone stood solid, taller than Joshua himself, and he realized it was not crowned like an obelisk, a monument type he had seen in books before. With no point at the top of the stone, it appeared to be squared off and flat, although Joshua based that assumption by what he was able to see in the darkness. The site the stone was placed was one of solitude, with no other stones nearby. The only things close by were trees, tall and aiming towards the sky. No flowers were placed around the grave, just wet grass that flicked at Joshua's exposed ankles.

It took him a minute to realize he was finally in the presence of his birthmother, and he felt a momentary absence of thoughts and words. He was not in the habit of some meaningful expression of his feelings fell flat.

Through the overwhelming exhaustion he noticed the dawn coming as the sun's light creeped through the neighboring trees. As the light began to approach the stone itself, Joshua felt a directness in his thoughts. He tried to collect the words into an honest expression of what he had never been able to say, and with a strained heave of his chest, he began to speak. He knew the words were his own, but the directness was shocking, even to himself.

"I want to understand," Joshua said with a heavy breath. "I don't even know you, and you left all this tragedy for me. You've hurt so many people, and most of all you hurt me. What kind of monster are you?"

It was difficult to force the thoughts forward, but the more he spoke Joshua felt the dam that had formed holding back so many feelings had begun to break. His heart quickened as a cold sweat beaded upon his forehead. He could feel the stress boil over, and he continued to release it.

"Why even bother to have me?" Joshua questioned with an outright tone. "You should've been focused on being a parent instead of your job or whatever else you've done that's hurting all these people. You've forced me into saving them from actions you committed before ending up here in the ground. So, now I must fix all of this, and I must figure out how. You couldn't even leave me anything to really help me know what all you've done and who you've done it to. Answer me. Just tell me why?"

The release had lowered the pressure in his mind, so Joshua's tone began to calm itself. His volume had been elevated in his speech, so he took a moment to breathe. He folded his arms in front of himself, not only to reflect the coldness in his body but also a sign of his anger and defiance. He began to speak again, this time with a definiteness he could only describe as the cold truth.

"Why is this Telena Goff following me?" Joshua asked angrily. "Some friend of yours stalking my every move? Is she going to be as destructive as you trying to hurt me as much as you have? Why is all this happening? You're not a mother. You're a monster. Monsters don't deserve to be mothers, so maybe you're exactly where you need to be. I won't have anything else to say to you until I get some kind of explanation."

Joshua became silent. He waited as if some voice was to come from the ground to answer the questions he had asked. His breathing was heaving his chest hard, and the frustration over the lack of response was overwhelming him. Time seemed to be nonexistent. The anger within him continued growing that his exhausted eyes strained with bloodshot veins.

While he waited, a ray of sunlight finally fell from the dawn's sky upon the top of the stone, and his eyes was drawn to the spot where the two connected. The copper marbled into the stone caught the sunlight, and it began to shine with an unnatural brightness and luster. The light seemed to warm the metal, as Joshua's chest began to feel the familiar feeling of the burning sensation from his pendant.

He looked down and held the stone in his right hand, seeing the familiar color of purple with white light radiating from its center. The pendant began to burn his hand, so he attempted to pull the pendant off his body with one strong jerking motion. Instead, as he gripped the stone, his mind became dizzy. He stumbled forward, reaching his left arm forward to place his hand on the stone for balance. His mind went into complete darkness.

He did not recognize this place as the Shardland. His gaze looked from left to right into the black space, and he could not find any shards displayed. His focus drew upward towards a black emptiness, and he felt out of control of the situation. Joshua was a spectator, and his concentration did nothing to change the place where his mind was.

Due to no action of his own, a green vapor began to appear above him, swimming high and filling the darkness with an emerald sky, clouds thick and rotating. Quickly, the clouds overtook all the blackness until there was nothing left above but a deep green sky that appeared like a storm. While he could not feel any air in motion, Joshua could see the sky churn, and within seconds the clouds separated to reveal four openings.

Downward from the openings shot four solid beams of energy that Joshua could only compare to straight lines of lightening as they came close to his sight. He focused downward seeing that the beams, although appearing to unite at some point beneath his gaze, never fully came together. They were angled and drawn close to each other like arrows in a quiver, and Joshua grew fascinated by their presence. Their color had the same hue and luster as the copper on the monolith when the sunlight enflamed it, and it continued to appear like electrified metal.

From his chest, the pendant, no longer in his hand, began to emit a beam of its own. Outlined in purple, a white light forced itself forward and split from one solid beam into four. The four, as if having hands of their own, wrapped and gripped the copper beams within a fraction of a second, which energized all the light emitted with a great power. Joshua continued to feel no control over anything that was happening, so he continued to view the spectacle of energy.

His focus on all the beams began to be difficult as the beams from the sky began to pulse. From the top downward, a movement began from one beam to another like piano strings being plucked one by one. The pulsing, once reaching the energy from the pendant, shook the stone's beam from the point of connection towards him. He attempted to mentally stop them from reaching him, but the movements of the energy were far too fast. The pulses left the beams and entered him.

As the beams returned to their still positions, Joshua felt movement as the energy raced from his chest, through his neck, and toward his mind. Instantly, he could feel something in his thoughts. It was letters. He was not able to hear the consonants or the vowels, but he could somehow feel all these letters scrambled as they entered his thoughts. He felt an energetic shock as they filled his mind, and almost as instantly as they arrived, they began to unscramble themselves.

Joshua concentrated, attempting to keep the letters separated so they could be pushed back the way they came, but he did not have the mental strength. His mind began to shake from stress. Something was within the pulses as well as letters. He felt the four different sources of the information that had come through the beams, and he finally realized what he was experiencing.

It was the words of four different people, and worst of all Joshua knew all four were in a panic. His mind continued to shake from the stress as the view of the beams grew more unclear. As it blurred itself into a solid mass of white and copper-colored light, Joshua began feeling his body being shaken. The tremors were uncontrollable, and Joshua felt them increase the more he left the light.

The sun's glare stung his eyes with a feeling of dry fire, and Joshua's eyes ached from the attempt to pry his own eyelids open. He could feel a hand on his cheek and a thumb on his chin holding his head and trying to shake him awake. Through the small crack in his vision, he could see his sight was back to Westview Cemetery. His neck pained to turn his head toward a darker image above him, and slowly he began to see features of a face and the red hair that eventually became the face of Brier Goff.

"Can you hear me?" Brier questioned with a concerned tone. "Are you ok, Joshua?"

He could not respond. His thoughts still jumbled with the words forced into his brain so much that Joshua could not put the words together that he was alright. He continued to feel the letters in his mind collect into words as he attempted to sit up. The dew on the grass had soaked through his shorts, and he shivered in the cold looking into Brier's green eyes unable to speak.

"Do you need to go to the hospital?" Brier continued asking. "What can I do?"

The words finally came to Joshua, and he felt the air pushing from his lungs to his mouth without him directly making it happen. He felt dazed, and as the words pushed forward he felt the pain in his head begin to throb at an alarming rate.

"I can't see anything," Joshua finally said, releasing the words brought together in his thoughts. The words repeated as they must have repeated originally. "I can't see anything."

"Let me get you to a hospital," Brier announced in a frantic tone. "Let me call a doctor."

"I can't see anything," Joshua repeated in the same monotone way he had said it twice before. He could hear the words coming from his own mouth as if it was a recording. "The entrance is sealed off."

"The entrance is sealed off?" Brier asked, looking into Joshua's eyes. Joshua struggled to show some movement in his eyes or face that could let Brier know the words were not his own. "What are you talking about?"

"I dropped my flashlight," Joshua explained, but not quite sure what he was explaining. Although the words continued at the same rate and volume, he felt as they unraveled from his thoughts that the words were coming from different people. "Wait, here it is."

"I don't understand what you're saying," Brier said looking even deeper into Joshua's eyes. Joshua could see Brier was concerned, but he was unable to express what was happening.

His heartrate began to increase, and the panic Joshua had felt before he had awoken had begun to quicken his breathing. His body felt pain, and soon all parts of him began to be in the worst pain he had ever experienced. He began physically to experience a full body tremoring that continued to intensify as he spoke.

"What is that?" Joshua asked as his eyelids rolled back into a frightening strained stare looking at Brier. He imagined the four people searching in the dark with a flashlight trying to find a way out of some dark place, but instead they had found something else, something terrifying.

He felt the panic of the four people racing into his

muscles until his body felt like it was ripping apart. His body began seizing with the shooting pain running throughout himself. He watched Brier move back slightly, watching him and not sure what else to do.

The final words finally came together, and as Joshua became aware that they had unified, he also became aware of what he was about to say. He quickly understood the pain he was experiencing, the pain of four people trapped in some dark unknown place. More frightening, he realized what they had become aware of seconds before their deaths. He released the words, feeling the pressure that had built up from his diaphragm erupt the air from his abdomen up through his body and across his vocal cords into a scream. The words came forth, and Joshua collapsed beside Brier on the cold wet grass into unconsciousness.

"IT'S DYNAMITE!"

ABOUT THE AUTHOR

WILLIAM K. MARCATO is a lifelong resident of north-central West Virginia. After receiving his Bachelor of Arts degree in English from West Virginia University, he continued his experimental research in paranormal psychic phenomena as well as his love for writing. Upon the passing away of both of his parents, he returned to writing full-time. His interest in Appalachian folklore and the ghost stories of West Virginia are motivating factors for his current subject of literary work.